WHAT IT TAKES BABE

THE PETE PETERSON TAPES PART I

Des Tong

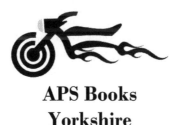

APS Books
Yorkshire

APS Books,
The Stables Field Lane,
Aberford,
West Yorkshire,
LS25 3AE

APS Books is a subsidiary of the APS Publications imprint

www.andrewsparke.com

A catalogue record for this book is available from the British Library

WHATEVER IT TAKES BABE

PROLOGUE
Friday, 24 October 1971

IT'S THE opening night of the brand new million-pound music club The Lexxicon. The coloured spotlights dramatically cut through the atmospheric haze enveloping the three figures standing centre stage. In the middle, wearing his new Anderson & Sheppard suit, multi-millionaire owner Gerry Fontana is looking great. He has few vices, but handmade suits from his favourite tailors in Savile Row are one. His latest, a dark blue, double-breasted cut from the finest Italian silk, fits him like a glove. With an open neck, white cotton shirt and the exquisite gold cufflinks bought as a wedding anniversary present by his wife Janine, he looks every bit the successful club owner. Even with slight lifts in his black leather Ferragamo loafers, Gerry is just five feet six inches tall. With cropped dark-brown hair and a bull-like neck, he is the image of his late father Antonio, an Italian immigrant from Tuscany.

At his right-hand side, his wife Janine, wearing a figure-hugging, backless, cobalt blue Yves Saint Laurent evening gown, looks stunning. At five feet ten inches plus her heels she towers over Gerry. But he is such a powerful character nobody notices, or if they did they would never have the nerve to comment. On the stage she seems noticeably excited at being involved in the events happening tonight, though not many there would know the smile is a mask hiding the conflicting emotions swirling around inside her head.

Over on the other side of Gerry, rock star Pete Peterson is the epitome of cool. Dressed in his trademark leather jacket and jeans he is secretly wishing he could smoke the joint in his pocket. He and his band The Flames are about to play their set, to celebrate the opening of the club.

Gerry's white Rolls-Royce Silver Shadow, registration GF1, is parked outside: a symbol of his wealth and power. The Lexxicon is the newest, and biggest addition to the nightclub scene in the city. Tonight, it's packed with punters, friends and celebrity guests from the world of music, sport and politics. Even the police are represented: by the Chief Constable, George Williams, and his aptly named right-hand man, DCI Law. All in all, it couldn't get much better for Gerry right now; his music management company, Fortuna Artists Management, are representing Pete Peterson, who has just signed a very lucrative recording deal with

Westoria Records in the States that morning. Things are on the verge of really taking off.

Looking out from the stage he can see the majority of the crowd consists of Pete's faithful followers, pushing right to the front, excitedly waiting for his performance. The atmosphere in the room is electric, and everyone there seems to sense that something big is going to happen before the night is over.

So much has been happening over the past few days, Gerry can hardly believe he is standing here soaking up the atmosphere. But behind the bravado lies a dark secret, which, were it to be revealed, could bring his empire crashing down, destroying everything he's worked so hard to create.

CHAPTER ONE

GERRY FORTUNA hadn't had an easy childhood. His mother, who had been born in the Black Country, had met his father Antonio when he was working as a waiter in an Italian restaurant in Birmingham. There wasn't much money and when Gerry was born things had become tight, even more so when his sister Estelle came along a year later. Gerry had left school at fifteen without any qualifications, deciding he'd be better off attending the University of Life. He'd learned to look after himself, mainly because being the smallest in the class meant he'd had his share of bullying, but his dad had taught him the basics of boxing and he'd always given as good as he'd got. He would have loved to have been a boxer and for a while attended a local gym, but lacked the dedication.

He found himself instead, attracted to the entertainment industry. Not that he could sing or anything like that, but as he grew older he got a kick out of going to clubs and watching how they worked. At the age of eighteen Gerry lost his mother to alcohol addiction and vowed never to touch a drop. But even so, he could see there was money to be made from supplying good quality entertainment and alcohol to people who wanted it.

He still kept fit and could always handle himself if there was any trouble – which tended to be a regular occurrence – and it was because of his reputation that he was approached by one of the Barton family who asked him to be the head doorman at their club The Cave. Tommy Barton had met Gerry in a club one night and they'd got on well. Although his family had a thriving butchers business with shops across the city, Tommy was more interested in music and clubs, so had been given the responsibility of running The Cave.

The Cave was one of the most popular clubs in the city and was always busy. In reality it was a room with a bar in one corner and a small, raised stage in the other where the bands played. Situated just off one of the main streets in the city centre it was accessed down a narrow alleyway, which made it easy to control who they allowed in. Gerry was the ideal choice and became well known as a fair but fierce doorman who took no nonsense. You didn't go to The Cave to cause trouble if you knew what was good for you! Working there had given Gerry the experience and the money he needed to fulfil his dream, and finally after much soul searching, he decided to take the giant step of opening his own club. He'd been on the lookout for premises for a while, and eventually found a big old warehouse situated five minutes from the city centre. It was structurally sound and had a large car park around the back. Along with a group of friends, many of whom were builders, Gerry set about converting it into a stylish nightclub. Thanks to his time at The Cave, he already knew the two features he wanted that would set his club apart from the others. First, a good-sized stage. The bands had always complained about the cramped stage in The Cave and if Gerry wanted to put on the best music, the bands had to feel good. He'd also built a dressing room, which The Cave didn't have. Secondly, and most importantly, the bar would stretch the whole length of one side of the club. The biggest bar in the city! He knew he would make his money selling booze – and he wanted to make sure the punters had every opportunity to buy it from him.

In September 1965, Gerry opened his new club – The Hideout – in a blaze of publicity. He'd invited all the influential people he knew, and on opening night the club was packed. With plenty of free drinks flowing, everyone was complimentary, and Gerry was confident that he had made the right decision. But once the initial euphoria died down, business was slow. The trouble was Gerry's main competition; The Cave, and the Coliseum – a big old music hall owned by an Irishman called Harry Castle. Both were well-established, and even though Gerry was a well-known character on the club scene, it had been a depressing couple of months with hardly any customers taking the short trip out of the city centre. But Gerry wasn't a quitter and gradually things began to pick up; they started to get a regular crowd, especially when he put on local bands. There were plenty of good groups around, but he made sure only the best played The Hideout. There was one band in particular called the Daybreaks, that he knew from his time on the door at The Cave. The lead singer Johnny Rhodes always insisted on using the cream of local musicians and they'd recently returned from a stint in the South of France. Word was, they were the tightest band around, and Gerry pulled out all the stops to get them on at The Hideout, before the Bartons or Harry Castle could book them.

On the first night they played, the club was packed to the rafters. The band was on fire. It was obvious to Gerry that this was one of the best bands he'd seen, but there was something else he spotted that really excited him. Although singer Johnny Rhodes was the focal point, the lead guitarist also had charisma. When Johnny allowed him to sing, he mesmerised the girls in the crowd, and his playing was fantastic. He enthralled Gerry, along with the many females in the crowd who stood there drooling.

"That lad's got something special." He leaned over to his friend Bobby the Boxer, shouting to make himself heard over the volume of the band. *One for the future*, he thought to himself.

At the end of the night as the band were packing up, he approached Pete Peterson, who was the youngest in the band.

"That was some nice playing tonight, lad."

Pete lit a cigarette. "Thanks man, glad you enjoyed it. Is this your gaff then?"

"Yes, I'm Gerry Fortuna, what do you think of it?"

"Cool place, man, good sound too," replied Pete. "Say, didn't you used to be on the door at The Cave? I'm sure I remember your face."

"Yes, I was, but they're the opposition now. I want you guys playing my club regularly; you're the best around and you bring in the punters. If you don't mind me asking, how come you don't sing more songs? You've got a good voice."

"Thanks man. Yeah, well, it's Johnny's band and he calls the shots, so I do as I'm told. Listen Gerry, it's been good talking to you but I gotta go. The van's about to leave and they won't wait if I'm not ready. I'll catch you next time, yeah?"

Pete picked up his guitar case and walked over to where a group of young girls were all waiting to speak to him. Gerry noticed how Johnny Rhodes seemed annoyed by the amount of attention Pete was receiving.

Yeah, he thought again, *definitely one for the future.*

CHAPTER TWO

PETE PETERSON had been playing in local bands since he was fourteen, and in 1964, aged sixteen, he was approached by legendary singer Johnny Rhodes.

Pete had only recently started work in a clothes store in the city centre, when Johnny walked in one Monday morning. Renowned for being a snappy dresser, he was wearing a smart, grey velvet, regency-style jacket, tight blue jeans and black leather winkle-picker boots. Pete recognised him straight away – he'd seen the Daybreaks playing at The Cave at the weekend. Johnny was looking at some new Slim Jim ties that had just come in. He chose a red one and approached Pete.

"Hi, you're Pete Peterson aren't you? My name's Johnny Rhodes and I've heard really good reports about your playing. I need a new guitarist for my band and wondered if you fancied coming down to do an audition."

"Wow, yeah," stuttered Pete, taken completely by surprise. "That would be great. When were you thinking?"

"Tonight at The Cave, d'you know it?"

"Yeah, I was in there the other night."

"Good, be there for seven with your guitar," said Johnny. He walked off, leaving the tie on the counter.

Pete's boss, Mr. Brown, came over as Johnny left through the revolving door. "Who was that?"

"Johnny Rhodes, Mr. Brown; he's a well-known singer."

"I've never heard of him. And tell him next time he comes in, not to handle the merchandise unless he wants to buy it. Whoever he is."

Pete's friend, who'd been to see the Daybreaks with him on Saturday, came over. "Was that Johnny Rhodes you were talking to just then?"

"Yeah, and he's asked me to go down to audition for his band tonight."

"That's fantastic, go for it mate. Just think. No. More. Mr. Brown!"

Pete hadn't thought of that. What would he tell his parents? He decided not to say anything yet; he probably wouldn't get the gig anyway.

That night after he'd had his tea, he made the excuse he was going for band practice with his mates. Instead he caught the bus into town with his guitar, and got off a stop before The Cave. He didn't want to be seen getting off the bus, and wasn't going to let on that he didn't have a driving licence.

It had all happened so quickly he hadn't had time to be nervous, but walking into the club and meeting the other members of the band, he suddenly wasn't quite so confident. They were all a lot older than him and much more experienced. They nodded as he came in, pointing to the amp that was there for him to use: a brand-new Marshall. He'd only ever seen one in the music shop in town; had never actually played through one. His hands were shaking as he tuned his guitar. But he needn't have worried; the guys were great, and in no time at all they were jamming on an old Chuck Berry song.

Johnny arrived, did the formal introductions, and soon they were going through some of the songs Pete had heard them play at the weekend. Pete felt it had gone really well and Johnny seemed happy, coming over to talk to him at the end of the session.

"That was great Pete, I was really impressed. How would you like to become a full- time member of the Daybreaks?"

"Wow, yeah I'd love to."

"Right, well I know it's a bit short notice, but we're off to the South of France next week for three months, so if you're up for it, the job's yours. Oh, and you'll need a passport," said Johnny. "You do have one?"

"Yeah of course," replied Pete. Luckily he'd been away to Lloret de Mar for two weeks the previous year with his parents, and had had to apply for one. *This is gonna be great,* he thought to himself as Johnny and the others began to pack up their equipment. *A trip to the South of France and I get paid as well!*

"So you'd better start learning our sets," said Johnny. "We're contracted for four forty-five-minute sets a night! Here's a list of the songs we'll be playing and all the keys. We leave on Friday night. The van'll pick you up and then we're driving down to Dover to catch the overnight ferry."

The following morning at the clothes shop, Pete announced he was leaving on Friday: Mr. Brown wasn't at all pleased. But Pete's parents were very supportive; his dad had been a pianist in the big band era and encouraged him all he could.

The van picked him up at teatime on the Friday, and his mum had given him a flask and some sandwiches as he climbed in the back. The guys had taken the rise out of him at first, but when he unwrapped the mini feast she'd prepared and offered it round, he noticed no one refused.

The crossing on the ferry had thankfully been smooth, and after clearing French customs they finally got under way. Pete had never experienced driving on the right-hand side before and was thankful it wasn't him in the driving seat. Their van wasn't the newest or fastest, and it had taken most of the weekend to get to St Tropez. By the time they finally arrived they were all shattered, but the sun was shining, and they had a huge villa provided by the club owners as part of their agreement. It even had its own pool surrounded by orange and lemon trees.

Pete quickly became an integral part of the Daybreaks and was soon doing his share of vocals with Johnny. The open-air club, Le Soleil, was amazing. Situated in a fantastic position on a promontory overlooking the Mediterranean, it was filled every night with beautiful women. On a couple of occasions it was rumoured there were famous film stars in the club - even Mick Jagger one night - but Pete never saw them. At sixteen he was the youngest in the band, and began to realise he could use his youthful looks to his advantage. The word went round St Tropez that the English band at Le Soleil was the one to see. With the club packed every night, some of the most attractive women Pete had ever seen were queuing up to meet him after the show.

It was the swinging sixties – sex was free and easy. Pete was enjoying himself. The other members of the band were also participating in the fun, although Johnny had caused a few rows: he seemed irritated by Pete's popularity. Johnny was the bandleader after all and didn't like being overshadowed. A problem was also becoming apparent: Pete's new- found enjoyment of drugs, which, like sex, were freely available.

He was usually fine during the gig, restricting his drug taking to marijuana after the show. Then one night he turned up the worse for wear – he'd recently been seeing a girl who had introduced him to cocaine – his playing was dreadful and he looked a mess. Johnny was furious and confronted Pete after the first set.

"What the hell are you playing at Pete?" he said as they came off stage into the dressing room. "Can't you see you're putting the whole gig in jeopardy?"

"Be cool man," mumbled Pete, but a couple of the other band members joined in.

"Can't you see what you're doing to yourself?" said Jim the drummer. "Your playing's rubbish and you look like shit! It's you who needs to be cool!"

"Wow, you're freaking me out man," replied Pete, but Johnny joined in.

"OK Pete here's the deal," he said. "You either pack in the drugs or you're out! The owners of the club are really strict, and if they see you on stage like that again we'll all get fired!"

This had an immediate sobering effect on Pete; he sat down and started to cry. "Guys, I'm sorry," he blubbered. "I don't want to lose this. I'll be cool I promise, it's all I've ever wanted to do."

By now it was time for the band to go back on for their second set, and they all left the dressing room except for Pete. It wasn't until halfway through the set that he came back on and started to play. Johnny approached him as they were coming off stage, but Pete put his hands up and stopped him before he had chance to speak.

"Guys, I just want you to know the drugs are history, and I'm back," he said with an exaggerated bow.

The Daybreaks finished their contract at Le Soleil without any further incidents. Pete limited his vices to sex and alcohol, which he enjoyed in abundance, and at the end of their three-month stint they returned to the UK.

Playing four sets a night for three months had been a great experience, and they were now one of the most solid bands around. Suddenly, they were being offered bookings at prestigious venues like The Coliseum, and supporting famous bands from all over the country, as well as returning to play at The Cave.

Another club had opened while they were in St Tropez – The Hideout. It was owned by the former head doorman of The Cave, Gerry Fortuna, and he had contacted Johnny to book the Daybreaks as soon as they returned home. He was a big supporter of the local music scene, renowned for his taste in music and his ability to spot talent. He made sure that the Daybreaks played the Hideout at least a couple of times a month, and they quickly built-up a following, which as far as Gerry was concerned was good for business.

Much to the chagrin of Harry Castle and the Bartons, The Hideout was becoming known in the city as the place to go to for the best music, and great local bands like the Daybreaks. By the end of the year, the club was firmly established as a top venue, and the business was flourishing. Gerry always tried to be one step ahead of the opposition, so he decided to expand. He opened up a new bar, converted from the old offices upstairs above the club.

Gerry wanted it to be exclusive and had designed a special entrance, which was accessed via a lift lined with cream leather. Two doormen would make sure the guests were suitably dressed, and the fixtures and fittings would give it a luxurious feel. It also meant he could justify charging more for the alcohol. He opened Georgie's – his private members' club – in April 1966. It was named after his favourite footballer, George Best, and after much negotiation the man himself came down and officially opened the bar. He turned up slightly worse for wear, which considering he was playing at the weekend, was surprising – but it didn't stop him drinking copious amounts of vodka and posing for photographs with all the guests.

It was a spectacular night with a 'who's who' of well-known faces from TV, sport and showbiz turning out. Even a couple of the Bartons had turned up, although Harry Castle had declined. Interestingly, Gerry had received an invitation request from the recently appointed chief constable, George Williams, so seeing it as his opportunity to build a relationship with the law, he had been more than happy to oblige.

Gerry had been fortunate that up to now there had been no major trouble at The Hideout. Of course there were always the lads who'd had a few too many on band nights, but that was always dealt with by his doormen. However, he'd heard rumours that a notorious gangster in London was planning to make a move on other territories. Gerry wasn't fazed, but it was a good idea to have direct communications with the local police; George Williams had been happy to chat at the opening night of Georgie's and had become a regular visitor.

Georgie's was a big success, and after a couple of months it was busy most nights, but unsatisfied, Gerry started to look for a gimmick to entice more customers. He liked the idea of topless barmaids. It was really popular in the clubs in London, and he decided to introduce one to Georgie's. He'd put an advert in the local press, but to date hadn't had much success. Then quite late on one Friday night, a club DJ he knew came in with a few friends. He made a point of giving free memberships to DJs as they were always useful to know. He was at the bar talking to George Williams and a couple of other men, when he couldn't help noticing the attractive redhead who came in with the DJ.

CHAPTER THREE

NINETEEN-YEAR-OLD Janine Burke was out of work again. It was the story of her life: she didn't seem to be able to hold down a job for more than six months. She'd just been fired from her job in Mepham's department store, where she'd worked on the make- up counter. It was a drag, because she'd always been able to keep up her glamorous appearance with the freebies she had access to. She'd lost count of the number of jobs she'd had since leaving school. The problem was her inability to get to work on time in the morning, mainly due to spending most nights out in the clubs. She loved music and dancing. Especially dancing. She could lose herself in the sounds. Her favourite music was Motown, and as soon as the DJ played the latest Tamla record, she was the first up on the dance floor.

Janine was a bubbly fun-loving girl born in Ballykobh, a small town in Southern Ireland, who had moved over to the UK with her family when she was ten years old. As far as she could remember, her dad had been a photographer for the local paper and regularly met with a group of men at her house to talk about what was going on. But he'd suddenly announced one day they had to pack up and come to England, and she'd had to leave all her friends behind. It had been tough at first, with the children at the new schools always making fun of her accent; even though, thanks to the Irish education system, she was far in advance with her schoolwork. But she was a tough girl, and along with her sister Jackie, had always given as good as she got. Her dad eventually found a job working for the local newspaper and was now the main photographer in the area. He still went to the Irish club a couple of nights a week for his Guinness, and often talked about the old country; although his interest in Ireland had waned since they'd left.

Janine was still living at home with her parents, and had had a succession of boyfriends, although her forceful character and occasionally fiery temper, ensured none of her relationships had lasted more than a couple of months. She was just under six feet tall, with shoulder length red hair, but her most striking feature was her amazing emerald green eyes. They could hold you entranced and Janine knew it; often using them to her advantage, especially when she wanted something.

One Friday night, as the club Janine was in was closing, the DJ (who had a bit of a thing for her), asked her to join him and a group of friends at Georgie's, the new place in town. Janine had been in The Hideout a few times, but never in the leather-lined lift that took you to the private members' club above, so she jumped at the opportunity. Better yet, the DJ was a member so she wouldn't have to pay. She was a little apprehensive; she'd heard that Georgie's was pretty exclusive, but she was wearing a smart new outfit she'd bought that week and felt good. The tan suede mini skirt she had on showed off her legs, and the matching fitted jacket was really stylish.

Stepping out of the lift, they were met by a large muscular doorman who checked them over before allowing them to pass along a corridor lined with photos of Gerry Fortuna and celebrities from the worlds of entertainment, sport and politics. At the end, another doorman welcomed them into the sumptuously decorated private members' club – its low lighting and expensive furnishings giving it an atmosphere of exclusivity. Once inside, it was everything Janine imagined a luxury club should be. The people, the clothes, the style. This was it! This was where she wanted to be!

There were several large booths around the edge of the room, and leather sofas spread across the rest of the club. The bar was along one wall at the back. Sitting with the DJ and friends in one of the booths, she recognised the owner standing at the bar; seizing her chance she walked over to him and the group he was with.

"Hello, Mr. Fortuna. I'm Janine Burke. I just thought I'd tell you what a fantastic club you have."

"Well, Janine, it's nice of you to say so," replied Gerry; her beauty had not escaped him. "Can I get you a drink?"

"That's really kind," said Janine. "I love champagne!"

Gerry smiled to himself, *she has nerve too*, and turning to the group of men he was with said, "Gentlemen, will you excuse me?" He went behind the bar to the chiller and removed a bottle of champagne from the top shelf. "Well, if you like champagne you'd better have some of this then," he said, removing the cork with no more than the barest hiss. He filled a glass and gave it to Janine, who he noticed, never took her eyes off him as she took a mouthful.

"Wow!" she said as she took the glass from her lips. "Jeez, that's better than the normal stuff I drink."

"Well, I only serve the best," said Gerry with a smile, guessing she had probably only tasted Moët before. 'Rock'n'roll mouthwash' as it was called in the trade.

"Sure I've had champagne before, but nothing like that," said Janine, taking another sip. "It's like nectar."

"Vintage Bollinger, Janine; best in the house," he replied as he put the bottle into a bucket of cold water and added a few ice cubes.

"Aren't you going to join me?" she asked. Gerry was pouring himself a glass of Coca-Cola.

"No thanks. I don't drink, but don't let me stop you," replied Gerry.

"That's a bit strange," she whispered to herself. "A club owner who doesn't drink. Don't think I've ever come across that before!"

Gerry heard her. "Well, it's a long story; remind me to tell you sometime," he said, pulling up a stool next to her. "So is this the first time you've been in Georgie's?"

"Yes, I've been dancing in The Hideout a few times but I've never been up here. It's a bit too expensive for me," sighed Janine.

We'll have to remedy that, Gerry thought to himself. "So what do you do for a living then, Janine?" he asked.

"Well to be honest, right now, nothing," she replied. "I've just been fired from my last job in Mepham's, so I'm looking for something new. Why, do you have any vacancies for a hard-working girl?" She raised her eyebrows and fluttered her eyelashes.

This could be my lucky night, thought Gerry.

"Well, I might have something that would interest a woman like yourself," he said. "I'm looking for a very special kind of person to work here, and it could just be right up your street."

"Go on then, I'm all ears."

"I'm looking to introduce a bit of glamour into Georgie's and I need a barmaid... with a difference." He wondered if he'd overdone the pitch.

Janine was curious. "So what's the difference?"

"She needs to be topless," said Gerry. "It's all the rage down in London, but we'd be the first in the city. I'm prepared to pay well. No funny business, all above board!"

14

He could tell she was quite shocked, but she did her best not to let it show. "Well, I'd have to think about it," she said. "For a start, what do you mean by pay well?"

"How does thirty quid a week sound? You wouldn't get that at Mepham's."

"Yeah well maybe, but I'm gonna have to put up with a load of your lecherous punters ogling me. I'd want at least forty quid."

This woman's got some balls and I like her, but let's see how far I can go, thought Gerry.

"Hmm, that sounds a bit steep to me, and I do have a couple of other girls in mind," he lied. Then, after a short pause; "What about thirty-five?"

"Would that be including a taxi home every night?"

Gerry smiled and nodded his head. "You know what, you drive a hard bargain! Yes, a taxi home every night."

"Then you've got a deal. For thirty-five quid a week, I don't care who sees my tits," said Janine, and shook Gerry's hand. It was a firm handshake too, something that Gerry's father had taught him was important. 'You can always trust someone with a strong handshake,' he'd said, when Gerry was young.

"Hang on, I thought you said you'd have to think about it?" asked Gerry, now playing with Janine.

"Yeah, well I did," she replied. "And as you said, I wouldn't get it at Mepham's. So, when do I start?"

"How about next week?"

"That suits me fine," said Janine. "And let's face it, the outfit's not going to be too much trouble, is it?"

They both laughed and Gerry topped up Janine's glass. "See you Monday, then. We open at ten o'clock." He smiled as she walked back over to her friends. Little did he know how his life was going to change.

The next day Janine met up with her younger sister Jackie in town. Suddenly, last night's agreement with Gerry didn't seem such a good idea. Jackie was always the sensible one. She married her childhood sweetheart shortly after leaving school and had two children. Like Janine, she was beautiful, but with short blonde hair and blue eyes.

"Jesus, Janine, have you gone out of your tiny mind?" exploded Jackie as they sat in the coffee shop where they met every weekend. "I mean, what are Mammy and Da going to say?"

"They don't have to find out," replied Janine. "Nobody I know goes in Georgie's, and if you keep your mouth shut it'll be fine. And anyway, I'm old enough to make my own decisions."

"Yeah well I think you might find our Da'll have something to say about it," said Jackie.

"Well the money's great. Twice as much as I've ever made before, so maybe I can finally get my own place and a bit of independence. I mean it's OK living at home, but I want a bit of freedom and this could be my opportunity. You're all right married to John, and with the kids it's all happy families. But I want something new, something exciting and I think I might have found it! You promise you won't say anything?"

"Course not! I wish it was me, you think playing happy families is a doddle? What I wouldn't give to be there too."

"So why don't you then?" replied Janine. "You've got a great figure; blokes still look at you. I've seen them. Just think, you and me, we'd clean up!"

"Whoa, are you mad! John would kill me, and anyway you're the showoff in the family. All I ask is that you're careful. You're going to be mixing with some pretty heavy people. That Gerry Fortuna has a reputation and some of his friends are well known around town."

"Sis, trust me, I can do this. And who knows, it could be the beginning of a new life!" said Janine as they hugged and said goodbye.

CHAPTER FOUR

IT WAS Monday evening, and Gerry was already in the bar with the two doormen stocking up, when Janine walked in. She was both excited and apprehensive about the situation she'd talked herself into. Sure, she'd had plenty of jobs where she met people; being a barmaid wasn't a problem. She'd been one once before in her local pub and had enjoyed it. She'd also been complimented on her figure many times by previous boyfriends – but to walk around in front of strangers without her top on was a completely new proposition.

As she pressed the button in the leather-lined lift to Georgie's, her heart was beating fast. But when the doors opened, and she walked down the corridor admiring all the photos of Gerry and his celebrity guests, she was in a different world. This was her chance. She could be meeting some of those celebrities, albeit with her top off.

Gerry snapped her out of her thoughts, "You got here then, babe?" he said from behind the bar. "We're just stocking up ready for tonight."

"Is there anywhere I can get changed?" asked Janine.

"What do you need a changing room for? All you've got to do is slip your top off! Oh, and by the way, there's a photographer coming in later to get a few snaps."

The look on Janine's face took Gerry by surprise.

"OK, lets stop right there!" she said, storming up to the bar and leaning into Gerry's face, her green eyes flashing. "We need to get a few ground rules sorted out before we go any further!"

Gerry heard a cough and the sound of footsteps, as the doormen discretely disappeared down the corridor leaving them alone. Traitors! he thought.

"Firstly we never made any agreement about a photographer. What's he gonna take my picture for?" said Janine.

"It's for the local press, a bit of publicity for the club."

"Oh Jesus, I can't be in the paper! My dad will kill me if he finds out!"

"Well that's a shame," said Gerry, realising he now had the upper hand. "And there was me thinking I was dealing with a professional. Instead

I've employed an amateur who has to get her dad's permission. Sorry love, this ain't gonna work, we may as well call it quits right now."

"OK look, just hang on," said Janine backtracking. She knew she might have slightly overstepped the mark. "You just took me by surprise saying about the paper. I won't have to take my top off for the photo will I?"

"No, course not, the Post isn't X-rated yet," laughed Gerry. "Look, calm down. How's about I bung you an extra twenty quid for the photo, and you can use my office to change in?"

"Well, that sounds better already. But one thing you'll need to get used to; I won't be pushed around."

Yeah, said Gerry to himself smiling, *those damn green eyes'll be the death of me!*

Gerry had smoothed the waters, and now with a glass of champagne in her hand, Janine was laughing as the photographer snapped away. He'd talked her into a compromise; she'd opened the top of her blouse a little more than normal, but it still looked decent enough that her dad wouldn't complain. At least she was happy, although Gerry wasn't bothered. Either way he'd got the result he wanted. With the photo session completed, Janine slipped into Gerry's office to fix her makeup and get ready. She had bought a new mini skirt made from strips of different coloured leather, from her favourite stall in the Oasis market. She was just checking herself in the mirror when Gerry walked in.

"Very nice, babe, very nice," he said, smiling at her reflection in the mirror.

Surprised, Janine's first reaction was to cover herself up. Then she realised she was about to walk out into the club topless and started to laugh.

"Come on," said Gerry, seeing the joke and laughing with her. "Your clients are waiting." He took her hand and led her out into the club, which was now packed.

"We've never been this busy," whispered Gerry in her ear. "You must be my lucky charm." *This is gonna be great,* he thought, scanning all the punters.

"Yeah, and don't you forget it", replied Janine under her breath. Then with her most alluring smile, she thought to herself, *I think I'm gonna like*

It had been fantastic publicity. The photo had made the front page of the Post, and word had quickly got round the city. Janine settled into her role as the main attraction, and business was booming upstairs at Georgie's. At the same time downstairs, The Hideout was gaining a reputation for great live music.

One night however, a minor incident made Gerry realise he would have to keep an eye on security. It had been a busy night with the Daybreaks playing to a full house, and usually the doormen made sure only members were allowed upstairs. But Janine became aware of a table of four young guys who'd had a few too many to drink. They'd been downstairs watching the Daybreaks and had somehow managed to gain access to her bar. It wouldn't have bothered her normally, except one of the guys was becoming a nuisance, constantly making references to her boobs, and getting louder as the night wore on. Gerry had been told what was happening and strode into the bar accompanied by a doorman and his friend, Bobby the Boxer. Bobby was well known locally and occasionally hung out at the club. Gerry walked up to the table and asked the guys to leave. Three of the group immediately acknowledged it would be a wise move to do as they were asked and got up to go; but the one who had been annoying Janine decided to take matters into his own hands and tried to confront Gerry. Before he had time to think, Gerry stood aside so the doorman and Bobby could grab the troublemaker by his arms and drag him out of the room to the emergency exit, where he was unceremoniously dumped through the doors and down the stairs. Janine had never witnessed this kind of situation before and was shocked that Gerry had calmly folded his arms and watched. Laughing, the doorman and Bobby returned, pulling the doors closed behind them.

"Hang on a minute, Gerry," said Janine. "I know he was a bit out of order, but there was no need for that!"

Gerry was annoyed that she'd interfered and decided to put her firmly in her place. "Anyone who comes into my club and doesn't behave, will pay the price, he was lucky he could still walk! Listen, in future, you mind your business and keep to your side of the bar and leave this side to me! And it's Mr. Fortuna. Now, a Coca-Cola for me and whatever the boys would like, Janine, please."

Janine was momentarily lost for words, but she'd noticed the punters were leaving. "Well, Mr. Fortuna," she snapped sarcastically. "That was certainly a great way to end the party!"

Gerry, Bobby and the doorman, at the end of the bar, were laughing and carrying on as if nothing had happened as Janine looked across at them and shook her head.

The relationship between Gerry and Janine had numerous ups and downs over the next few months. Gerry soon discovered Janine's fiery temper; if things didn't suit her she wouldn't hesitate in saying so. On more than one occasion they'd had blazing rows across the bar in front of the customers, and word was spreading that they were becoming a separate cabaret show on their own. This concerned Janine at first, but when Bobby the Boxer told her that people were starting to come on the off chance of seeing a row, she realised she could use it to her advantage.

"Listen Janine," Bobby said one night, "the boss really likes you; I've watched him. Don't get upset when he has a go at you; have a go back. He respects you and I think he enjoys it. I know I do, and I've watched the punters and they do too."

So, she started to encourage a disagreement every now and then, especially if there was a decent crowd in, and even though there might be the odd glass broken, it was worth it to keep the punters happy.

Bobby was a friendly guy who was beginning to make a name for himself on the local boxing circuit. He had become a good friend of Gerry's and was a regular in Georgie's; and because he was usually in training he didn't drink alcohol, which was handy when there was trouble. He'd helped the doormen downstairs sort out a few rowdy customers once or twice. In fact when Janine thought about what he'd said, and a few things that had happened recently, she realised that maybe she was becoming fond of Gerry too. Firstly, he'd decided that she didn't need to work topless anymore. The gimmick had started to fade and he wanted her to be herself. Also, he'd started to give her the occasional lift home instead of letting her wait for a taxi. He was good company, and riding home in his Rolls-Royce or Rollie as he called it, was really nice. She made sure she kept everything on a professional level though, always making him drop her at the end of her driveway. She'd finally left home and had her own bedsit in a nice area of Edgerton, overlooking the reservoir. It wasn't cheap, but since she'd managed to get Gerry to pay her a good wage, she could afford it, and had lovingly furnished it with second-hand bargains she'd found in the local market.

Things had been running pretty smoothly for Gerry with both the club and the bar turning over a good profit, but as with most things, he suspected it wouldn't last. It was a Tuesday night, and there were only a few guests upstairs, mainly regulars and friends of Gerry's. Downstairs was closed as there was no band on, so Gerry on such nights had given his doormen the night off as it was so quiet. He would take care of things himself if necessary. He was sitting in the corner at a table with Bobby, when two men wearing long black coats walked into the bar, stopped in the middle of the room and looked around. Suddenly, one of them whipped out a long-handled sledgehammer from under his coat and smashed it down on a table, sending glasses flying everywhere. A few of the customers screamed. The other opened his coat, revealing a sawn-off shotgun. He walked up to the bar and pointed the weapon at Janine. He had a prominent scar running from the corner of his mouth to his ear.

"Well, this is very cosy," he said, leaning on the bar waving the gun in the air before firing it into the ceiling above Janine's head.

Gerry tensed, on his guard, waiting to see what happened next.

"Good evening all. My name is Sammy the Scar, and my friend here is Harry the Hammer – for obvious reasons." They both laughed at their little joke, which really riled Gerry. "Now I have your attention, I bring a message from our boss, Mr. Jimmy Walsh. He would be very happy to meet Mr. Fortuna with a view to discussing his future security arrangements, thus avoiding any repeats of tonight's little episode."

Gerry noticed Janine was standing rigid behind the bar, and all the blood had drained from her face. He glanced at Bobby, and without saying a word they both leapt up from their table, moving across the room with lightning speed.

Bobby grabbed hold of the sledgehammer, wrestling Harry to the floor. With all his training Bobby was supremely fit, and quickly gained the upper hand, and a punch to the man's throat with frightening speed and accuracy, rendered him unconscious.

At the same time, Gerry had dived across the bar at Sammy, knocking the shotgun from his hands; without thinking he instinctively grabbed up an empty bottle on the bar, smashing it over Sammy's head, punching the dazed and defenseless man's face relentlessly. Bobby who had rushed over to help now found himself trying to stop Gerry, who, uttering deep growls, seemed in a trance. He shrugged Bobby off, but Janine screamed at Gerry to stop.

Using all his strength, Bobby finally managed to pull Gerry away from what was now a bloody mess slumped against the bar. Gerry stood there breathing heavily covered in blood. He didn't understand what had happened to him, but he knew he was excited. His heart was racing, but strangely he felt sexually aroused, and it showed.

Bobby had the presence of mind to go behind the bar to make a phone call to Mick, one of the doormen who lived close by. He rushed in moments later and stared at the mess, but at least Gerry had calmed down and was back in control. Now he had to get things sorted out and quickly.

"Janine, don't just stand there, make sure all the guests are OK, then get them out," he barked. "Bobby, you and Mick help me get these two bags of shit downstairs. That Jimmy Walsh is gonna regret the day he tried to muscle in on my patch!"

It took them the best part of an hour to restore some semblance of order to the bar, and later, after Gerry had changed into one of the clean shirts he kept in his office, they decided to leave the rest of the clearing up until the next morning.

In Gerry's car on the way home; Janine was still concerned about what had just happened. "Listen, Mr. Fortuna, what happened tonight needs to be reported to the Police," she said.

"Don't worry, babe, it's all under control." Gerry was trying to sound relaxed even though he was far from it. "But I will give my friend, the chief constable, a call. Oh and it's Gerry now we're out of the club."

"OK, Gerry then." said Janine. "But that was scary. We could have been hurt. I've never been so frightened in all my life. He pointed that gun straight at me!" She was looking at him in a way he found strangely enticing.

"It'll take more than a couple of jumped-up fancy boys to bother me," he said, and reached over to rest his hand on her leg. "But it's nice to know you're concerned."

He wasn't quite sure what happened, but an electric shock shot through him as he touched her. She looked back at him and he knew she could see how excited he was. Suddenly, she was shouting at him. "Pull over, pull over now!" He saw a side street to their left and turned into it.

"Get in the back," she ordered.

For once Gerry did as he was told without any argument. Janine quickly slipped off her knickers and climbed in pulling the door closed behind her. Feverishly working on his zip, she had his erection in her hand in seconds, and before he had time to think, she had straddled his legs and lowered herself onto him.

She didn't know how long it lasted - it could have been seconds; it could have been hours - but Janine's pent-up emotions finally burst and she shuddered to a climax. She climbed off Gerry and saw he was still excited. As she lowered her head, there was a smile on her lips. *You might fight like an animal, but I know how to tame you Mr. Gerry Fortuna!* she thought to herself, as she slowly teased him until he was totally spent.

As he drove Janine home, Gerry wondered how things could ever be the same between them. What should be his next move? Whatever happened, he knew his plans had to include Janine.

The following morning at Janine's insistence, Gerry phoned the Chief Constable, George Williams, who set up an official meeting at the club that afternoon. George turned up with a new DCI called Ray Law, recently transferred from Liverpool and suggested he become the liaison between him and Gerry. Ray Law was a tall, young, good-looking black guy, and Gerry noticed how he seemed to watch Janine's every move. *Something I'll need to keep an eye on if DCI Law is to be a regular visitor,* he thought to himself.

Getting down to the subject of the specific incident, Gerry's show of force had obviously made Jimmy Walsh think twice about causing any more trouble. George had spoken to his opposite number in the Met who'd arranged a similar meeting in London. While they were discussing what happened the previous night, a message came through to George, that Jimmy Walsh had suffered a mysterious loss of memory about there ever having been any incident in the first place.

Gerry finally explained that he'd been receiving threats for quite a while and had chosen to ignore them. Obviously thinking Gerry would be a push over, Jimmy Walsh had sent a couple of his soldiers up onto Gerry's patch, and was planning on moving in. Fortunately, after what had happened, a truce was now agreed, and no further trouble would be coming from down South. Gerry could relax for the time being, but as George Williams pointed out; "In your line of business, you never knew where the next threat will come from!" Years later, those words would come back to haunt him.

Gerry and Janine were now seeing a lot of each other outside of the club, and word was going round that they were an item. This pleased Gerry; even though he was ten years older than her, it didn't seem to matter – they were having fun. He eventually asked her to move in with him. It seemed like a good idea at the time. Except he hadn't predicted his sister's reaction – she still lived in the house they'd been left by their father. Estelle or Stella as she was known, was a year younger than Gerry, and had taken their mother's alcohol-induced death badly. Unfortunately, because Gerry hadn't been around to look after her, she too had started to drink; mostly vodka.

Gerry had never really had a serious girlfriend before, only lots of casual relationships, which had never lasted more than a couple of months. Stella had suddenly realised that for once he was serious about someone and she felt threatened. She had taken an instant dislike to Janine, and verbally abused her at every opportunity about their age difference. Gerry had explained about Stella's demons and Janine did her best to avoid her, but he was becoming more and more depressed about the situation and finally decided something had to be done.

"Never had you down as a cradle snatcher, Bro," Stella slurred one evening as Gerry and Janine were leaving the house. "And a Paddy too."

Gerry stopped in the doorway and turned slowly, giving her an icy look. "OK Stella this has gone far enough. I've had about as much as I can stand," he said. "I want you to listen very carefully to what I'm about to say."

Stella looked at him with bleary eyes, holding a tumbler of vodka.

"I didn't want to have to do this, but you give me no choice. I've made arrangements for you to be cared for. I can't have you abusing Janine anymore. For once in my life I feel like I have the chance of a serious relationship with someone, and you're not going to spoil it. So tomorrow, I'm taking you to see the place where you're going to live from now on."

Stella was silent as she stared at him. Then she stood up unsteadily, spat out the word "Bitch!" and wobbled out of the room without looking at Janine.

During the drive into the club Gerry never said a word, and Janine knew it was best not to comment. The following day he took Stella to the place he'd arranged for her, and by the end of the week she had moved out of the house and had her own room in a luxurious care home in the countryside. It had been a big decision for Gerry, and Janine could see it had upset him, but she did her best to support him when he needed her and the rest of the time allowed him space to deal with it in his own way.

Fortunately, Gerry soon found something to take his mind off his personal problems. After one of the regular jam nights at The Hideout, Gerry had come into the club with Bobby and noticed Pete Peterson slumped at the bar, drowning his sorrows.

"All right then, penny for them!" said Gerry. He and Pete had become good friends.

Pete lit a cigarette and drew deeply on it. "That bastard Johnny Rhodes has just announced he's leaving to join the Blues Rebels, and now I'm back to square one."

Gerry pulled up a barstool and sat down next to him. "Look lad, how many times have I told you, you don't need a lead singer. You can do it yourself. Why don't you look around the scene in the city and pick the best young players and form a new band? The time's right for a different sound and you can be the one to make it. You can use the club to rehearse any time you want. All I ask is you play a gig here every so often."

Pete looked at Gerry and put down the glass he was nursing. He thought for a moment. "You know what? That's a bloody good idea. I was recently talking to Tony and Billy Waters, the twins in the band that played here the other night. They're dying to try something new – great players and young too."

"So what are you waiting for?" said Gerry.

25

Pete got in touch with the twins the next day and put Gerry's idea to them. Over a cup of coffee they started to make plans. "The way I see it, we've got nothing to lose," said Pete. "I'm tired of playing the same old covers every night, and now Johnny's left, the time is right to start something new. I've written a load of songs that he wouldn't listen to, but I know you guys would be perfect."

Tony was skeptical. "What about this Gerry guy? I've heard plenty of stories about him from when he was at The Cave. People say he's a bit of a thug. Do you trust him?"

"Gerry's cool," replied Pete. "He's a big music fan and he digs what I do. Plus, he's offered us the use of the club for free, to rehearse any time we want."

"Seems good to me," said Billy. "I'm up for a change, and I know Jess Peters is bored shitless with that crap band he's with. We should give him a call. He's a great rhythm player and sings too."

Tony still wasn't convinced. "So what's the catch then, man? There's always a catch. When it sounds too good to be true, it always is."

"You're such a cynical bastard at times," said Pete. "All Gerry said to me was we could repay him by playing a gig here every now and then. Look we've got nothing to lose; are you up for giving it a go?"

Billy nodded and turned to Tony. "Bro what do you think? You'd kick yourself if you missed out."

"OK, I'm in," said Tony.

"Cool, I'll give Jess a call tonight," said Pete. "This is gonna be fuckin' big guys!"

Within a week the band was formed, and they started to rehearse some of Pete's original material. True to his word, Gerry gave them a set of keys to the club so they could come and go as they pleased. He came down a couple of times to watch, and one night after a rehearsal took Pete aside to have a chat.

"It's sounding amazing, lad, just like I thought it would. I told you you didn't need a lead singer. You're the main man. The one thing you need now is a strong name."

"Yeah, well we've been talking about that, and we thought The Flames sounded pretty cool," said Pete.

Gerry thought for a minute. "Hmm, The Flames. I love it! So now what we need to do is get you some gigs, and I mean proper gigs. There's only so long you can keep playing the clubs you've been doing up to now, including here. I know just the man to do it – he'll get you into some of those big venues down in London, that's where the real action is!"

Again, Gerry was true to his word, and the following week announced he'd invited Anders Neckermann, a Svengali-like character who was rapidly gaining a reputation in the music industry for finding and nurturing new talent, to come and hear them. It just so happened he was based in the same street as the famous Flamingo Club in Soho.

Anders turned up dressed head to toe in crushed red velvet; but more importantly he loved the band; so much so that he came up from London again the following week to sit in on their rehearsal. The first thing he did was encourage them to work on the new sound they were creating, suggesting they get away from the traditional vocal harmonies heard in so many of the Merseyside recordings, and look for an edgier rock style. Then together, they devised a much more exciting stage show involving smoke and pyrotechnics, which he felt suited the name The Flames.

The following month Anders got them their first gig at the Flamingo and they took the place by storm. Pete's songs were a breath of fresh air, and the music press loved them.

"That was amazing tonight guys." Anders had just about squeezed into their tiny dressing room. "There's a friend of mine here from the NME, and he's freaking out! For sure he's going to give you a great write up."

"That's great, but it would be a lot better if we could get a bigger dressing room," Tony moaned from the corner.

"Yeah and a few proper beers, instead of this lager crap they gave us," Billy chipped in waving an empty bottle.

"OK, OK, give me chance here, guys. It's your first gig; you're lucky I managed to persuade them to give you anything. Next time will be better, you'll see. The manager's already asking for you to come back. Trust me, it's gonna be big!"

Soon enough they were filling the Flamingo every week and all the big record labels in London were beginning to take notice. You couldn't open a copy of the NME or any other music publication without spotting a photo or review of The Flames. Anders certainly knew how to get a band into the press; his latest stunt - getting Pete photographed walking out of a top London hotel with Sophia Loren - was nothing short of sensational. The truth of the matter was, Anders had tipped the head porter fifty pounds to let him know when the film star and her entourage were due to leave and then he and Pete were waiting in reception with a photographer. All it took was for Pete to hold his nerve and walk up to her asking for her autograph, holding her arm while posing for the camera. It was all over in thirty seconds, but Anders had a worldwide scoop and Pete had his face on the front page of every national daily, with headlines claiming their ongoing relationship. Pure genius.

Suddenly, The Flames, and more to the point Pete Peterson, were becoming household names.

In 1968, under Anders' direction, they recorded their first album. It was well received and made the Top Ten; and they started planning their first major headline tour.

CHAPTER FIVE

WHILE PETE and his new band The Flames were setting the music scene alight, Gerry had an announcement of his own that he knew would surprise everyone. He'd been feeling for some time that his relationship with Janine was getting stronger, and he had made the decision to put it on a much firmer foundation. He'd secretly invited a few of his closest friends to Georgie's with the excuse it was a business announcement involving him and Janine.

On the night, Gerry had put on his best suit, which had intrigued Janine – he usually dressed quite casually when he was in the club. Then, when everyone had arrived, he stood up and asked Janine if she'd come round to the front of the bar. As the room went quiet, Gerry got down on one knee and produced a small box from his pocket. Inside was a huge solitaire diamond ring. With his heart pounding he asked her if she would marry him.

Janine had been stunned and momentarily speechless. Gerry thought he was going to have a heart attack. Then grabbing hold of him, she kissed him crying, "Yes, oh yes!"

Everybody cheered and Gerry shouted for drinks all round; he went behind the bar himself to crack open bottles of Janine's favourite Vintage Bollinger Champagne. He still refused any alcohol himself even though it was a special occasion, honouring the promise he'd made because of his mother. He felt sorry that Stella wasn't there to celebrate with him, but he knew it would only have caused trouble – and tonight he wanted to be happy.

The wedding was a star-studded affair, with the ceremony taking place at the cathedral in front of four hundred guests. In the weeks leading up to the event, Janine had almost driven Gerry crazy with her attention to detail in the planning. Their legendary arguments in Georgie's were happening on a nightly basis, and in the end he'd allowed her time off to deal with the arrangements, while he concentrated on the day-to-day running of the clubs.

Gerry too had been a pain, not knowing what he wanted to wear. Finally a customer recommended the exclusive London tailors, Anderson and

Sheppard, and eventually he'd settled on an amazing charcoal grey suit. He asked Bobby the boxer to be his best man. They'd struck up a firm friendship since the violent episode in Georgie's and Bobby had taken his responsibilities very seriously, liaising with Janine regarding all the arrangements. Nobody had ever known Bobby's surname, which turned out to be McGregor – and he surprised everyone by wearing a traditional kilt representing his family's official McGregor tartan.

When the big day finally arrived, Janine had looked incredible in an exquisite white Givenchy wedding dress made from the finest silk. Her sister Jackie was maid of honour, and had worn a trendy, cream Mary Quant shift dress with matching shoes. The outfit had caused major rows between her and Janine. Janine had wanted her to wear a full-length silk dress, but Jackie argued she would get more use from her choice, than a posh bridesmaid's dress that she'd never wear again. Janine wouldn't admit it, but she thought her sister looked beautiful. Her father had proudly walked her down the aisle, and then sat with her mother who was wearing the biggest hat anyone had ever seen.

Gerry and Bobby looked fantastic, and even though they were both noticeably shorter than Janine, it was never mentioned. Subtle arrangements had been made for Gerry to always be standing on a higher step when the official photographs were being taken.

Afterwards, a lavish reception was held at a magnificent sixteenth-century manor house in the Cotswolds, with the guests ferried from the cathedral in a fleet of coaches. The food was amazing and the speeches entertaining, with Bobby's being particularly amusing. He'd revealed later, that before he became a boxer he was a comedian performing in the local clubs. To finish off the night, the entertainment was provided by Pete Peterson and The Flames.

Gerry had been especially pleased that Pete had agreed to perform at the reception. They had just recorded their first album, and the following week were setting off on their maiden UK tour; so the guests were to be given an exclusive premiere of their brand new show as devised by Anders Neckermann.

Just because it was a wedding, they hadn't skimped on any of the production – complete with pyrotechnics. The performance was fantastic, and Gerry was sorry to leave before the end, but a chauffeur-driven limousine was waiting to whisk him and Janine to a private jet to take them to the South of France. Sadly, leaving early meant they missed the hilarious sight of Janine's father, stripped down to his trousers and braces dancing at the front of the stage with Janine's sister, while her mother slumped at their table swigging champagne straight from the bottle.

The couple were staying in a luxurious villa complete with its own private pool. It was perched on top of a hill just outside Cannes overlooking the Mediterranean, and even though Janine sensed Gerry had been nervous about leaving Bobby in charge back home, he finally managed to relax. They'd found a tiny street in the centre of Cannes which was lined with fabulous restaurants where they dined every night, feasting on fresh seafood and meat all cooked to perfection. Janine had loved the local aperitif she'd been introduced to; Kir Royale, made with creme de cassis and topped up with her favourite champagne.

During the sunny days by the pool, workaholic Gerry had spent his time lying on a sun lounger dreaming up new schemes; while Janine had read books, and built up a fantastic tan, to enhance her red hair and green eyes.

"Come on Ger, get in the pool, it's fabulous," Janine called as she floated lazily on a pink inflatable bed. "Give the plans a rest for once."

Gerry stood up and stretched before running and jumping in, causing a huge wave which caused Janine to fall in the water.

"I suppose you think that's funny," she spluttered, swimming to the side of the pool as he powered away in a strong crawl. Twenty lengths later he emerged dripping wet and walked over to where she lay soaking up the sun. It was fortunate they weren't overlooked, as she hooked her fingers into his trunks pulling them down in one quick movement. She teased him to an erection all the while looking up at him with a tantalising smile. *There's something about those eyes I can't resist,* he thought to himself, as he picked her up and walked back into the pool. Leaning on the side, she threw her head back as he untied the laces on either side of her bikini bottoms allowing them to float away. He lifted her legs up and pushed himself deep inside her. She used her heels on the cheeks of his bottom to control the speed of his thrusts and eventually with water splashing everywhere they climaxed together, sinking into the cooling water of the pool.

Back in the villa, Janine poured a glass of chilled champagne for herself and an ice- cold Coca-Cola for Gerry but his mind was once again on the plans he was formulating.

It had been an idyllic week, and they returned to a new home. Before the wedding, Gerry had bought a brand-new penthouse apartment on the top floor of a new development right in the heart of the city. It had the most amazing panoramic views from the huge balcony and was equipped with all the latest appliances. Janine loved it.

Gerry had decided to sell the old house now that Stella was settled in the care home. It held too many sad memories; he wanted to move on and start a new chapter in his life with Janine. Apart from their clothes, which had been packed and moved across to the new apartment, everything else was sold with the house. Although sorry to see it all go, Gerry was happy to draw a line and look to the future.

He already had the idea for his new music club planned out. There was a buzz in the city for soul and reggae music, which was becoming more and more popular and he was eager to cash in on the trend. He wanted to open a new venue called Rudi's, playing predominantly black music and featuring a Jamaican DJ called Mr. C (or Charles as he was known to his friends). Mr. C was gaining a name for himself in the clubs, and by getting him at Rudi's every night Gerry felt sure he'd bring his following with him. That way he'd have The Hideout concentrating on the latest pop and rock bands, while Rudi's could feature the new soul and reggae acts.

A couple of weeks later Gerry dropped a huge bombshell. He was closing Georgie's. It had been slowly losing custom over the past year, and he wanted to concentrate his energy and money on the new project. In his mind Janine didn't need to work there anymore, and there were plenty of other things for her to do. Or so he thought.

"What do you mean, you're closing Georgie's? What am I gonna do now?" she'd exploded, when he told her his plans over breakfast one morning. "Do you expect me to sit on my arse all day doing nothing?"

"I'm sorry babe, it's a business decision I need to make. The place has been losing money over the last year and I want to concentrate on Rudi's," explained Gerry as calmly as he could. "I'll keep it going until the end of the year, and we'll have a huge party on New Year's Eve as a send off. Then if you want, you can help with booking the bands at The

Hideout, they're always moaning they need another pair of hands."

"Yeah, well we'll have to see," she replied. "I don't like working in offices, I never have. I much prefer meeting people, that's why I enjoyed working behind the bar."

"Look I'm not keen on the idea of Mrs. Gerry Fortuna serving pints in one of my clubs. It was fine before we were married but things are different now," said Gerry, getting his coat and walking out the door. "I'll see you at the club later." *That didn't go as well as expected*, he thought, as he made the short trip to his office at Georgie's.

One of his plans was to convert Georgie's back to offices again, so he could get out of the tiny room he had at the moment. He'd convince Janine she could work in there as well. In the meantime, she could amuse herself going out with her pals. He didn't mind her going on the occasional trip down to London if it kept her happy and he was too busy sorting out the paperwork and plans for Rudi's. She'd understand once it was all sorted.

But Janine was becoming frustrated. She burst into tears after he'd left, and phoned one of her friends. They spent the rest of the day getting drunk. *Gerry won't be too pleased, but he can stick his club,* she thought, through her alcoholic haze.

When she'd married Gerry, they were a dynamic couple who were always seen out and about. Their sex life was wonderful, and he gave her whatever she wanted. But suddenly things had changed. Apart from his night off, which he spent relaxing in front of the TV watching films, she rarely saw him; and fur coats and champagne were no longer enough. She wasn't working any more, and even though he'd suggested she could help book the bands at The Hideout, she'd said no. She'd started going out more and more with her friends, and having the occasional trip down south which was fun: but she was bored. She wanted some action and Gerry didn't seem interested any more.

New Years Eve was a sad night at Georgie's. Janine had been out and bought a new red trouser suit specially for the occasion and had invited a few of her friends along. The club had been full, and now after they'd all gone it was just a cold and empty room. Lots of champagne had been drunk, mainly by Janine and her pals, and tears were shed as they locked the doors for the last time.

Gerry had tried to reason with her, saying that bigger things were just around the corner, but she was a nightmare to talk to after so much champagne. A few friends had come back to their apartment for a nightcap, and Gerry could sense Janine was up for a row.

"Sho what you're tryina shay, is I'm a lady'v leisure then, Ger, thad it?" Janine tried to pour herself another glass of champagne and was spilling more than was going in her glass.

"Look babe, I keep telling you there're big things on the way. 1969's gonna be great for us. Rudi's will blow 'em all away, you mark my words," said Gerry. "Let's have a toast!"

Bobby McGregor was there, along with Pete Peterson, George Williams and his wife, and a couple more of Janine's friends.

"C'mon then, lez drink to your success, 'n me doin' fuck all," said Janine, stumbling towards Gerry who was his usual sober self. He just managed to catch her before she fell over the sofa. "An' don' forget good old Georgie's," she mumbled as she slid rather ungracefully into an armchair, spilling her glass of champagne over her trouser suit and passed out.

Conversations stopped mid-sentence. There was an embarrassed silence.

"Time to go," George Williams suggested diplomatically to the others, and one by one they said goodnight to Gerry, wished him a Happy New Year again and left him alone with a snoring Janine.

Gerry surveyed the scene in their apartment. Tidying up could wait until the morning he thought, as he walked over to the huge window, which took up almost one side of the lounge. Sliding it back, he stepped out onto the balcony. She can think what she likes, he thought to himself as he took in the panoramic view, but Gerry Fortuna's gonna be the biggest name in this city. He stood there gazing out at the lights, suddenly feeling cold with just his shirt on. Turning back, he noticed Janine curled up on the armchair, and instead of trying to get her into bed, he covered her with a blanket and kissed her gently on the forehead. Turning off the lights, he climbed into their king-sized bed and closed his eyes. Yes, he thought to himself, this is just the start.

CHAPTER SIX

IN JANUARY, Pete decided to make a permanent move to London. He was getting fed up with the amount of travelling every week down to the Flamingo in Soho, and he was being asked more and more to perform on other artists' recording sessions, with the new breed of musicians he was getting to know. He'd already sung and played guitar on a couple of hit albums, and was enjoying the capital's bohemian lifestyle, although his band mates had noticed he was taking a lot of drugs again.

He'd made friends with a guitarist who was in one of the new bands on the psychedelic rock scene and was sharing a big old house in Kensington with him, a rock drummer and a bass player. The nights they weren't gigging were spent jamming and experimenting with various drugs which the drummer stashed in his ever-present shoulder bag.

The subject of drugs had also cropped up - in connection with Gerry's application for a licence for Rudi's – at recent meetings with George Williams and the council's licensing committee. There were concerns that more and more drug use was going on in clubs, and the police were regularly raiding venues in a bid to clamp down on it. The black music scene had a bad reputation, of which Gerry was well aware, and he was keen to make sure Rudi's didn't become part of it.

As for Janine, she seemed to have finally settled down, working a few days a week in The Hideout helping to book the bands – although she was out of the office more than she was in - spending time with her friends. It suited Gerry though. He was up to his eyes with the statutory planning forms for Rudi's, and everything else that went with opening a new club. He'd finally found the ideal premises a stone's throw from the railway station, just around the corner from their apartment. It was an old clothing warehouse, consisting of two large rooms, which he intended knocking into one. He'd convinced Mr. C that it would be a great career move to work at Rudi's, and word was already going round the city about the great new soul and reggae venue about to open.

Gerry had also met a very talented jazz musician playing at The Hideout, called Alex Mitchell. He prided himself on being able to spot talent, and just as with Pete Peterson, he felt that Alex had something special.

Along with the bass player and drummer, the Alex Mitchell Trio had wowed audiences and Gerry was impressed. Alex was an amazing pianist but as Gerry discovered, he also had a vast knowledge of the music industry, which Gerry felt he could use to his advantage.

It so happened there was a big charity event coming up at the Town Hall, that Gerry had agreed to organise. He'd been talking to Anders Neckermann about booking The Flames for it. With Rudi's taking up so much of his time, he decided to get Alex involved in helping him with the planning. There was the added bonus that Alex and the trio would open the first half of the show.

The timing couldn't have been better: The Flames had had their first number one in the charts the previous week and were hot property. Anders had tried to pull the gig, because the money Gerry had originally agreed to pay them was half what they could now command with a hit record, but Pete intervened and said they would honour the commitment. There had been a queue of fans stretching around the Town Hall when the booking office opened, and tickets for the show sold out within hours of going on sale. Alex had worked hard, and Gerry had been impressed with the way he negotiated great deals on the sound system and lighting. He'd also persuaded the other acts on the show to reduce their fees in aid of a charity which helped people with alcohol and drug problems, a cause close to Gerry's heart.

The charity show was a huge success. A capacity audience had been treated to an amazing night of entertainment; starting off with the Alex Mitchell Trio, followed by two well-known local bands. Bobby McGregor compèred the event, resurrecting his comedy act especially for the night and wearing his kilt for an extra laugh. After the interval, The Flames had taken the place by storm, finishing with their chart-topper, which had the whole audience out of their seats, dancing.

Gerry and Janine sat in the balcony with the Lord Mayor, George Williams, and their respective wives but during the interval Janine excused herself.

"Listen Ger, I'm gonna have to get some fresh air," she said. "I'll see you later."

She didn't return to her seat for the second half, but Gerry wasn't unduly worried – he had a good idea where he would find her later.

At the end of the night Gerry and his guests had gone backstage, thanking all the bands and people involved in the show. There were lots of handshakes and photographs for the local papers as they mingled with The Flames and Alex in the Green Room. Pete Peterson was noticeable by his absence, which Gerry thought strange, although one of the band had mentioned he was disappearing a lot lately.

In fact Pete had decided to get away for a quiet drink as soon as The Flames had finished their set. It had been chaos when they'd played their number one single; the crowd had gone wild and Pete just needed some space. After walking around for a while, he found himself back outside his old stomping ground, The Hideout.

Walking through the door, Pete noticed Janine sitting at the bar on her own. Spotting him, she beckoned him to sit next to her. Although a little intoxicated, having consumed the best part of a bottle of champagne on her own, she was still pretty much in control of herself.

"What happened to you at the gig tonight?" said Pete, pulling up a bar stool and lighting a cigarette.

"I needed some fresh air and a drink," she replied. "And with the greatest of respect, I've seen The Flames so many times I think I know the songs better than you!"

"Yeah, point taken," Pete replied, drawing on his cigarette.

"Can I have one of those?" asked Janine.

Pete was surprised. "I didn't know you smoked."

"Sure, there's a lot of things you don't know about me," said Janine, keeping her eyes on Pete while he lit her cigarette. She leaned in and brushed his arm with her breast. She drew deeply on the cigarette and blew smoke into the air above their heads.

"How long have we known each other?" she asked, breaking the silence and pouring him a glass of champagne.

Pete thought for a moment. "It's got to be three years now; ever since you first started at Georgie's."

"Ah yes, the good old topless days! Amazing to think that every male member of the club's ogled my tits at some time or other!"

Sipping his champagne, Pete smiled. "And very nice they were too!"

Janine smiled back. "Still are," she said, and leaned on him again.

Is she that drunk? thought Pete, as he tactfully moved away.

"Well, I'm sure that's something for you and Gerry to share," he said, attempting to be diplomatic.

"Yeah, well between you and me, there's not been that much interest from old Gerry for quite a while now." She took another mouthful of her drink and poured the rest of the bottle into their glasses.

Pete was starting to find the conversation a little uncomfortable. He regarded Janine as a friend, but even more so as Gerry's wife; he'd been present on a couple of occasions when Gerry had reacted to someone paying a little bit too much attention to her, and the outcome hadn't been pretty.

Janine didn't seem bothered by his obvious embarrassment and carried on flirting. "You know, I fancied you from the first time you came into the club. And then when you played your guitar – Mmm, sex on legs," she cooed.

"Well, it's always good to know that I'm hitting the right spots with the opposite sex," he replied. He was now intrigued as to where the conversation was heading.

"Hitting the right spots?" she said loudly. "Babe, let me tell you there's been plenty of times I've watched you play and wanted you there and then!"

Pete nearly choked on his champagne as she reached over and touched his leg moving her hand nearer his crotch. Taking all his courage, and possibly his life in his hands, he leaned over, looking her straight in the eyes. "So, what are we going to do about it then?"

Janine calmly leaned back, opened her handbag, and pulled out a scrap of paper and a lip pencil. "Write your phone number on there and I'll call you next week. I'll make some excuse about seeing some old girl friends down in London. Think you can handle that?"

"Try me," he said, and they clinked glasses.

Their timing was perfect – just as they emptied their glasses, Gerry and his guests came bursting through the door.

"See, I told you she'd be in here." Gerry ushered everyone in and noticed Janine's empty champagne bottle.

"Alright babe, need some more bubbles then?" he asked, reaching into the chiller to take out a new bottle of Vintage Bollinger, expertly removing the cork.

"You're gettin' good at that Ger," said Janine, slightly slurring her words.

"Here you go Pete," said Gerry, filling their glasses. "Get some of that finest French bubbly down yer neck!"

He can be such a prat at times, thought Janine, but smiling sweetly she slipped the piece of paper back in her handbag.

Pete raised his glass, and as he took a mouthful he wondered if he'd done the right thing or just made the costliest mistake of his life. He'd noticed Janine smiling as she slipped the paper back in her handbag. *Perhaps she'll forget when she sobers up. Only time will tell, but next week could be interesting.*

Gerry was asleep when Janine left the apartment on Thursday morning the following week. She'd showered and dressed as quietly as possible so as not to wake him. The last thing she wanted to do was explain where she was going and why so early. Yesterday she'd been shopping, and spent ages choosing a few special things she hoped Pete would like. Living in the city centre had its advantages, one of which was proximity to the railway station. Dressed in a smart navy-blue trouser suit and pale-blue silk blouse with a new bag over her shoulder, she had only had a five-minute walk to catch an early train.

She bought a first-class ticket and relaxed with a coffee while going over her purchases.

There was an attractive businessman sitting across the aisle from her who had looked over a few times, which on any other day would have been interesting to pursue, but she ignored him and concentrated on making plans for the day ahead. She'd give Pete a call as soon as she'd sorted out the hotel. There was a place she'd stayed with Gerry on a couple of trips, and she'd got to know the manager, who was very discreet. She caught a taxi from Euston straight there, and after asking to see the manager negotiated a special deal for the penthouse suite.

Pete had been up until the early hours jamming with a few friends in the house he shared in Kensington. They'd consumed a fair amount of alcohol and various drugs from one of his housemate's never-ending supply, so when the phone rang at ten thirty the next morning, he was still asleep. The knock on his bedroom door, telling him Janine was on the phone, soon got him down the stairs in his T-shirt and underpants.

"Hey Pete, it's Janine. I didn't get you out of bed did I?" she asked, in her lilting Irish brogue.

"No, no I'm just up," he lied. "You sound great, where are you?"

"Well, I caught an early train and I'm in the Metropole hotel in Knightsbridge, do you know it?"

"Yeah, that's the one near the museums - very expensive. I was there last week for a music awards do."

"Well then get your arse over here now. I have a room that's costing me a fortune and we have some unfinished business to attend to. Meet me in the bar, and don't be long."

"OK give me an hour to get myself together," blustered Pete, realising he had no shoes on and was barefoot in the cold hallway.

"An hour! Do you treat all your women like this? I've just sat for ages on a crowded train to get down here."

"Sorry, yeah, look I'm on my way."

"Hurry up, babe." She put the phone down.

Pete raced up the stairs and in the mess that was his room, grabbed the cleanest clothes he could find. The communal bathroom was free for once; he dived in the shower and was out on the street flagging down a taxi in record time. It had all happened so fast he hadn't had time to consider the consequences of what was happening. He had never believed she would call him after their meeting in The Hideout last week. But she had, and he was incredibly excited. As the taxi pulled up outside the Metropole and the top-hatted doorman opened the door to welcome him, he knew there was no going back.

The hotel was one of London's most expensive. He walked through the opulent marble-floored foyer and followed the sign to the bar, trying to act as casual as possible. He'd never seen so many flowers. Everywhere he looked there were huge vases of fresh blooms; the smell was intense. He felt the eyes of the cute little blonde receptionist on him as he passed and vaguely remembered her from the other night at the awards ceremony he'd attended with Anders Neckermann. Her number was on the slip of paper she'd given him as he left, still in his jacket pocket.

The bar was bright and modern; Janine was sitting on a bar stool smoking a cigarette. She smiled when she saw him walk into the bar. There was an empty champagne glass in front of her and as he walked up she crushed her cigarette in the ashtray.

"You look amazing," he said, kissing her on the cheek. "Can I get you another drink?"

"The only thing I want is you," she said, slipping off the stool, heading out of the bar and across the reception to the lifts.

From the corner of his eye Pete noticed the look on the receptionist's face. *Nothing like a little jealousy*, he mused.

As soon as the lift doors closed Pete put his arm around Janine and pulled her to him – she gently pushed him away.

"Just be patient," she said, straightening her jacket.

The lift finally reached the top floor, and as the doors opened Pete realised by room, she had meant penthouse.

"Wow nice, you don't mess around do you?"

"The champagne's in the bucket, babe – do the honours," said Janine, disappearing into the bathroom.

Pete closed the door and looked around. It was a huge suite and he was in the lounge, which had a luxurious cream leather sofa and two matching armchairs. There was a fully stocked bar in the corner, on which stood a bottle of champagne in an ice bucket.

Through a pair of double doors on the other side of the lounge was the bedroom, housing a king-sized bed with sensuous black silk sheets, and a sliding picture-window leading out to a balcony which offered a fantastic view across the city. He popped the cork and filled two crystal flutes and was still admiring the view as Janine walked out of the bathroom wearing a stunning black silk basque, stockings and stilettos. She crossed the room, took a sip from the glass he handed her, and went over to sit in the chair by the window, seductively crossing her legs.

Pete was momentarily lost for words. Trying to remain as cool as he could, he excused himself and rushed into the bathroom. He slipped the small wrap of silver paper from his jacket pocket and hurriedly scooped up a small amount of white powder with his fingernail. He held it to his nostril and sniffed sharply. While it burned its way into his septum, he quickly stepped out of his clothes and walked back out into the room wearing just his boxer shorts to revel in the erotic sight of Janine as she drank her champagne.

He knelt in front of her, and as she uncrossed her legs he caressed her inner thighs and gently kissed her moist lips. As she softly moaned he began to lick and stroke her until she arched her back and pushed herself off the chair forcefully onto his mouth.

Stepping out of his shorts he took her hand, guiding her onto the bed. Before she had chance to lie down he gripped the hem of her basque jerking downward so she had to remain kneeling, and pushed himself slowly inside her from behind. She gasped and backed onto him but before she had time to relax he flipped her over onto her back, kissing her mouth and sucking her tongue as he entered her again.

They took turns in leading, until after a while they both knew they could hold back no longer. As Janine screamed out, he felt like the top of his head had just blown off, and they lay on the bed soaked in sweat.

"Oh, my sweet Jesus, I've been waiting so long for that," purred Janine as she reached over and poured another glass of champagne from the bottle in the ice bucket at the side of the bed. Pete lay back and watched her as she drained the glass in one go.

"You certainly enjoy that bubbly," he observed, lighting a cigarette.

Leaning over and taking it from him she drew deeply and blew the smoke out. "Yeah well, we're not all Guinness-swigging bogtrotters yeh know! Some of us have class," she said, leaning down to kiss his limp manhood, making him sit up with a jolt.

Later as they finished the tray of smoked salmon and caviar, washed down with another bottle of champagne, she began stroking him again. Pete could feel himself becoming excited, and jumping up went into the bathroom to find the wrap he'd left in his jacket. He scooped another small amount with his nail, but he didn't know Janine had followed him and was standing in the doorway watching as he snorted the cocaine.

"What the fuck is that?" she demanded taking him by surprise. He spun round sniffing, looking shocked to see her.

"Ah it's nothin' babe, just a bit of toot to keep me goin'," he mumbled.

"I didn't know I was gettin' involved with a fuckin' junkie," she exclaimed. "What the hell's goin' on Pete?"

"Look it's nothing, babe. It just gives me a boost when I need it. I didn't hear you complaining before."

"So do you take that all the time?" she asked. "I've read about marijuana and how that can be addictive, but what does that stuff do to you? I mean it can't be good for you."

"Look, it's not a problem. OK?" said Pete. "I know what I'm doing, and like I said, it just gives me a kick. Don't worry." He looked down at his growing erection. "Now I seem to have something that needs your attention, so are we going back to bed or what?"

"Hmm. Well, well, well," she said smiling.

When Gerry finally went into the kitchen to fix himself some breakfast that morning, he noticed Janine's note on the table saying she'd gone down to London for the day to see one of her friends for lunch and a bit of shopping, and not to wait up. He had a busy day ahead with the builders and architect at Rudi's, so the fact that she was out of the way was a bonus. Throwing the note into the bin he smiled to himself; she'd probably be going to some extortionately expensive restaurant in Knightsbridge, and then spending the afternoon wandering around Harrods before having a bottle of champagne in one of the bars nearby, ahead of the last train home.

Sitting at the breakfast bar looking out over the city, he could see the roof of Rudi's, which was a short walk from their apartment block. Finally, everything was on schedule, and he was happy with how it was looking.

They'd taken the dividing wall out between the two rooms in the former clothes warehouse making a really big area; and with the supporting beams in place, work was well under way on the stage and DJ podium. Mr. C was supervising his performance area personally and had incorporated two cage-like structures for the go-go girls he wanted as part of his set up. They were the latest attraction on the club scene, and there wasn't a shortage of good-looking girls desperate to audition for a job. Gerry was happy to leave that in Mr. C's hands, although one or two of the builders had offered to help out.

The bar was taking shape. They were also making a big feature of food in Rudi's – authentic soul food - black-eye peas and rice, grits, chitlins, cornbread and fried chicken - would be served in a separate restaurant area. Not exactly to Gerry's taste – but Mr. C was all in favour. Gerry preferred the burgers and chicken and chips they served at The Hideout, but was happy to go along with something different providing it pulled in the punters, and he didn't have to eat it.

They were all going to the local Caribbean restaurant for lunch to try some of the dishes, although Gerry would have preferred Janine to have gone in his place. Her taste in food was far more adventurous than his, and he hoped he could get something plain and not too spicy; but Mr. C had gone to a lot of trouble arranging the trip so he couldn't let him down. As it turned out, it was a wonderful meal, and Gerry was confident that the food would be a big hit in the club. Despite his misgivings, he enjoyed it, and afterwards talked enthusiastically with the chef about how they were going to organise the kitchen.

Janine woke with a start. It was dark outside, and for a moment she didn't know where she was. Then turning over, she saw Pete gently snoring, reminding her of their amazing lovemaking. Switching on the bedside light she saw the three empty champagne bottles and the remains of the food they'd ordered; they must have fallen asleep.

Pete had woken when she turned on the light.

"Where you going babe?" he said, stretching his long body. "What time is it?"

"Time I was making a move," replied Janine, as she walked over to the bathroom. "If I don't get that last train there'll be murder at home."

"Can't you just call him and say you missed it and you'll be back tomorrow?" he said, lighting a cigarette as he got out of bed. He stood naked in the open window, looking over the lights of London.

"You have got to be joking," she shouted from the bathroom as she turned on the shower. "Today has been beautiful and I want to do it again, but I don't want to give him any excuses to ask questions."

Suddenly, she felt Pete behind her in the shower, his hands soaping her body. "Oh God, you are unbelievable!" she said as he slowly bent her over.

She didn't resist.

Later, as she sat at the dressing table wrapped in one of the hotel's plush dressing gowns, putting her makeup on, she noticed Pete was quiet and withdrawn.

"Look babe," she said, turning round to face him. "Let's get the ground rules sorted before we go any further. I'm married to Gerry and he takes care of me in the way I want. I'm high maintenance but he puts up with it, for whatever reason. I don't know and I don't ask. You and I could have a nice little scene down here with no ties. That would suit me fine, but if you have a problem tell me now, and we'll call it a day with no hard feelings. What do you say?"

"Well, if you put it like that I don't really have much choice do I?"

"No, you don't! But I'd kill you if you said no," she replied with a smile. "Oh, and you can stay here the night if you want. The room's paid for so why not enjoy it."

"Do you want me to come to the station with you?" Pete asked as Janine put on her trouser suit.

"No babe it's OK, but you could do me a favour and look after my underwear until next time. I'd hate to have to explain that away if Gerry found it."

Fifteen minutes later she climbed out of the taxi and hurried to catch the last train, at the same time as Alex Mitchell was walking out of the station bar.

"Hey, Janine hang on," he called, running to catch her up.

"Alex," she looked surprised. "I didn't know you were in London today. Come on, we need to hurry if we're going to catch the train."

They made it with a couple of minutes to spare, although Alex only had a second-class ticket, so he made his way down the train as it pulled out of the station.

Sitting down in her comfortable first-class carriage, Janine thought how lucky she was that Pete hadn't come to the station. It was a close call and one she would make sure didn't happen in the future. She looked up as a man sat down opposite her; it was the businessman she'd seen that morning. Coincidences happen for a reason, she thought, and this time returned his smile. She'd ignored him on the way down, but now she took in his expensively tailored suit, fitted white shirt and tie, and expensive gold cufflinks. His aftershave wafted across the table.

"Hello again. How was your day?" he asked. "Hopefully better than mine."

"Well, you could say that," Janine replied. "What was so bad?"

"Ah just a wasted journey and a meeting that was a complete disaster, but I don't want to bore you with my troubles. Can I buy you a drink?"

Janine thought what a cute smile he had. "Well, I usually drink champagne," she said, "but a glass of wine would be fine."

"No problem. Champagne it is," he replied, standing up. "I'll be back in a sec." He strode off down the carriage returning shortly after with a bottle of champagne and two glasses.

"Cheers," he said, passing her a glass. "How rude, I don't even know your name. I'm Richard; Richard Kennedy"

"Hi, Richard Kennedy, I'm Janine. And thanks for this."

"Good old British Rail," he laughed, filling her glass. "The waiter nearly fell over when I asked for champagne. I don't think he's ever had to open a bottle before. So, what brings you down to London then?"

"Oh, nothing exciting. Just a day out with an old friend," she said. "A spot of lunch and some shopping."

"Well judging from the lack of bags you didn't do too well on the shopping front?"

Smiling to herself, Janine thought back to Pete, behind her in the shower. "Ha! No, but the rest of the day was fun. Anyway, you never said what you do."

"Well, I'm a property developer, and on a good day I can sell my company's apartments and suites to rich foreigners living in London. Sadly though, today wasn't one of those days." He took a large mouthful from his glass. "More champagne?"

"Thanks," she offered up her glass, and he filled it. "Must be a lot of money in that," she asked with an inquisitive look.

"Yes well, today apart, it can be very lucrative if you get the right buyer."

"Do you have a card? I might just be able to put some business your way," she said, wondering how old he was.

He took out his wallet and gave her an expensively embossed business card. Just then there was an announcement that the train was arriving into the station and people started to ready themselves to get off.

"So do you have a number where I can reach you?" he asked almost shyly. "Maybe another bottle of champagne sometime?"

"Don't worry Richard, I'll call you," Janine replied, putting his card in her purse. She squeezed past him making sure he felt her breast as she leaned into him. "And that's a promise." She kissed her fingertip and gently pressed it to his lips leaving him standing in the aisle. *Sooner than you think Mr. Richard Kennedy*, she thought as she stepped down from the carriage.

She'd seen Alex as she made her way down the platform, but hadn't given him the chance to catch up and speak to her. Gerry might like him, but she wasn't a big fan. She couldn't put her finger on it, but there was something about him she didn't like. Back at the apartment, she let herself in without a sound, and leaving her trouser suit over the back of a chair, crept into the bathroom to clean her teeth. Gerry was asleep and snoring loudly as she slipped into bed beside him. She was aching after making love with Pete, but at the same time felt intrigued by Richard Kennedy. *A property developer with penthouses and suites? Now that could be interesting.* Definitely something she would have to follow up, and with that on her mind she drifted off to sleep.

Pete had taken up Janine's offer of staying in the room and had wandered down to the bar for a nightcap. As he was walking from the lift, he spotted the receptionist again. She had her coat on ready to leave.

"Hi, you just finished?" he said.

There was a flicker of recognition on the girl's face.

"You're Pete Peterson from The Flames aren't you?" she said. "I remember you from last week."

"I don't suppose you fancy a drink? I hate drinking alone."

"I'd love to, but I'm not allowed to be seen with guests in the hotel. Maybe another time?" she said, starting to leave.

"Hang on a minute," said Pete. "How about in my room? I'm in the penthouse suite and it's awfully lonely on my own. Is there a service lift you could use? You could say you're coming up to answer a guest's request if you're caught. I won't say anything. Promise." He gave her his most convincing smile.

"Well, I could get into trouble, but it is very tempting, and I've never been in the penthouse."

"Cool, listen give me ten minutes to get a bottle of champagne and I'll see you up there," he said, walking over to the bar.

Wow, a drink in the penthouse with Pete Peterson! she thought to herself as she took her coat back to the cloakroom.

He'd just finished pulling up the sheets on the bed and tidying round when the buzzer on the door went.

"Hey come on in. Champagne?"

"Fantastic, thanks," she said, walking past him into the suite.

Pete filled a glass and taking it, she stepped out onto the balcony.

"What do you think of the view?" he asked as he came out and stood beside her, putting his arm around her waist.

She turned to him and kissed his lips.

"It's lovely, but I'm cold out here. How about we drink this inside?" she said as she took his hand and led him to the bedroom.

CHAPTER SEVEN

GERRY WAS in a good mood during breakfast the next morning. The plans for Rudi's had all been passed, and with the builders and decorators working flat out, his proposed opening in June was fast becoming a reality. Janine was doing her best to listen, and look interested, as he told her all about the visit to the restaurant yesterday. She nodded her head and smiled when it seemed appropriate. The best thing was, he wasn't bothered about what her day had been like in London, and as he left for the club she gave him a peck on the cheek and sighed with relief as the door closed behind him.

So, Mr. Richard Kennedy, let's see what you're all about, she thought to herself as she turned on the shower and stepped under the needles of hot water.

Two hours later, dressed in a figure-hugging black mini dress, she made her way to Le Metro, one of her favourite wine bars, conveniently situated just around the corner from Kennedy Developments. She'd called the number on the card and he picked up on the third ring, sounding surprised, but pleased that she'd called. Le Metro was his suggestion and he was sitting in a corner booth with a bottle of champagne and two glasses already waiting for her.

"I thought you might be OK with this," he said, standing as she reached the table.

"Bollinger, my favourite," she said as she sat down next to him. "How did you know?"

"I just know these things," he said, filling her glass. What Janine didn't know, was that Richard had been in Georgie's one night with a group of clients, and had overheard Gerry say that Vintage Bollinger was her favourite champagne. "You look amazing!" he said.

Janine took the compliment with a smile.

"Thanks for your call, it was quite a surprise," he continued lighting a cigarette. "Oh sorry, would you like one?" He offered her the pack.

She took one and touched his hand as he held his lighter for her. She drew on the cigarette and allowed the smoke to slowly drift from her lips making eye contact as she did so.

"Well, I have to admit I'm fascinated by what you said you do, and an

49

offer of champagne is too good to refuse," she said.

"Are you interested in property then? I'd be happy to show you some of our best apartments. If that's what you mean."

Janine took a sip of her champagne, savouring the biscuity taste. "Yes, I could be. What do you have in mind?" She inspected him across the rim of her glass.

He was intoxicated by her eyes. "How about I show you one of our top apartments right in the city centre? It's a luxury penthouse with an amazing view and it's two minutes from here." Taking her hand, he led her out of the bar; leaving behind the bottle of champagne, their glasses hardly touched.

The next thing she knew they were in the lift on the way to the penthouse and he was kissing her neck. She could feel his excitement as she leaned against him. The doors opened directly into the apartment – she slid his jacket off and was pulling at his tie and shirt buttons before the doors closed. They stumbled across the lounge into the bedroom, and she pushed him back onto the bed pulling down his trousers and boxer shorts in one swift movement. Before he had time to move, she took him in her mouth, teasing him for a while until he suddenly pushed her dress up around her waist. Lifting her up and rolling her onto her back, he pulled her knickers to one side and pushed himself deep inside her. She was so excited she found herself climaxing almost immediately, wrapping her legs around his waist as she cried out. She could feel he was still erect.

Pushing him off the bed she knelt down as he stood over her, held him with both hands, using her lips to excite him until she felt him start to shake and groan. "I wish we'd brought the rest of that bottle with us," she said, wiping her mouth.

He walked unsteadily across to the kitchen. "No problem. We have everything you desire, madam." He re-appeared in the doorway with a chilled bottle of Bollinger and two glasses, naked apart from his black socks.

Janine burst out laughing and lay back on the expensive Cashmere rug at the bottom of the bed. "You are one hell of a guy, Richard Kennedy."

Gerry's good mood had quickly evaporated when he opened the

envelope on his desk at The Hideout. In it was a single sheet of paper, with a message:

$ BEWARE THE ROTA

He was tempted to rip it up, but remembering the meeting with George Williams and DCI Ray Law after the last bit of bother, he decided it made sense to give them a call.

A couple of hours later at the station, the two policemen were telling Gerry about current rumours of an American drug cartel called Rota Bocan which had originated in Miami and was run by an Irish American called Benny Mulligan. The cartel was attempting to muscle in on the UK drugs trade although there hadn't been any reports of problems in their area so far. The concern was Gerry's proposed opening date, only weeks away. As a precaution, Ray Law suggested they keep an eye on the situation, and if there were any more developments Gerry was to contact them immediately.

Making his way back to Rudi's, Gerry was deep in thought as he passed Le Metro bar just in time to see Janine walking in and greeting a property developer he knew - Richard Kennedy.

I must remember to ask her about it later, he thought, then immediately went back to thinking about any enemies he had who might be behind this latest threat.

He quizzed Mr. C as soon as he arrived about anyone he knew that might bear a grudge, but the DJ was as puzzled as Gerry. Mr. C said he would ask around his circle of friends if they knew anyone causing trouble, but all of his contacts were right behind the club and eagerly waiting for it to open. It was a complication that Gerry could do without, but he would have to ignore it for now and concentrate on making sure everything else was on course for the grand opening.

Although Gerry wasn't into the black music scene, he knew who the big names were, and was impressed they'd managed to book Junior Walker and the All Stars to appear. The tickets were already sold out and even after paying for the main act, Mr. C and all the bar staff, Gerry would still make a tidy profit from the opening.

That night, as he and Janine were finishing the steaks she'd bought from the market on her way home, Gerry suddenly put his knife and fork down. "I didn't know you knew Richard Kennedy," he said.

Janine's stomach tensed and she felt sick. "Yeah, I met him on the way down to London, and he was on the same train on the way back," she said, trying to remain calm. "We got talking and he said he was a property developer, so I thought he might be interesting to know, especially as you're always looking at new projects."

"He's a good guy. I bought this apartment from his company. Sells a lot of stuff to foreigners based in London. You thinking of getting into the property business then, babe? Do you good to get involved with something. It'll keep you busy."

"Ah Jeez, you never know," she replied. "He showed me a penthouse apartment in the city centre that's available."

"Oh, what was it like?" asked Gerry.

"Tasty!" She smiled to herself. "Very tasty!"

It was the grand opening night at Rudi's and the city was buzzing. The sell-out crowd was predominantly black, although there was a smattering of white soul fans mixed in. Junior Walker was incredible, and Mr. C's caged go-go dancers were a huge success.

Thankfully since the one-line letter, Gerry had received nothing more, and the show went off without any major trouble. The police had agreed to take a relaxed approach about drugs on the opening night, although Ray Law had warned him that it was an exception, and they wouldn't be as lenient in the future.

The whole drug scene sickened Gerry. He understood alcohol, and although he didn't drink, he accepted that booze was business; he was the first to admit that it was promoted wholeheartedly in all his clubs. But drugs were another thing. They were illegal, and he couldn't afford to have anything illegal in his clubs. The drugs culture was dangerous, and the people behind it even more so; Gerry already had enough potential trouble if the Rota Bocan letter was a genuine threat.

Gerry had convinced Mr. C to let the Alex Mitchell Trio play a set to open the show, and despite his concerns, they'd gone down really well. It helped that the other two musicians in the trio were both black, but their choice of material and the sheer brilliance of their playing had won the audience over so much, that Mr. C had suggested they play a regular weekly spot.

The twenty-four-year-old bass player Wynton Brown had been born in the UK to Jamaican parents, while twenty-five-year-old drummer Thomas Wilson Jr, was from Chicago, Illinois. The music they played was predominantly by black artists, and although Alex had been born in the Midlands to a middle-class white family, he'd always loved American Jazz, especially the likes of Charlie Parker, Oscar Peterson and Charlie Mingus. Alex, Wynton and Thomas were great musicians, and together they had a fantastic understanding of each other's playing. When they were on stage it was as if they were on another planet, and their music was a special kind of bond.

Off stage however, they all lived completely separate lives. Alex had a tiny apartment in the old part of the city, Wynton lived with his girlfriend in a small flat, and had a laid-back attitude which reflected in his playing style, while the more opinionated Thomas shared a small, terraced house with his brother James.

Janine was in her element, and the minute Junior Walker and the Allstars started the intro to 'Road Runner' she was down on the dance floor. Gerry was happy to see her enjoying herself; although there had been moments recently that he had thought she was becoming a little too familiar with Richard Kennedy. Recently divorced, Kennedy was regarded by some as one of the movers and shakers in the city with an eye for beautiful women. One of whom, it seemed, was Janine.

Janine for her part, seemed to be quite taken with the property development business, and regularly went down to London to view apartments and suites. She hadn't had any success yet, but still seemed enthusiastic when Gerry had discussed it with her. He'd been so involved in setting up Rudi's, he seemed to have lost his focus on their personal life. They'd had such a vibrant marriage and he was worried it was slipping away. They only ever saw each other at breakfast and the occasional dinner. The rest of the time was spent rushing about, with him splitting his time between the office at The Hideout and Rudi's, and Janine meeting Richard Kennedy for viewings, or taking trips down to London.

He decided one way of relieving some of the pressure would be to appoint a manager to run Rudi's for him. He'd been impressed with the way Alex Mitchell conducted himself, and although Janine wasn't keen, Gerry made the decision to offer him the job. Since Alex seemed to get on well with Mr. C, who had been his first choice but had turned the job down. Gerry called Alex and asked him to come in the office for a meeting.

"What do you think then, could you combine the two?" said Gerry, to a visibly shocked Alex.

"Wow, I really don't know what to say Mr. Fortuna. I mean are you sure I'm the right man for the job?"

"I wouldn't ask you if I didn't think you could do it."

"I mean if the trio can play there a couple of times a week, and then on my night off we can pull in another gig, I don't see a problem. And you're sure Charles is OK with it?"

"Mr. C? He's fine. In fact, I originally sounded him out about it, but he wasn't interested. Plus, he really rates you as a player so there's no problem. If you have no other concerns, the job's yours. How soon can you start?"

"Well, there's a couple of trio gigs in, but other than that, straight away."

"Good; then let's get the paperwork sorted and you can get on with it." Gerry stood and shook Alex's hand.

Alex Mitchell suddenly found himself in a position of power. As manager of Rudi's, he would have control over all the money that was coming in and going out – and he needed money. It didn't take him long to work out a way to use his new position to his advantage. One of the things he knew, was that when an artist was booked to appear at the club, he had to deal with an agent who took a percentage of the fee, a commission. As a musician he hated agents, thinking of them as leeches on his hard-earned money. So, he worked out a way that he could cut them out altogether. He invented a fictitious agency based at a false London address. He booked the artists through it, making sure he always spoke to them personally. Then he made sure the fee paid to the artist was always substantially lower than the fee paid to the agency by the club. A typical scenario might be that Rudi's would pay Alex's agency five hundred pounds for an artist and Alex would pay three hundred to the artist. The artist was happy and Alex made two hundred. It was that simple – and with at least two artists a week playing at Rudi's, Alex's little scam quickly started to pay dividends.

Alex had also been approached by his drummer Thomas, who had offered him a payment for allowing him to pick up a package once a week from the club, no questions asked. It was an offer Alex couldn't refuse even though he suspected that it was drug related. The parcels were coming from Florida, and there were rumours about a Miami-based drug cartel trying to move in on the Birmingham scene. Although he knew he was playing with fire, the financial gains were huge, and as long as he could keep Gerry from poking his nose in, he'd be fine.

As for Mr. C, he didn't seem bothered about anything apart from his record collection and his go-go dancers, all of whom he personally interviewed; and judging by the turnover of dancers, that kept him pretty busy.

CHAPTER EIGHT

WITH THE weight of Rudi's off his shoulders, Gerry decided he'd like to get involved in the artist management side of the business. He'd been upset at handing over Pete Peterson and The Flames to Anders Neckermann, even though at the time he knew it was impossible – but he'd always thought he'd like to try again at some stage, and now seemed like the right time. They'd had a relative amount of success since they signed, but after their first hit and tour nothing seemed to be happening. He got the impression from talking to the band when they played at the charity gig earlier in the year that Pete was becoming unhappy with how things were.

Gerry planned to convert the old Georgie's club into a suite of offices, so he thought he'd base Fortuna Artist Management there. And what better way to launch the company than with the stellar signing of The Flames?

His first task though, would be to convince Pete that moving from Anders Neckermann to FAM was a good idea. His trump card was Janine. She always seemed to get on well with Pete, and if she could convince him it was a good idea, Gerry felt sure Pete would agree. The rest of the band shouldn't be a problem especially if money was involved.

Janine couldn't believe it when Gerry asked her if she'd go down to London to talk to Pete about his plan. She'd managed to see him a few times over the last few months, each time a sex-filled day at the Metropole, but this was a bonus – she had Gerry's permission. Maybe she could even do an overnight stay saying they went to a gig.

"I'm on the early train down to London tomorrow," she told Gerry over dinner. "I'm in first class but I got a reduction by booking in advance and smiling sweetly at the guy in the ticket office. Pete's talking about us going to a gig to see some new band so I might stay over at the Metropole if it gets late. OK?"

"Whatever it takes babe," said Gerry, finishing his steak.

The next day, sex with Pete was the best it had ever been. Probably because they both knew she didn't have to rush back on the last train. She'd called him as soon as she arrived in London and he was waiting for her in the bar at the Metropole. He'd avoided the receptionist on his way in, as they wouldn't be taking advantage of a free night this time. Janine had wafted in looking amazing, and within minutes they were in bed. Later that evening, drinking another bottle of Bollinger, they'd discussed Gerry's proposed offer to The Flames, and in principle Pete was happy. Things had become strained with Anders; especially after a publicity stunt he pulled went spectacularly wrong, and ended up costing the band, and in particular Pete, a lot of money in lost royalties.

"Look I'm cool with it," he said as he lay back on the bed. Janine had come back from the bathroom and was pouring herself a glass of champagne. "But I can tell you now, the biggest problem is gonna be Anders. He can be a stubborn bastard at times. Do you want some of this?" he said, offering her the joint he'd rolled while she was in the loo.

"No, I don't, and to be honest I'm getting concerned about the amount of drugs you're taking," she said. "Jeez, I mean God knows what you're like when I'm not here. You're beginning to look a mess babe, and if you turn up looking like that when you meet with Gerry he'll go crazy. You know what he thinks of drugs."

"Don't worry about me," he said, reaching over and pulling her down in the direction of his groin. She soon had him moaning, and a few seconds later he exploded in her mouth. "Fuck me, Janine, you give a great blow job," he said, gasping for breath.

"Yeah, I know," she said, picking up her glass and swallowing the champagne in one. Gripping the top of the headboard she pulled herself up, smiled and crouched over his face. "Now it's my turn!"

Then the buzzer went. Pete climbed off the bed and pulling on his robe walked over to the door. He opened it to reveal the receptionist.

"We didn't order room service did we?" called Janine.

"Well, it all depends," he replied, taking the girl's hand and pulling her into the suite. "Janine, this is my friend Suzy, and I think the evening is about to get a whole lot more interesting."

Janine and Gerry were talking over dinner the following night. "Pete's cool with the idea," she said. She'd arrived back mid-afternoon absolutely shattered. The previous night had been one of the most outrageous experiences of her life. She had always had an open attitude about sex, but Pete and Suzy had blown her mind on more than one level. They had also taken a lot of cocaine, convincing Janine to try some. It hurt her nose, and she'd upset Pete when she sneezed and blew his line onto the carpet. Next time she'd stick to champagne. What had Pete called it? 'Ménage a trois'.

"So, what else did he say?" Gerry snapped her out of her reverie.

"He's pretty pissed off with Anders after that crazy stunt landed them in court. It's cost Pete and the band a lot of money. The one thing he said though, was that Anders can be really stubborn."

"A pile of cash waved under their nose usually does the trick in my experience," replied Gerry. "You look knackered babe, why don't you get an early night? Pete keep you out on the town all night, did he?"

"You could say that," she said with a laugh. "You coming?"

"Sorry, babe. I'm going to that boxing night with Bobby. Don't you remember? It's a big fight for him."

She wandered over to the bedroom. "Ah yeah I forgot. Try not to wake me up if you're late, I've got an early meeting with Richard tomorrow and I want to be fresh. There's a new development he's involved in and he wants me to see it."

Gerry was buttoning up his white dress shirt. "You seem to be spending a lot of time with Richard lately."

"Yeah, I think he fancies me," she said laughing.

"Just as long as that's all it is," he replied, standing in front of the mirror trying to fasten his bow tie. "I hate these dress dos."

"Don't forget Ger, most blokes have seen my tits at some point, and that was your idea. Come here; let me do it," she said, kneeling up on the bed and pulling him close to her. She kissed him tenderly on the lips holding him close. "Are you sure you have to go tonight?"

"I don't think it would look good if the main guest wasn't there," he said. "Plus, Bobby is relying on my support and I can't let him down."

"Of course not," she agreed, tying his bow with a perfect knot. "But maybe I could relieve a bit of that tension before you go," and she reached down to lower his zipper.

Later, as he closed the bedroom door behind him, Janine lay back on the pillow and was asleep in seconds.

When Gerry called Anders Neckermann at his Soho office the next morning, the secretary said Anders could fit him in at the end of the week. Gerry had decided to drive down in Rollie – he wasn't a fan of British Rail and hated sitting in a carriage with a load of other people, even if it was first-class.

Anders' secretary, a well-dressed young man, showed Gerry up to the office, which was on the second floor of an old building a few doors down from the Flamingo Club. Boxes of records were piled up on the floor, and gold and silver discs adorned the wall behind his desk. Anders, dressed in a shocking-pink silk shirt with frills down the front, and matching crushed-velvet trousers, was on the phone sitting with his feet up on the desk. He beckoned Gerry to sit on the chair in front of him. After a couple of minutes he finished the call and turned his attention to Gerry, who by now was close to losing his temper and walking out.

"Gerry!" Anders exclaimed in his usual exaggerated manner. "How are you? What brings you here my friend?"

"Well, I don't enjoy being kept waiting, so I'll get straight to the point," Gerry replied. "I'm setting up a new management company and I want The Flames to be my first signing. Let's face it, you've done nothing for them since their first album, and that stunt you tried to pull has cost them a fortune. I know for a fact Pete wants out, and without him there's no Flames."

Anders stood and paced around the office. "Are you crazy? There's no way I'll let them go." He laughed loudly. "How much do you think I've spent on them? Eh? You think you can just walk in here, Mr. Big Clubman, and call the shots?"

"This bundle of readies in my hand says maybe you should think again," said Gerry, waving a large wad of five-pound notes.

"Readies! Readies!" shouted Anders. "You think you can buy me off with readies? Eh? Go fuck yourself! Or in fact, go fuck your wife for a change, instead of letting Pete Peterson do it!"

Gerry jumped off his chair and grabbed Anders by the throat. "What did you just say, you piece of shit?"

"You heard me," spluttered Anders. "From what I hear, Mr. Big

Clubman can't get it up! Pete Peterson's been screwing her for you."

Gerry dragged Anders over to the open window and pushed him backwards over the sill holding him by his shirt frills until he was hanging over the street below.

"I tell you what we're gonna do," he said, as Anders dangled precariously two floors up. "I'm gonna pretend I didn't hear what you just said, and you're going to sign a release clause in The Flames' contract. That way, I'm not going to drop you from this window. Does that sound like a good deal?"

Anders forced a strangulated laugh, so Gerry pushed him further out, his feet starting to scrabble for a grip.

"I said, does that sound like a good deal?" Gerry's voice had suddenly become menacing.

"OK, OK, I'll sign, I'll sign!" spluttered Anders, and just as his secretary rushed through the door, Gerry pulled him back through the window.

"Good timing young man. I think our meeting has come to a satisfactory conclusion, don't you Anders? I happen to have the release form here – all it needs is your signature at the bottom."

"Yes, yes, sure," said Anders, straightening his jacket. "My secretary can witness it."

Ten minutes later, Gerry sat in Rollie, with the signed release form in his hand. He laughed out loud. *Didn't even cost me a penny*, he thought, as he started the engine and drove slowly out of Soho. But one thing bothered him; what Anders had said about Pete Peterson and Janine. Was it true, or just attempted bravado?

I'll have to handle this very carefully thought Gerry, as he gritted his teeth and stared at the motorway ahead, stamping his foot down hard on the accelerator.

CHAPTER NINE

GERRY HAD signed The Flames – and the reaction in the music press had been mixed. The reporter from the NME who had championed the band when they first emerged, now questioned whether they could cut it in the tough music world by signing to a small-time operation from the sticks; whereas one of the other magazines had commented that Pete Peterson's writing on the next album would be a major factor in their future.

Gerry had decided that he would deal with the Pete and Janine situation, if there was one, later. He was already busy working on plans for a huge UK and European tour to coincide with the release of The Flames' new album Pete had been writing in London. The dates would keep him and the band on the road for a good part of the next year.

In the meantime, Janine had organised a party to celebrate the formation of Fortuna Artist Management and its new signing. It was déjà vu for her as they were in the old Georgie's where she'd first met Gerry; although without the bar where she'd had such good times meeting so many people, everything now looked completely different. She shuddered when she remembered the occasion she was threatened with a sawn-off shotgun.

On the night, she'd invited a great cross section of guests, including the band members, their wives and girlfriends, and Bobby, who was his usual bubbly self talking to Richard Kennedy over in the corner. Richard had glanced at Janine a couple of times but she'd made sure to be very professional and just acknowledge him being there. George Williams had come accompanied by his wife, and DCI Ray Law had made an appearance, although he had not looked his usual calm, relaxed self. He'd made a fuss of Janine when he arrived, but then asked if he could have a private word with Gerry, and they'd gone off to Gerry's office. Pete had turned up late looking a mess. Janine had been worried about him and the rumours that his drug-taking was getting out of control.

Since the last time they were together in London, he'd been in the studio finishing the new album and things hadn't been going well. Pete had been allowed to produce it himself and had been arguing with the band and the recording engineer about the final mixes, which meant the release date had been put back. Now, unless the situation was sorted out quickly, the tour dates that Gerry had been working so hard to finalise, could be in jeopardy. It had been a risk letting Pete produce his own songs, but Gerry had shown faith in him, and from the bits Janine had heard, it was sounding OK – but not great. The trouble was, Pete had started to believe in his own publicity, and this – coupled with his excessive substance-abuse – meant he was becoming unmanageable. Janine had kept Gerry away from the studio as much as she could, but he'd been concerned about the rumours and the state Pete had turned up in was not going to help.

It was a Monday night, so Rudi's and The Hideout were both closed and all the staff were there enjoying themselves on their night off. Mr. C had volunteered to bring some sounds along and was spinning his latest favourites, accompanied by a couple of the latest go-go dancers who were getting everyone up dancing. Alex Mitchell had arrived with a handsome young black man, and they seemed quite close. Alex introduced his guest as James, the younger brother of his drummer Thomas, who was also there with the bass player Wynton. Janine had never warmed to Alex, and she'd told Gerry she didn't like him after the first time she'd met him. She couldn't put her finger on what it was that made her uneasy about him, but there was definitely something that bothered her.

Gerry and Ray Law had finally reappeared and were talking with Ray's boss, so Janine decided it was time to relax and mingle with the guests; but before she had time to get herself a glass of champagne she was called into action.

A few music journalists had also been invited along and were eagerly trying to get a word with Pete about the new album; but he wasn't in the mood and had already told one of them to "Fuck off back to London!" Janine tried to intervene but he hadn't finished yet.

"And tell your bosses they can wait with everyone else for their copy," he shouted. "You're all the same you scum. You journos, you build something up just so you can knock it down again. Well, this album's gonna prove you're all a bunch of wankers who know fuck all!" The room had now gone quiet hanging on his every word. "You want a quote?" Pete was now in full flow. "The Flames are gonna set the fuckin' world on fire! Print that you bastards!"

Janine and Bobby were now standing either side of Pete. They grabbed his arms, steering him out of the room into Gerry's office, and closed the door.

"Bastards! They know fuck all." Pete stomped around the office. "I need another fuckin' drink," he said to no one in particular.

Janine was waiting for Gerry to come storming in, but instead he opened the door and walked into the room with a beaming grin on his face.

"That was genius Pete," he exclaimed. "If that doesn't get the front-page headlines on every music paper, I'll eat my hat! Now before you say anything else and destroy the moment, get your arse back in the studio and finish that album."

Gerry turned on his heels and walked out leaving Janine, Bobby and even Pete open-mouthed.

The following morning, Gerry was deep in thought when Janine came into the kitchen for breakfast.

"You OK, Ger? Great party last night."

"Yeah, Pete stole the show, and from what I hear he'll be all over the music press this week."

"Well, that's great news don't you think?" But she could see something was wrong. "So, what's bothering you?"

"Just what Ray Law had to tell me last night when we were in my office. He's had reports that there are a lot of drugs circulating in the city, and the main point of distribution seems to be Rudi's. He hasn't got any concrete evidence yet, but they're keeping a close watch on what goes on there."

"Have you spoken to Alex about it?" Janine asked. "Surely he must know something. He's there most nights and seems to have links with all the main players in the city."

"Yeah, well I'm meeting him later this morning along with Charles. I've got to get this sorted out quickly before word gets round, or we'll start to lose the punters."

"Ger, I've told you before there's something about Alex. I just don't trust him," she said.

"Look, babe, I hear what you're saying, but I have to sort this out myself. Trust me, if he is behind this or anything else that affects the club, he'll wish he'd never been born."

He stood up and kissed her on the forehead as he picked up his jacket and left.

Janine sat drinking her coffee looking out of the window, thinking. Why did she have this feeling about Alex? She didn't even know him. Maybe she should do a bit of investigating. There was someone she could ask and she just so happened to be meeting him that afternoon.

Janine and Richard Kennedy lay naked in bed in one of his apartments, overlooking the Arts Quarter of the city. Outside the rain was beating against the windows, but inside it was warm. He was propped up on one elbow watching Janine drink the champagne he'd brought with him.

"We're good together, don't you think," Richard said, gently stroking her hair.

"Ah Jesus, don't be giving me the love thing just because we have a good time in bed." She put her glass on the bedside table and turned to face him. "Look, I like you a lot, but I'm married to Gerry. You've known that all along. OK, it might seem strange I'm here in bed with you, but that's the way it is. I'm not going to leave Gerry. He treats me well and I'm happy with that, and as long as we're not stupid we can continue to have fun. But don't think of falling in love, because it ain't gonna happen!"

"Wow, where did that come from?" Richard sat up straight. "It was only an observation. Love and commitment are not on my agenda right now so you can relax. I've not long been through a very costly divorce, so getting tied up in another relationship is the last thing on my mind."

"Well, that's grand, and I'm sorry I overreacted," she said smiling. "And yeah we are good, I just don't want to spoil it, that's all." She became more serious. "Listen there's something I want to ask you. You're into jazz and you've mentioned how you like Alex Mitchell and his trio. What do you know about him?"

"Hmm, funny you should ask," he said, pouring more champagne. "He contacted our office recently, enquiring about one of our luxury apartments. I thought at the time it was a bit out of his price range."

"Well Gerry gave him the job as manager at Rudi's," said Janine.

"Yeah but even so, he'd need to be earning top dollar to afford the place he was looking at, and even Gerry doesn't pay those kind of wages. So why the interest in Alex Mitchell anyway? What's he done?" he asked, gently squeezing her left nipple between his fingers.

"Ah, it's probably nothing," she said, reaching over to stroke him back to life. "So how about we finish what we came here to do in the first place?"

Alex Mitchell felt like he'd spent his whole life taking orders. His father, Sergeant Major Alexander Mitchell, had been invalided out of the army after the war, and had insisted on maintaining a strict discipline in the house with both Alex and his mother. Although for the most part Alex had despised the rules and regulations, one thing he had to thank his father for was making him practice his scales on their old upright piano in the parlour every day. At the time as a young boy, he had hated being indoors while all his friends were outside playing football but now, when he sat down at the piano and played, he knew it had all been worthwhile. Alongside his bassist and drummer, he made wonderful sounds that were finally being recognised. The only trouble was, jazz didn't pay, and Alex had grand designs on where he was going in the world – and for that he needed money. Rudi's had given him that opportunity, and using all his acumen he'd set up a couple of scams on top of the generous wage Gerry Fortuna paid him. So far he'd managed to keep his boss away from the action, but he knew from the look on Gerry's face at the previous night's party, there was a problem. Alex didn't know the other man coming out of Gerry's office, but he looked like a policeman and that could only mean trouble.

Alex was sure the agency was safe. He always dealt with that personally and there hadn't been any problems with any of the artists; so it had to be the arrangement he had with Thomas. He'd been nervous about getting involved with anything to do with drugs, but the money he was being paid to turn a blind eye was too good to refuse. All he had to do was be at the club when the shipment, disguised as a box of records arrived, and keep it in his office until Thomas came to pick it up. For that simple duty he would be paid fifty pounds in cash.

Gerry had called him first thing and told him to be at the office for a meeting with him and Mr. C at ten o'clock, which was fortunate, as there wasn't a scheduled drop that day.

When Alex arrived, Charles was already there along with the man Alex had seen with Gerry the previous night, and they both looked serious.

"Right, guys let me introduce you to DCI Ray Law. He brought me some rather worrying news last night which I wanted him to share with you straight away," he said.

"Thanks Gerry," said Ray. "We have learned through a couple of our informants, that there's a serious drugs war threatening to blow up. On the one hand we have the Jamaicans who've been at it for years but with whom we've never had any trouble. Then, on the other hand, we have a new team calling themselves Rota Bocan, who we believe to be a drugs cartel based in Miami. Their boss is a man called Benny Mulligan. By all accounts he's a heavy character originally of Irish American descent, who you don't want to get on the wrong side of. Up to now we've always been happy to let the Jamaicans get on with it, mainly because they've kept themselves to themselves and haven't bothered anyone else. The trouble with the new lot is they're greedy bastards and they want to take over completely. Understandably, the Jamaicans aren't happy about it. At the moment it's been limited to a couple of threats, but that's not going to last. The reason I asked Gerry to call a meeting with you guys is there's a rumour that Rota Bocan are using Rudi's as a distribution hub."

"I've spoken to all my guys and no one knows anything," said Mr. C. "I mean we all like a little spliff now and then, but nothing like what Mr. Law here is saying."

"What about you, Alex, have you heard about this?" Gerry asked.

Alex was desperately trying to remain calm as the others looked at him. "Nothing at all. It's been going great. In fact we've got two sell-out gigs this weekend. Desmond Dekker on Friday and Wilson Pickett on Saturday. We try and make sure we have a mix of reggae and soul to keep everyone happy. But there's never been any trouble in the club."

"We need you both to be our eyes and ears," said Ray. "Let's try and nip this in the bud before anything serious happens." Ray gave them each of them one of his cards. "You can contact me any time."

Gerry still seemed uneasy. "I hate druggies, and I don't want my clubs associated with drugs of any kind," he said, putting his hand on Alex's shoulder. "Can we have a word before you go?"

Once in his office, Gerry sat down behind his desk and beckoned Alex to take a seat.

"You sure everything's kosher down there, son? Don't hide anything from me."

"Everything's great Mr. Fortuna. Business couldn't be better," Alex replied, feeling more confident. "In fact, bar takings are the best they've ever been."

"I don't give a shit about the bar takings!" Gerry banged the desk with his clenched fist. "If I find out anyone's involved in drugs and using my club, they better hope DCI Law gets to them before I do because if I catch them they're fucking dead!"

Alex drove straight to Thomas's terraced house after the meeting. His brother James was already there and they could both see that Alex was rattled.

"You look like you've seen a ghost. Are you OK?" James asked, reaching out to touch Alex.

"I need to speak to Thomas now," said Alex, ignoring the comforting hand. "Maybe you shouldn't get involved James."

"We're family," snapped James. "What concerns Thomas concerns me."

Thomas stepped between them. "OK you two, chill out. Alex what's the problem? I've never seen you so stressed."

"I'm out Thomas! I can't do this anymore! Tell them! You need to get someone else!" Alex was shaking.

"Wow, be cool man," Thomas said. "What's going on, what's happened?"

"It's Gerry, he knows! The police have been down and they're watching the club. They know! They know it's me! Gerry's gonna kill me! I'm out! Tell them I quit! Tell them!"

James was holding Alex by the arms trying to calm him down. "Bro, you've got to help him," he said.

Thomas was thinking. "You're gonna have to let me speak to them Alex," he said. "They won't like it. People don't just quit."

"I don't care whether they like it," Alex was in tears. "I'm out! I quit!" He shrugged off James and ran out of the flat. Jumping in his car he drove off at high speed, narrowly avoiding a bus, which slammed on its brakes and blew its horn.

"Shit! Shit! Shit!" exclaimed Thomas. "This is not good. No one ever leaves Rota Bocan. Mr. Mulligan is not going to like this! You're gonna have to talk to him, James. This can only end one way and that's bad."

Over on the other side of town, Mr. C had driven to an insalubrious area of Hawksworth, consisting of once luxurious detached houses which were now in a sorry state. He'd entered one that had most of its windows boarded up and deep reggae bass sounds vibrating from the basement.

Inside there was no lighting, so carefully treading on bare wooden boards through the high-ceilinged hallway, he walked into what used to be a tastefully decorated drawing room. In the darkness, Mr. C could just make out an old man sitting in a threadbare armchair by the fireplace. The man motioned for Mr. C to sit on a straight-backed chair across from him. He was smoking a fat joint made with the finest ganja, which he passed to Mr. C who took a deep draw on it, holding the smoke in his lungs.

"So, what is the news Charles?" The old man asked.

"Man, we got trouble with these greedy yanks," said Charles, as he exhaled the acrid smoke, feeling the buzz from the weed. "The lawman, he's cool; he don't want no trouble. I don't trust that Alex though. He's a slime ball. He never gives a straight answer to Mr. Gerry. He's got his fingers in the pie. I know it." He passed the joint back to the old man.

The air was now thick with smoke, and he could hardly see across the room.

"Dem want war, dem get war," replied the old man, taking a long pull on the joint, releasing a dense plume of smoke that completely enveloped him. "But first we need a plan," he said thoughtfully. "I speak to the Association; they will know what to do. Best you go now. I will call you. Take care."

Mr. C drove away, unaware that he was being photographed from a battered old Transit van parked across the road. The photographer was Joe Burke, one time IRA commander from Ballykobh, now part of a new cell of sympathisers based in Birmingham.

CHAPTER TEN

JOE BURKE was in his darkroom, developing the roll of film he'd just taken, mixing the chemicals to allow him to print off the copies from the negatives currently in the developing tank when he heard the phone ring in the hallway.

"Now, how's it going? The prints? No problem, I have them on the go here," he said into the mouthpiece. "Grand, I'll be there first thing in the morning." He replaced the receiver.

"Who was that dear?" his wife asked from the kitchen. The smell of the ham and cabbage smiling in the pot on the hob, made Joe's stomach rumble.

"Ah just yer man from the club, asking for the photos from last week's do," he replied. "I said I'll take the prints round tomorrow."

"Well just you make sure you get your money," she said. "You know what you're like, always forgetting to ask them for it. Those prints cost you a fortune by the time you add up all the costs of the paper and chemicals. We can't afford to keep doing stuff for free."

"Jesus, I know, Sadie; you don't have to go on. Now you take care of what's on that cooker while I finish off in my room."

He went back into his dark room and closing the door he switched on the red lamp to finish the printing safely. Gently immersing the photographic paper in the trays of liquid, he watched as the images of Mr. C entering and leaving the house, became visible. *There you are you bastard*, he said to himself as he hung the photos up on the wire stretched across the room. *Just what exactly are you black feckers up to?* Then turning off the light, he closed and locked the door, leaving the prints to dry.

Joe and Sadie Burke lived in a smart semi in Alderton, an area on the outskirts of the city favoured by the Irish immigrants who'd moved over in the mid-fifties. Most of the men were involved in the construction of the new road system, but Joe had a well-paid job as the chief photographer on the daily newspaper. He also had a decent sideline doing weddings and other weekend functions.

"Have you seen our Janine lately?" he asked his wife as they ate their dinner later.

"No, but she called Jackie the other week inviting her to the opening of Gerry's new club; Rudi's I think it's called," she said, helping herself to another boiled potato.

"I don't know why he has to open another feckin' nightclub, especially one for the blacks," said Joe. "He should keep his nose out if you want my opinion."

"Ah Joe, why don't you leave it," she said. "He seems to know what he's doing, and our Janine seems happy enough according to Jackie. She was telling her how she's got herself involved with some property developer selling big apartments to foreigners."

"Well at least she's not showing her boobs to every gobshite in town anymore. Closing that club where she worked is the one good thing he's done," said Joe.

"I wish you wouldn't swear so much, Joe, especially at the table."

"And why doesn't she speak to us?" Joe railed, standing up to clear the empty dishes. "Is she too busy to call her Mammy & Da now?"

"Jesus, Joe, what's got into you? You're like a briar tonight," said his wife. "She'll call when she's ready."

The following morning, Joe and his three fellow Association members, Michael Brennan, Niall Fitzgerald and Sean Whelan, sat around a table in the back room of St Mary's, their local Irish club, studying the prints Joe had brought. The four of them, all originally from Ireland, were now living in the city, and although it wasn't yet eleven o'clock, there were four half-empty glasses of Guinness on the table.

"Our Janine's gobshite of a husband employs this black fecker as one of them disc jockeys at his new club," said Joe, prodding one of the photos he'd taken of Mr. C. "These were taken yesterday afternoon. Thing is, what's he visiting Old Errol for?"

Michael spoke. "According to Seamus, Errol called last night saying there's big trouble brewing between the Jamaicans and the Yanks. He wants a meet. Seamus's boss, DCI Law, has been talking to Gerry Fortuna warning him they're keeping an eye on that new club of his over by the station. Rudi's it's called."

"So, what do we know about these feckin' Yanks?" asked Joe. There was silence at the table. "For feck's sake somebody must know something." He stood up, finishing his pint and putting the empty glass on the bar, beckoning the barman for another.

Niall spoke up. "There's a black guy who plays drums with yer man from Rudi's, Alex Mitchell. He's been spoutin' all kinds of shite lately. I like the jazz you know, and went to see them play in a pub in town. Full of it he was afterwards, to anyone who'd listen. Talked about how this Rota Bocan were here and gonna take over."

"Hang on there," Joe said, sorting through some photos in his case. "Is this him?" he asked, pointing to a picture taken outside the entrance to Gerry's club.

"Yeah that's him. Bit of a cocky fecker if you ask me," said Niall.

"Well, the day I took that, he was only there a matter of minutes, and came out carrying a parcel. Could be nothing, but maybe we should keep an eye on him."

DCI Raymond Jackson Law had been born and raised in Toxteth, Liverpool by his parents, Delroy – who was originally from Barbados – and Joan, a petite brunette from Kirkby. They'd met at the Grafton Rooms where they both liked to go dancing every week. They married in 1944, and Raymond, their only child, was born the following year.

Growing up in the fifties, Ray (he hated being called Raymond - his mother was the only one he allowed to call him that) was an attractive young man who inherited more of his mother's European looks than his father's. His light brown skin and wavy black hair coupled with his looks, made him an instant hit with the girls, especially when they discovered he was built with porn star proportions. Many a lucky female had gasped in ecstasy when Ray stepped out of his boxers.

Growing up he had mixed with the gangs of black guys from the area, at one time becoming the singer in one of the many close-harmony groups popular at the time. He had a good voice and, like his parents, enjoyed dancing. However, his father had wanted him to get a good education, and after passing all his exams with flying colours, he had been encouraged to study for a law degree at Liverpool University. Following graduation Ray then surprised everyone by opting to join the police force instead of becoming the lawyer his father had hoped.

Being a police officer in Liverpool during the sixties was tough and not without its problems, but he'd excelled. As a result, his passage through the ranks had been rapid, and when he was offered a posting with promotion to DCI in the Midlands, he jumped at the opportunity. Birmingham was an up-and-coming city with lots of new development happening, and depending on which way you looked at it, plenty of crime.

One thing Ray never refused, was a challenge.

Ray had been fortunate that during the first week in his new job George Williams had taken a shine to him; recognising his experience and ability in the field. As a result, one of the first jobs he was tasked with was acting as the Chief Constable's liaison officer with a successful club owner called Gerry Fortuna, who was a personal friend of George. There had already been a violent situation at one of his clubs, that the owner had dealt with himself. It had possibly been unlawful, but because there had been no comeback from the other parties involved, the police were willing to overlook it.

Only now there was a drugs problem at Mr. Fortuna's new club. Ray had worked with the drug squad whilst he was on Merseyside and it was one of the main reasons why George Williams had got him involved. It didn't help, however, that Ray found Mr. Fortuna's wife incredibly attractive – things were about to get a whole lot more complicated.

Ray had had a long chat with Gerry Fortuna at the party to celebrate the opening of his new offices and the formation of his management company. It had been a lively affair with Pete Peterson turning up out of his brain, sounding off to all the music journalists who were present. Ray hadn't had chance to enjoy the night, as his main objective (apart from taking the opportunity to flirt with Janine) had been discussing the latest information they'd received about Rudi's, and the possible coming drugs war between the Jamaicans and Rota Bocan.

Ray knew, from his experience in Liverpool, that if you had one team in the city who were the known drugs dealers you could control them, and until recently the Jamaicans had quietly got on with it without causing anybody any trouble. The problem now was that Rota Bocan were intent on not just taking a share, but flooding the market with cheap drugs and controlling the city. The Jamaicans were not happy and tensions were rising.

The day after meeting Mr. C and Alex Mitchell at the club, Ray's thoughts were confused. Gerry had arranged for them all to gather in his offices and Ray had outlined his concerns about Rudi's being a hub for the drugs. Mr. C had seemed pretty genuine especially when he openly admitted he liked the odd spliff, but the reaction from Alex Mitchell had concerned him. Mitchell had avoided answering Gerry's question and Ray had sensed his unease. Afterwards on his way home to the smart little apartment he'd been lucky to find in a quiet, leafy part of nearby Barlowe, Ray decided he'd do a little more digging on Alex Mitchell, when he was back in the office first thing in the morning.

Ray enjoyed living on his own with none of the pressures of sharing his space with anyone else. His apartment was in a recently built block of four, and he was lucky to have a garage where he could keep his treasured White 1.6L Lotus Twin Cam Escort. He wasn't looking for any kind of relationship - although he thought to himself he'd like to find out more about Gerry Fortuna's wife. For now, he was quite happy putting his feet up, watching football on his new colour TV, with a couple of beers and the fish and chips he'd picked up from his local chippy.

CHAPTER ELEVEN

IT WAS the beginning of the Christmas holidays and Gerry had closed the offices down until after New Year. Nobody in the music industry did anything other than party from the start of December and he'd decided to join them. He'd been working flat out since signing The Flames to FAM, booking their UK and European tour which was due to kick off in March next year. Pete Peterson had finally got his act together and finished the album, which would be released the week before the first date of the tour. He'd managed to confirm most of the press and publicity, so he felt he was due a well-earned rest.

The Hideout was fully booked with office parties every night, and the catering ran like clockwork with turkey dinners churned out with military precision. The only dark cloud was the situation with Rudi's, which was still rumbling on. Ray Law had been in touch to say they were keeping it under observation, but as yet had no firm leads, although Gerry sensed there was something Ray wasn't telling him.

Their major concern was the huge seasonal concert that had been arranged for Christmas Eve. It was a sell-out with a thousand tickets sold, and Alex Mitchell had been working for weeks booking the acts through his agency – he stood to make a lot of money from his share of the commission. He'd managed to persuade a couple of well-known Jamaican reggae artists to play, as well as a chart-topping soul band with support from local acts. It promised to be an amazing night of music.

Gerry had decided to drop by the offices to pick up a copy of The Flames' album, when he noticed a large envelope had been pushed through the letterbox. Thinking it was a contract, he ripped it open and froze. On a single sheet of paper, he saw the message:

$ YOU WERE WARNED

He picked up the phone and called George Williams.

Sitting around the table in the back room of St Mary's Irish Club, Joe Burke and three fellow members of the Association, studied the photos spread out in front of them, their four glasses of Guinness hardly touched.

"There he is again," Joe pointed at one of the photos. "That's every week for the past month, and the only other person in the club is yer man, Alex Mitchell. It has to be the drop. Look at the parcel, it's exactly the same as the ones from last week and the week before."

"And every time, straight after, there's a flood of the stuff out there. Errol's guys are saying they can't sell it as cheap as these bastards!" Niall took a mouthful of his Guinness.

Michael stood up. "OK! So what are we going to do about it then?" He took his pint and drained the glass.

"First we think carefully about our next move," Joe said with a calming voice.

"How about we get another one of those letters off to yer man Fortuna. That'll make them think it's the Yanks stirring up the trouble," said Niall. "The first one had him runnin' to the cops right enough."

Sean, the quiet one of the four, suddenly spoke. "Did yer see there's a huge concert at Rudi's on Christmas Eve? Loads of big stars, all the tickets are gone."

"What are you sayin', Sean?" Joe looked across at him.

"I have a friend who has access to Semtex," Sean replied with a menace in his voice. "Maybe we could give them bastards something to think about?"

"Ah now that's serious shite yer talkin' there." Michael sat down again.

"It's not serious when it affects our territory," Sean replied. "Them fuckin' Yanks think they can just walk in an' take over; I reckon we let 'em know who's boss round here! What d'you say Joe?"

"I don't know, Sean. Like Michael says, that's serious shite alright. It's a long time since we had anything to do with explosives, and Semtex is bad stuff. I wouldn't know where to start with that!"

"So maybe you leave it to the experts then," replied Sean becoming serious. "My friend Frank deals with it all the time, and he's over here working on the roads. I was having a jar with him the other night and got talking about our situation. Said he's more than happy to help. He's from Cork and still supports the cause."

"What the fuck were you doing talking about our business, Sean?" Michael jumped up. Sean stood up and stared him down.

"OK calm down you'se two," Joe stepped in between them. "Michael's right, Sean; you'd no right discussing our business. However, I'm thinking it won't do any harm having a chat with your friend. How about you ask him to come along. It'll be December next week and if we want to do something to that concert we need to move fast."

Janine hadn't seen Pete since the night of the party, when after his outburst she and Bobby had finally managed to get him into a taxi back to his hotel. Gerry's attitude had surprised them all, and Pete had done as he asked, returning to the studio to finish the album.

Janine had to take a trip down to London to pick up some artwork for one of Richard's properties, and with the memories of the outrageous events from her last visit still on her mind, she called Pete at his house.

"Hey babe, yeah it's all cool," he said, sounding slightly stoned. "Why don't you come round? Jump in a cab, you're just around the corner!"

"Well, OK, but I can't stay late. I have to be back tonight." She climbed into the taxi wondering if she was doing the right thing.

The house Pete shared with the other musicians was a five-minute trip, just off the High Street in Kensington. It was an old three-storey Victorian terrace with a basement which would originally have been used by servants.

Janine rang the bell and the door was opened by a girl wearing a tie-dyed kaftan and not much else. Her long brown hair hung in ringlets down her back and she was smoking a joint.

"Oh hi. I'm looking for Pete," said Janine.

"Yeah sure come in," said the girl, wafting away down the hall. "Pete! Lady here to see you!" she shouted up the stairs, disappearing into what appeared to be the kitchen.

Pete appeared at the top of the stairs wearing nothing but a tight-fitting pair of jeans. "Babe! Come on up. Mind the mess."

The place was a tip, with drum cases and amplifiers piled up in the hallway; but standing there, Pete looked every inch the rock star. Janine's stomach did a skip as she climbed the stairs. He held her in his arms kissing her at length on the lips. Maybe just one more time she thought as they went into his bedroom.

It was a mess with clothes piled everywhere, and a huge sheet pinned up over the window. The bed looked like it hadn't been made for ages, but Janine didn't care. It didn't take more than a few seconds to slip Pete's jeans off, and as she held him in her hand rubbing gently, he unbuttoned her skirt and she stepped out of her knickers. Her jacket was the last thing to be shrugged off.

She pushed him back on the bed and climbed on top, gasping as she lowered herself onto him. They played with each other knowing just how far to go before stopping and starting again until finally they couldn't hold back and they both exploded, Janine crying out, and then getting a fit of the giggles as she realised everyone in the house had to have heard them.

Lying together afterwards, Pete said he thought they might have some champagne somewhere and as he got up to go downstairs, Janine noticed a box of chocolates at the side of the bed.

"Hey, can I have one of these chocolates," she called as he was leaving the room. "Yeah course, but just the one," he replied closing the door.

They were delicious and Janine had eaten three before Pete returned with a bottle of Moët Chandon.

"Sorry, this is all we've got," he apologised, seeing the look on her face; "I know, rock 'n' roll mouthwash! Hey how many of those truffles did you eat?"

"Only three," she said. "Why? They're really nice."

"They might be nice, but they're also filled with dope, and if you've eaten three you're gonna be well out of it. Maybe you ought to think about staying here tonight," he said. "That's some heavy shit you've just eaten."

"I can't do that. What would I tell Gerry? He didn't like me coming down in the first place. He's not happy about me working with Richard." She was sounding worried.

"Yeah, well from what I've heard you've been doing a bit more than working with him!" Pete laughed. "But hey, rock 'n' roll, babe. In the meantime, we need to get you to the station before that stuff kicks in." Pete went to help her up, but she wouldn't move.

"Come on." Pete tried again but Janine was staring at his guitar, which was on a stand in the corner of the room. "What's up?"

"That snake over there just smiled," she said, pointing. "It keeps looking at me."

"Oh shit," exclaimed Pete. "Now we're in trouble."

Half an hour later he managed to get her on the train back to Birmingham. She seemed a lot better in the taxi and he'd told her not to speak to anyone on the way back. He'd found her an empty first-class compartment and pulling down the blinds he gave her a quick kiss and closed the door, jumping out of the carriage just as the guard blew his whistle. He'd almost collided with a man in the corridor as he made his way out of the carriage. Pete thought he recognised him but couldn't place his face and thought no more about it as he climbed into a taxi.

Janine was just putting a cigarette in her mouth as the door slid open and the man Pete had seen in the corridor walked in.

"Need a light?" he said leaning over and lighting her cigarette with his lighter. He was small, with a friendly face and had a slight Birmingham accent. "Say aren't you the lady who used to work in Georgie's?" he said as Janine blew out a plume of smoke. "I used to be a regular. Shame it closed down, I really enjoyed going there."

Janine smiled and nodded taking another draw on her cigarette. She was doing her best to concentrate on what he was saying but finding it hard to focus. He sat down in the opposite corner of the compartment rambling on about the leather-lined lift and something else, but it was all a blur to her.

By the time she'd finished her cigarette she noticed he'd left but hadn't seen him go. She was just relaxing back in her seat when the door slid open and he returned with another man. The second man, who was taller than his friend, pushed the door closed and flipped the catch to lock it. The first man no longer looked quite so friendly, and Janine suddenly became very aware of her situation, trying to remain calm. The drugs in her system were no longer having such an effect and her senses were becoming pin-sharp again.

The first man spoke. "My friend here and I used to love you serving us at Georgie's. You have the most beautiful breasts, Janine. It was a shame you covered them up. We came every weekend just to see them."

Janine smiled and slowly reached inside her handbag to find the pointed metal tail comb she always carried with her. To her relief her fingers touched the cold metal teeth and she gripped it tightly.

The other man was speaking now. His voice was quite threatening. "I've always wanted to touch your breasts. They looked so perfect; let's play a game – we'll pretend we're back at Georgie's and you're serving us. No one will know except us three. Here, I'll help you with your top," he said, standing up and moving towards her.

As he did so, Janine noticed the first man had unzipped his trousers and was already rubbing his small, erect penis. She glanced back just as the other man made a lunge for her, and in one swift move she pulled the sharp metal comb from her bag and stabbed it into his hand. The man screamed as blood poured down his arm, while Janine turned and aimed between the first man's legs with the pointed toe of her stiletto, delivering a painful kick to his testicles. The second man was angry now and grabbed her shoulder with his other hand spinning her round, but Janine was ready, remembering something she'd seen Bobby do at the club one night. She clenched her fist and punched the man as hard as she could in his throat. It took him completely by surprise and he collapsed on top of his groaning friend. Calmly, Janine picked up her handbag and stepping over her two debilitated assailants, flipped the catch on the door and slid it back. She turned round surveying the scene.

"That was fun guys. I hope you'll allow me to serve you again, yer dirty pair of feckers."

She made her way to the restaurant car where she bought herself a glass of champagne, which she drank straight back in one go. She ordered another, but this time sipped it slowly until the train pulled into the station back in Birmingham.

When she thought back to what the two men had said, she vaguely remembered a couple of guys who used to ogle her – she had dismissed them at the time as a pair of weirdos. She definitely wouldn't make the mistake of travelling alone in a compartment again, but she decided against mentioning the episode to Gerry. There would be too many questions asked which she couldn't answer.

CHAPTER TWELVE

ALEX MITCHELL lay with his head in James' lap, stretched out on the sofa. They were in Alex's cramped apartment, which was damp and in desperate need of redecoration.

Alex hated it and constantly complained to his landlord who always promised to do something about it but never did. It was on the bottom floor of a block built in the fifties which was already showing signs of wear. Until recently he couldn't even consider looking for somewhere else, but since his new job at Rudi's (and his scams on the side), he'd been thinking about moving up market. That was until the meeting with Gerry Fortuna and DCI Ray Law.

James' brother Thomas, the drummer in Alex's trio, had promised he would speak to the Rota Bocan about allowing him to cancel their agreement, but so far he'd heard nothing back.

"I tell you; Thomas won't let you down," James said, stroking Alex's hair. "It'll be fine, don't worry."

"This is serious; I'm really scared," said Alex. "If Gerry gets the slightest whiff of me being involved, he'll kill me. He said so!"

"That's just him though. All bluster. He wouldn't really do it. Don't worry, we'll sort it." James said, trying to calm Alex.

"And that policeman, he's onto something. I got the impression he knew more than he was letting on. And then there's this big gig coming up. Shit! If anything goes wrong with that I'll lose a load of money!" Alex stood up.

"Listen man, just relax. The gig is gonna be amazing. Look at all the work you've done and the acts you've got booked. Stop worrying. Let me do something to take your mind off things." James reached down to open Alex's trousers.

"Oh God, I can't relax. Not now, man," said Alex.

"Oh, definitely now," whispered James, as he pulled Alex towards him. Alex let out a low moan but just then the telephone rang.

"Fuck!" exclaimed James.

Alex picked up the receiver, zipping up his trousers.

"Yes….Yes of course. What time? OK, I'll be there; no problem." He put the phone down. "That was Thomas. They want a meeting. Tomorrow morning at ten. Your place."

"Well, that's good news don't you think? At least they're willing to talk to you."

"Well let's hope so. I just know I need to get out before it's too late."

"So, stop worrying Alex, and come here. We have unfinished business." As he spoke James reached up and unfastened Alex's trousers again. This time he didn't complain.

There was an extra pint on the bar in the back room of St Mary's, as the four men listened to Sean's friend Frank outlining his plan.

"Yer have to use the element of surprise," he said. "They'll be expecting something to happen on Christmas Eve at the big concert. I guarantee the crowd'll be full of cops. So, we wait. Let them pat themselves on the back when nothing happens. Give 'em chance to relax, enjoy the festivities. By the time the New Year arrives they'll have forgotten all about it. Then BOOM! We'll blow the shite out of 'em."

"That's all well and good, but what about the loss of earnings over the Christmas holidays?" Michael said.

"A small price to pay to be rid of them for good," replied Sean. "I think Frank's plan will work. What about you Joe? Niall?"

"We'll need to make sure Errol's in on this," said Niall. "His guys are the ones who're suffering."

"No," said Frank, picking up his pint and swallowing half in one go. Wiping the froth from his mouth he carried on. "The cops'll automatically bring in all the usual suspects and you can't guarantee they'll keep their mouths shut. The less any of 'em know, the better."

"So, say we decide to go ahead, how do you intend on doing it?" asked Joe.

"Well after talking to Sean, I went down to have a look around the place the other night. The security is useless. The eejit doormen were too busy lookin' at the arses of the young lasses to be bothered about me. It wasn't too busy and I managed to check out various storage areas that were easily accessed. Anyway, there's a pile of cases under the back of the stage that don't seem to be in use. Looks like they've been there a while because they were covered in dust. It would be simple to put my device inside one."

"How would you detonate it?" Joe asked, becoming interested.

"It'd have to be done with a timer. There's that much electrical equipment, I wouldn't trust a remote control." Frank replied.

"And how would we get it in the club? There has to be someone there all day, like that manager guy." said Michael.

"Aye but they have to have cleaners as well," said Sean. "Molly, my cousin works there; she's a grand lass and she's still loyal to the cause, God bless her."

"Would you trust her to do it?" Joe asked.

"Of course. I'd train her personally. All she'd have to do would be to set the timer and flick a switch which would activate it, then put it in the case and close the lid," replied Frank. "If anyone asks her what she's doing, well she's cleaning, that's what she does and she'll be back home in Cork on holiday before anyone notices she's gone."

"OK Frank, thank you for your time," said Joe. "I'll need to discuss this with the others, and we'll let you know our decision. Sean, please show your cousin out."

DCI Ray Law was sitting at his desk, surrounded by scraps of paper covered in his scribble. He'd spent all of his time since the meeting at Gerry Fortuna's, trying to find information on Alex Mitchell, but with no luck. As far as he could tell, Alex was squeaky clean, without even a speeding ticket to his name. His musicians however were a different kettle of fish.

Wynton Brown had recently been cautioned for possession of a small amount of cannabis when his vehicle was pulled over for a faulty rear light. One of the hazards of being a musician travelling home late after a gig, was that traffic police would stop anything suspicious just to relieve the boredom. Wynton had been unfortunate. What should have been routine, turned into something else, because of the telltale drug fumes when he opened his window for the officers.

Thomas Wilson Jr had also appeared in his search, after he was arrested during a protest march about the death of civil rights activist Martin

Luther King – he made a note to follow that line of enquiry further. He wasn't sure why, but his instinct told him Thomas was a person of interest.

On a hunch, Ray called Gerry Fortuna's home number and Janine answered the phone. Yes, she was free that afternoon and would be happy to speak to him. After a quick lunch in the canteen, he set off with a spring in his step to their apartment.

Janine answered the door wearing a pale-blue silk blouse and cream slacks, with flat pumps. He had found it difficult to take his eyes off her before when he was in her company, and being on his own with her threw him completely.

"Hey Ray, come in," she said warmly. "Would you like a drink? Beer? Scotch? I've got some chilled champagne if you'd like a glass."

"Oh no, no thanks," he stuttered. "It's very tempting but I'm on duty. This is actually an official visit. I'd like to ask you a few questions if you don't mind."

"Sure, no problem. I haven't done anything wrong have I?" Janine gave him a sexy smile. "At least not yet."

"Ha, no; not yet but I live in hope," he replied. There was a slight pause and their eyes met briefly before he spoke again, breaking the silence. "Anyway, as you're probably aware there's a major drugs problem developing in the city, and we're led to believe it's centred on Rudi's. After the last meeting with Gerry, the DJ - Charles I think his name is - and the manager, Alex Mitchell, I decided to do a bit of checking up. In particular I was interested in Alex, but strangely I can't find anything on him. It's as if he doesn't exist, certainly in the eyes of the law – and I thought I'd get your opinion. I noticed your reaction to him at the party."

"I can't stand him," she said forcefully. Ray's eyebrows shot up. "I don't know why; I just don't trust him. I've told Gerry what I think, but he went ahead and made him manager of Rudi's. He gives me the creeps."

"He was with a well-dressed young black guy that night, and they seemed pretty close. Do you know who that is?"

"According to Charles, he's the brother of Alex's drummer, Thomas. That's really all I know. Oh, hang on! There was something I heard the other day from my friend Richard Kennedy. He was at the party. You must know him; he has a property development company here in the city. Well anyway, he mentioned that Alex had contacted his office looking to rent one of his expensive new luxury apartments. He thought at the time it might have been well out of Alex's price range, even with the money he's earning from the club."

"Hmm, so he's got money to throw around. That's very interesting," Ray said thoughtfully, writing in his notebook. "Did Richard say if he'd heard any more from him?"

"I don't think so. According to Richard, he was just looking round at the time. Are you sure you don't want a drink? I'm going to have a glass of Bollinger; can I not tempt you?" She picked up a cut glass champagne flute and pinged it with her fingernail.

Ray would have loved a drink with her, but needed to follow up on this interesting piece of information.

"I'm sorry, I need to get back to the office. Maybe another time?" he suggested, standing up to leave.

"I'll hold you to that," she said.

As he walked out of the apartment he hoped there would be another time to take her up on that offer.

When Ray arrived back at the police headquarters, there was a message waiting on his desk: Ring George Williams - URGENT.

He picked up his phone and dialled. The Chief Constable answered on the first ring. "My office, now, Ray." He sounded terse.

Ray took the stairs up to the top floor, two at a time, knocking on the solid oak door moments later.

"Come in," George's voice answered and as Ray entered, "Don't you ever get out of breath?"

"New fitness regime sir. What's up?"

"Gerry's had another letter with the dollar sign again. It says 'YOU WERE WARNED'. We've got to take it seriously this time. Especially since they've got that bloody concert coming up on Christmas Eve. It was delivered to his office. You'd better get over there right away. Where have you been anyway?"

"I was over at Gerry's apartment, talking to the wife, Janine, following up a lead. Had a hunch, and it turns out the manager of Rudi's seems to have a bit of spare cash. He's looking at luxury apartments all of a sudden." His thoughts turned to Janine. "Have to say, she is one classy lady!"

"Had a hunch, eh! Take my advice. Don't go getting tangled up with Mrs. Fortuna." George leaned back in his chair. "She's a classy lady alright, but just remember she's Gerry Fortuna's wife. Do yourself a favour and keep your distance."

"Don't worry boss; they call me Mr. Professional," Ray laughed as he left the office. George shook his head as Ray closed the door. *I hope you know what you're doing lad, I really do!* he thought.

Alex arrived at Thomas's small, terraced house at exactly ten o'clock. He'd been up early, showered and dressed, leaving James asleep in bed. Thomas opened the door, wearing just his dressing gown. He invited Alex into a tiny front room, made even smaller by the drum kit set up in the corner.

"Where are they? I thought they said ten o'clock," Alex said nervously.

"Be cool man," replied Thomas. "They phoned just before you arrived. They said they're not happy with your request, but they have decided to let you leave the agreement." Alex breathed a sigh of relief. "However," Thomas continued, "you can't go until after New Year. It's a very busy period over the holidays, and they need to make sure their shipments arrive safely." Alex started to protest but Thomas held up his hand. "Look man, there is no room for negotiation on this. Trust me. Be thankful they're allowing you to leave at all."

"How long after New Year?" Alex asked.

"They will let you know," replied Thomas. "They said there'll be another shipment tomorrow and one the following week as usual."

"OK. Fine. I just have to make sure Gerry doesn't come snooping around. He was pretty wound up about it at the meeting with the policeman the other day."

"Listen to me," said Thomas. "Just be cool and don't do anything different. If you panic he'll get suspicious and start asking questions. All you're doing is getting records sent over from the States. That's all anyone needs to know. Anyway, how's my brother? I hope you're treating him well."

"He's fine," said Alex, standing up to leave. "Are you OK for the rehearsal this afternoon? Don't forget we're playing at the gig on Christmas Eve and I want to go through a couple of new numbers."

"Yes, that's fine. I'll be there. And Alex. Don't hurt James, he's a gentle soul."

Thomas smiled to himself as Alex left. What an idiot. Does he really believe Benny Mulligan would let him leave just like that?

Ray Law and Gerry Fortuna were in Gerry's office examining the sheet of paper that had arrived in the post that morning. The dollar sign was crudely drawn and the writing big and clumsy.

"You know, there's something about this that's not right," Ray said. "It just doesn't seem like something the Rota Bocan would do. I mean just look at the letters. It's like something a kid would send, not an outfit like them."

"Whoever it is, they're obviously trying to scare us," said Gerry. "Do you think we should cancel the Christmas Eve gig, just in case."

"Hell no!" Ray exclaimed. "That's exactly what they want you to do. Look, we'll put undercover officers in the crowd and double the surveillance teams. We'll make such a show of force they'd be stupid to try anything."

"Well, OK, if you think it'll be safe, I'll take your word, but I think we should have another meeting with Alex and Charles."

"Talking of Alex, just how much are you paying him?" Ray asked. "I've heard he's been looking at renting an expensive apartment. Seems a bit strange he's got cash to splash around all of a sudden. Have you noticed a change in him recently?"

"To be honest since I made him manager, I've left him alone to get on with it. But it's interesting about the apartment, I certainly don't pay him that much. Who told you about it?" Gerry asked.

"Your wife said that he'd called Richard Kennedy's office enquiring about one of his new deluxe penthouses. I spoke to her earlier at your apartment," Ray replied.

"My apartment, really?" Gerry looked annoyed. "I had a hunch," Ray explained, slightly flustered.

"Well, I'd appreciate it if you would speak to me first, next time you have a hunch," Gerry said forcefully. "Janine has made it quite plain that she doesn't like Alex, but I don't want her involved in all this, so keep her out of it. I'll arrange another meeting with Charles and Alex down at the club. That way we can have a look round while you're there. Would tomorrow morning suit you?"

"I've got a meeting with George Williams at nine o'clock; could we make it say ten?" Ray thought it best to speak to his boss first.

"Fine. I'll arrange it now," said Gerry, picking up his phone.

"Thank you sir, and sorry about the misunderstanding with your wife. It won't happen again." Ray shook hands with Gerry. He breathed a huge sigh of relief as he left the offices. *That'll teach you Ray*, he thought, walking back to the office. *George Williams was right; he would definitely be playing with fire if he pursued anything with Janine.* Still, he couldn't help thinking it would be worth it though.

At the same time Ray Law was meeting Gerry, Mr. C made another visit to Errol in the house with the boarded-up windows. The downstairs rooms were in darkness, but he was able to see his way through to the drawing room where the old man sat in his armchair smoking. He beckoned Mr. C to sit on the chair in front of him and passed him the joint. Mr. C took a long pull on it, holding the smoke in his lungs before passing it back. The reggae music from the basement below seemed louder than ever and he strained to hear the old man speak.

"I spoken to our friends 'bout our problem," Errol said. "Dem say not to worry, it be sorted soon. Everyting cool."

"That's as maybe, but my guys is worried 'cause it costin' them money. The Yanks're sellin' the shit so cheap they almost givin' it away," Mr. C said, exasperated.

"Patience my boy," Errol was calm. "Dem say it all be back to normal real soon. Dem say the Yanks won't know what hit 'em. Boom!"

"They're not going to do something to the gig on Christmas Eve are they?" Mr. C asked, concerned.

"Dem not say. Dem just tell me they take care of the problem. Our problem is their problem dem say." The old man took another deep draw on the joint and passed it back. Mr. C could feel the effects of just one hit already and wondered how the old man managed to smoke so much. He was starting to feel light-headed and he had to drive home, so he took a token hit and returned it.

"Ha-ha, the ganja is strong, yes?" Errol laughed. "You tell your guys to have faith. Errol always look after dem before and he look after dem again. You go tell dem. You be careful Charles."

Mr. C picked his way out into the daylight again. He felt really stoned as he climbed into his car and drove off cautiously. Once again the camera shutter clicked as his movements were captured by Joe Burke sitting in the parked van further down the road, in the driveway of an empty house.

"Don't you'se worry," Joe mumbled to himself. "We'll take care of your problems. It'll cost you mind."

Alex had arrived home from the club. He was tired and just getting ready to go to bed when the phone rang. It was Thomas telling him the package would be arriving at eleven the next morning and he would be calling for it at half past. Alex was immediately nervous. He knew Gerry would be at the club at ten o'clock with the policeman snooping around, and he didn't know how long they'd be there. Charles would also be there, and he tended to hang around sorting his records once he was in the club.

"Can't you change the time?" he asked. "I've no idea how long it'll take, and if Gerry or that policeman get a whiff of something suspicious they'll start digging."

"You'll just have to get rid of them won't you," Thomas replied. "There's no way I can change the time of the delivery, it's already on the way. You worry too much. I'll see you tomorrow." He hung up.

"I don't need this pressure," Alex shouted, slamming the phone down. James put his arms around him. "Come to bed, it's late and you're so tense. Here let me help you relax."

"God, you seem to think sex is the answer to everything," Alex said, pushing him away.

James sat on the bed with a sad child-like expression looking up at him.

Alex backed down. "I'm sorry. It's just really difficult at the moment. I wish I'd never got involved in the first place. Come here, I know you're only trying to help."

James started to unbutton Alex's shirt. "I just love you so much."

"Yeah me too," said Alex, as their lips came together.

The following morning Ray Law was sitting in George Williams' office drinking a cup of fresh percolated coffee. It was from the machine he kept ticking over all day, and much better than the awful stuff he usually drank from the canteen. It was just after nine and they were going over the plans Ray had suggested for the Christmas Eve gig at Rudi's. It would involve a large team consisting of both undercover and uniformed officers – and George was concerned about the overtime bill.

"I'm sure we can get Gerry Fortuna to contribute towards it," said Ray. "I mean at the end of the day it's his club that's causing the problem."

"Well, you may be right, but Gerry's not known for throwing his money around. I think you should leave it to me to have a word with him."

"Come on, he must be making a fortune. All the tickets are sold and they're not cheap. OK he's got some good artists on, but even so…"

"Yes, well as I say, let me speak to him," George replied. "Anyway, you'd better be getting over to the club. One thing I do know about Gerry; he hates people being late."

Alex had arrived early and made sure everything was tidy in his office ready for the others. Charles arrived next and started sorting through his records just as Alex knew he would. At exactly ten o'clock, Gerry walked in with Ray Law. Alex was doing his best not to appear anxious although he couldn't relax, and hoped it wouldn't be too obvious to the others.

Ray Law said, "Right, well the reason we wanted to meet you down here is that Gerry has received another letter. The same as the last one, but this time it says 'YOU WERE WARNED'. We're still none the wiser as to who sent it, but we're treating it as a serious threat. Obviously our main concern is the gig on Christmas Eve ….."

"Surely we can't pull it at this late stage?" Alex interrupted a little too forcefully. "Everything is confirmed. It'd be a nightmare cancelling all the acts I've got booked."

"If you'll let me finish," Ray answered, just as forcefully. "We've advised Mr. Fortuna not to cancel the show. However, I am going to insist you increase the normal amount of security you have, as a precaution. My team will be actively involved on the night, both undercover as punters in the crowd, and as high-profile uniforms outside. Whoever is behind these letters is trying to scare you, but if we stick to the plans I'm drawing up we should be fine. Alex, I will need a list of everyone who will be performing on the night, and anyone else associated with them. Anyone helping with equipment will have to have a pass. Also, a list of all the staff working that night.

"Charles, I need you to spread the word around all your contacts that if they hear anything on the grapevine about shipments of drugs arriving, to get in touch with me. They can go through you if they're not happy speaking to me direct.

"We are led to believe there's a gang of Americans calling themselves Rota Bocan, who are trying to flood the city with cheap drugs and disrupt the usual supply chain. Do either of you know anything about this?" Ray looked directly at Alex.

Alex felt the sweat run down his back. He didn't know if it showed, but he could feel himself going pale.

"Alex, maybe you can show Ray and me around the place," Gerry suggested.

"Sure, no problem," Alex said, relieved. "Follow me." He set off into the main room switching on the daytime lighting with Ray and Gerry behind while Charles went over to his DJ booth and put a record on.

"For fuck's sake, turn that off," shouted Gerry, just about making himself heard over the intro to 'Cloud Nine', the latest single from the Temptations. Charles turned the record off and went back into the office.

Ray was amazed that during the day, the club, lit by a few normal light bulbs, was in fact just a big square box with the walls painted black. The banks of coloured lighting at night made all the difference in terms of atmosphere. At least now he could see clearly as he wandered round the back of the stage.

"What are these for?" he asked Alex, pointing to a pile of cases underneath covered in dust.

90

"I think they were what the sound system came in," he said. "They've been there since we opened."

"Well, you could do with getting them moved somewhere else. They're a fire hazard."

"No problem. I'll get the cleaner to shift them," Alex said, looking at his watch. It was a quarter to eleven.

Suddenly, Charles shouted from the doorway. "Alex there's a parcel just arrived for you. I've put it in the office."

Gerry looked at him and was about to speak when Alex said, "Ah, that must be the US imports I ordered. New tunes that the trio are learning. Latest Coltrane and Miles albums, absolutely brilliant. I'll let you borrow them sometime, Gerry."

"Me?" said Gerry. "I can't stand jazz. Right. Are we about done here Ray? I need to get back to The Hideout. There's a delivery of turkeys arriving. Two hundred Christmas dinners over the next few days. Bloody mayhem!"

"I think that's enough for now," said Ray. "If you can send that information through, Alex, I'd be much obliged."

Gerry and Ray left the club and Charles went back to sorting through his records.

Alex was still feeling pale half an hour later when Thomas turned up for his package. He said they couldn't talk because Charles was still there and might overhear their conversation, so he accompanied him to the door, stepping outside as Thomas left with the package. Neither of them spotted the Transit van parked in a side street across the road.

"So, I would say without a shadow of a doubt, that the shipments arrive at the club and the manager is in on it, because there he is with the black guy leaving with the same package as before. I've timed it – it's eleven o'clock every week, on the same day." Joe was once again spreading out the photos he'd taken on the table in the back room of the Irish Club. Michael, Niall, Sean and Frank were sitting around the table.

"I say we go ahead with Frank's idea," said Niall. "But on the understanding it's only the club and those two yokes that we take out."

"Don't worry about that. As I said before, I'll make sure that Molly knows exactly what to do – the timer will be set for eleven o'clock in the morning, which is when yer man will be there collecting the stuff." Frank leaned back in his chair. "There is one thing we haven't discussed yet. What this little exercise will cost."

"What are we looking at then?" Joe asked.

"Well, I can get the Semtex from a contact, so that shouldn't be too bad. Then there's Molly's fare home and a little sweetener to keep her quiet, and of course my costs." Frank thought for a moment. "A grand should do it."

"That's an awful lot of feckin' money," Michael said.

"Aye, and it's an awful lot of money I'll be savin' for you an' all," said Frank. "Take it or leave it boys."

"He's right," said Sean. "Those bastards are bleedin' us dry. I say we do it."

"OK, let's see a show of hands," said Joe. "All those in favour?"

Reluctantly, Michael was the last to raise his hand, but eventually it was unanimous.

"You'll have the money tomorrow," said Joe. "So, they make the drops on a Thursday morning."

"No problem. Molly will plant it on the Wednesday morning at eleven o'clock when she's there cleaning, and it will be on a twenty-four-hour timer for the following morning," said Frank. "I'll make sure she's had plenty of practice by then. Don't you worry; she'll be fine."

Later that night, Sean's cousin Molly snuggled up to Frank in bed. The attractive, slightly plump, thirty-year-old divorcee had welcomed the extra income for taking Frank in as a lodger, while he was in the UK working on the new road system on the outskirts of the city. It hadn't taken long for him to work his charm on her, and after being alone for so long, she welcomed the company – and his energetic lovemaking.

"Don't worry; it'll be easy. All you have to do is follow my instructions," Frank said, sitting up. "The timer has a switch on the front. You just make sure you push it to the right and then lock it in one of the cases under the stage."

"I don't know Frank. I mean what if someone asks me what I'm doing?"

She sounded nervous.

"There's nothing to worry about. If anyone questions you, tell them you've been told to tidy the cases under the stage. But you said there's only you cleans in the big room. Trust me."

Frank reached over and unbuttoned her nightie. She sighed as he slid his hand between her legs.

"I trust you, Frank. I do," she whispered closing her eyes.

The evening paper Frank had been reading slid off the bed, open at the entertainment page, revealing the advert for the new regular Wednesday jazz night at Rudi's, starting in the New Year.

CHAPTER THIRTEEN

CHRISTMAS EVE at Rudi's was chaotic. Not only did Alex have to organise the six artists, their musicians and all the associated personnel who were appearing that night, he also had to liaise with Ray Law and the undercover officers who were mixing with the sold-out audience, all of whom were eager to enjoy every moment.

For once he'd decided not to play in the show, but his musicians, Thomas and Wynton, were there – Thomas with his brother James and Wynton with his girlfriend.

Thomas had gone to the bar with Wynton to get some drinks and while they were waiting to be served, he said, "You want to buy some blow, man? Real cheap."

"Didn't know you were into that shit," Wynton replied.

"Yeah well I'm not, but some friends of mine are, and they got some really good stuff," said Thomas.

"I'm cool at the moment," said Wynton. "But maybe I'll give you a shout in the New Year."

"Like I said, it's real good stuff and cheap, man." Thomas turned round and it was his turn at the bar.

Wynton thought to himself that maybe he should have a word with his friend Mr. C; he was sure he'd be very interested in what Thomas had just told him, especially as it was he who Wynton usually bought his drugs from.

DCI Ray Law was sitting in Alex's office coordinating his team. He'd got ten officers – six men and four WPCs – circulating in the club dressed as punters. Outside he had four highly visible officers – two on the door with the bouncers and two sitting in a car across the street.

Gerry had been against Janine going, but she had insisted. No way was she going to miss a night of dancing to some of her favourite music. Reluctantly, he'd agreed and was slouched on a chair alongside Ray Law keeping an eye on the proceedings. "I must be crazy sitting here with the possibility of something going off," he said.

Ray looked up from the TV monitor he was watching. "Don't worry, everything's under control. What can possibly happen? There're cops everywhere you look. They'd be crazy to try something tonight."

"Yeah, well until I'm home safe in bed, I won't relax," Gerry said, looking around. "Where's Janine? Has anyone seen my wife?"

Alex had come into the office. "She was at the front of the stage dancing the last time I saw her. It's crazy out there."

Wynton and Thomas had returned from the bar with the drinks, and after a couple of minutes Wynton excused himself to go to the toilet, but instead made his way over to Mr. C's podium. One of the bands was on stage, which meant he had a break and was using the time to sort the records ready for his next set. Catching his eye, Wynton beckoned him over, and leaning close so as to be heard over the noise, told him what Thomas had just said. Mr. C raised his eyebrows and slapping Wynton on the shoulder said he'd pass the information on to Errol.

"You done good my man. Errol will be pleased. Here's a little something to make the festive season more enjoyable."

Unaware that they were being watched by one of Ray Law's undercover officers from the corner of the room, Mr. C slipped a small wrap into Wynton's hand as he left to return to the others.

The officer made a note to report the action to his boss later.

Janine was having a great time at the front of the stage doing what she enjoyed most, dancing. She hadn't realised how much she'd missed going out and letting her hair down. The music was fantastic – all her favourites. And to see artists whose records she'd danced to so many times, performing live on stage, was incredible. She knew Gerry hadn't wanted her to go, but she had desperately wanted to be there – and the fact that DCI Ray Law was in charge was an added bonus.

Janine had been surprised by Ray's visit to the apartment, but had found herself fascinated by him. She'd also noticed that Gerry had become strangely possessive recently, trying to get her to become more involved in the business. She was now an equal shareholder of his clubs and managing director of FAM with Gerry as chairman, which meant she was a very powerful woman in the city. As a result, the situation with Richard Kennedy had become tricky, and she'd had to calm it down much to his annoyance. In fact, he was starting to become a pain and sadly in the New Year he'd have to go. But right now, Mr. C was playing the new Temptations single – she closed her eyes and started moving to the rhythm.

Gerry was watching from the back of the stage. He was glad Janine was enjoying herself, even though they'd argued about whether they should come or not. Janine had been adamant and eventually he'd agreed, as long as he was there too. They didn't go out together much anymore like they used to, and he'd decided to make an effort to change things. Since he'd appointed Alex as manager at Rudi's it had certainly relieved some of the pressure of running both his clubs, but now with Fortuna Artist Management representing Pete Peterson and The Flames, he'd replaced one headache with another. Managing The Flames was a full-time job, with something or someone always needing his attention. Pete was a very demanding character, and with him living in London it made things difficult at times. Pete had a habit of disappearing for days on end just as Gerry was setting up a string of interviews, which meant either one of the other band members stepping in or having to reschedule. But Pete was gradually becoming so big a personality, he was overshadowing the rest of the band, which Gerry could foresee causing problems.

Hopefully, once the tour was underway in the New Year things would become easier, although there was one concern that Gerry had around Pete's growing reputation. It was common knowledge that he was becoming the archetypal rock 'n' roller with an insatiable appetite for sex and drugs, so Gerry had to find someone he could trust to keep him under control.

Gerry had wracked his brains trying to think of the right person. Then it hit him. Bobby McGregor! He'd be perfect. Bobby understood the entertainment side, he was tough and Pete respected him. All Gerry had to do was convince him to do it. He'd speak to him over the holidays.

Suddenly, Gerry's attention was snapped back to the present. The music had stopped and the audience was beginning to leave. It was one o'clock on Christmas morning, and thankfully due to Ray Law's hard work, the night had gone without a hitch. Making his way back to the office, he saw Janine pouring out glasses of champagne for all the staff. Gerry joined in the celebrations, even though he found himself drinking a glass of Coke along with Ray Law who was still officially on duty. Could they have been overreacting to the letters he'd received, or would their threat come in some other form?

With the worry of the Christmas Eve gig over, Ray Law had spent a relaxed few days back in Liverpool with his parents. George Williams had sanctioned his leave, insisting he get as much rest as possible. Ray was doing his best. He'd called up a few of his old friends and they'd got together for a few beers in one of his old haunts, the Philharmonic on Hope Street. It was a well-known watering hole, and he was enjoying meeting up with guys he'd not seen in years. Someone had produced a guitar, and they'd sung some of the songs they used to do together before he'd left to go to university. He'd gone to the bar and was waiting to be served, when he overheard a conversation between a couple of characters known to be involved in the local drugs scene, talking about the situation down in Birmingham. Ray listened as nonchalantly as possible. They talked about a shipment arriving the following week, which the Rota Bocan intended to circulate so cheap, it would put the Jamaicans out of business. They turned away and left the bar as he was served.

Ray joined his pals, thankful that the two men hadn't recognised him – but unfortunately, the encounter meant he would have to cut short his holiday and get back to the office.

After driving back down first thing, he called Mr. C and asked him if he knew anything about the shipment due to arrive the following week. Charles said he'd heard nothing but would put the word out amongst his contacts. Ray also put a call in to Alex Mitchell, but he wasn't at his flat or at Rudi's, which was annoying. Ray was reluctant to call Gerry because he knew he would overreact, so he called George Williams instead, arranging to meet him the following day, New Year's Eve.

Things had calmed down following Christmas Eve, George Williams had stood down the team Ray had put together – so he was concerned that Ray had asked to meet him urgently.

It was a cold day outside but the office was warm, and they were drinking mugs of freshly made coffee.

"So, you think the conversation you overheard was for real?" George asked, warming his hands on his mug.

"As sure as I can be. They're well known in the 'Pool as suppliers, and they seemed pretty positive in what they were saying," replied Ray blowing across the top of his mug to cool the strong black liquid.

George put his hands in front of the heater rubbing them together. "Hmm, so what are your thoughts? Have you spoken to anyone else yet?"

"Well, I spoke to Charles, sorry, Mr. C the DJ, and he said he'd heard nothing, but would put the word out amongst his contacts."

"What about the manager of the club?"

"Alex Mitchell? No, I tried both his flat and the club but no luck. I decided not to involve Gerry Fortuna for the moment. I think he'd be more a hindrance than a help."

"Yes, you're probably right there." George thought for a moment. "Well, if it's not supposed to arrive until next week, there's not a lot we can do apart from keep our ears to the ground for any whispers. I spoke to Gerry last night, and he said he's only opening The Hideout tonight for a private party, so I think we can relax for the time being. But it was right of you to flag it up. What are you going to do later, then? Any plans?"

"No not really. I did have an invitation to a party back home, but I'm not driving all the way back up just for that."

"Well in that case, you'll come with us to The Hideout. It's Gerry's private party with only a few special friends invited. In fact, I think he's got the Alex Mitchell Trio playing, so you could probably catch a quick word with him at the same time."

Ray started to object but George insisted.

"Sorry I won't hear any excuses. Oh, and don't forget, the delicious Janine will be there playing hostess with the mostest! You do have a dinner suit don't you?"

Ray nodded.

"So, that's it then. We'll see you there at eight o'clock."

Janine looked stunning in a tight-fitting, emerald-green, evening gown, which matched the colour of her eyes. She was pleased to see Ray Law walk in with George Williams and his wife and came over to greet them.

"I'm sorry to be a gate crasher," said Ray, slightly embarrassed. "George here insisted I come."

"Don't be silly, I'm glad you're here," said Janine, giving them all polite pecks on the cheek.

Their host was over by the bar with a few people Ray didn't recognise. "Come on in, come on in," Gerry called. "Drinks are free. Help yourself."

Maybe it won't be so bad, thought Ray as he poured himself a glass of champagne.

"Mmm, my favourite drink too." Janine pressed up against him as she reached over for a glass. "You have good taste, DCI Law," she said, before wafting off to join more new arrivals.

The Hideout looked very festive with streamers and balloons all around the walls. There was a long table down one side, covered in all kinds of party food. Ray wasn't too adventurous when it came to eating. He preferred simple things like steak and chips, so he decided he'd leave the vol-au-vents, cheese and pineapple cubes, and the exotic-looking canapés, to the other guests.

The two black musicians from the trio were setting up their equipment, and Ray remembered the snippet of information one of his undercover officers had told him on Christmas Eve about Wynton Brown having already registered in his search before and judging by what had happened between him and Mr. C at the club, it was obvious he was a regular user. Maybe Ray should have a quiet word with him and the drummer in case they knew anything.

Alex hadn't appeared yet, but Mr. C was in the corner playing some background music. He'd brought a couple of dancers with him, but they were sitting down for the moment. They'll probably be more energetic as the night wears on, Ray thought.

Alex Mitchell finally arrived with the young black guy Ray had seen him with at the FAM launch party. He was talking with his musicians as Ray wandered over.

"Hello guys, I'm looking forward to hearing you play."

"Yeah it should be a good night," Wynton said as he plugged in his Fender bass. He played a couple of silky runs across the strings and turned round to adjust the tone on his amplifier.

Thomas, already behind his kit, played a quick paradiddle on his snare drum before leaning forward to tighten the fittings on his cymbals. Alex was equally engrossed in setting up his Wurlitzer piano and played a melodic sequence of notes that Ray thought he recognized, but he decided against making a comment. They were obviously not interested in talking to him and he got the feeling he was encroaching on their space, so he made his way back to the bar and to George Williams and his wife.

"Are you not having anything to eat?" George's wife asked. "It's delicious." Judging by the amount of food piled up on her plate, she'd obviously not had anything before they came out.

George saw Ray's look and motioned for him to follow him. "She just loves canapés," he said smiling. "Did you manage to speak to Alex or the musicians?"

"No. They're in their own zone and I thought I'd leave them to it. Maybe later."

The chimes of Big Ben rang to bring in 1970, and everyone in The Hideout linked arms to sing Auld Lang Syne. Janine had somehow managed to manoeuvre herself next to Ray in the ring of guests and turned round to give him a kiss at the end of the song. He felt embarrassed that she wasn't with her husband and broke away quickly, but not before he'd seen Gerry out of the corner of his eye watching them.

"That was naughty," he said, edging away from her.

"I know," she said, giving him a sexy wink.

George Williams had also noticed and stepped in between them to give Janine a kiss just as Gerry came over. "Happy New Year, and let's hope it's a peaceful one," he said, reaching out to shake Gerry's hand.

Just as Gerry was about to say something, a row broke out in the corner of the room behind Mr. C's decks.

Mr. C was pointing a threatening finger in the drummer's face. "You tell your Rota Bocan, we not goin' to take no shit. We gonna sort dem out once and for all!" He was shouting at Thomas.

George looked to Ray who quickly moved over to the group.

"OK guys; show's over; let's all calm down," Ray said in his most authoritative tone, a near miracle considering he'd drunk the best part of a bottle of champagne. "I don't know what the problem is, and as it's a private party and I'm here as a guest, I don't really care but cut it out."

"Dem Yanks gonna pay," Mr. C said under his breath. He sucked his teeth.

"I said that's it!" Ray was more forceful this time.

He turned to speak to Thomas but the drummer had disappeared out of the club along with Alex and his young black friend. Wynton was quietly packing up his equipment, but obviously knew what was going on so Ray approached him.

"You want to tell me what just happened?"

"Twas nuttin' man. Just a misunderstandin'."

"Well, the report I received on Christmas Eve, of you receiving drugs from our friend here, wasn't a misunderstanding, Wynton. So, do you want to tell me what happened, or do I get you down the station where you'll be searched? Somehow I don't think you'd want that. Am I right?" Ray was now right in Wynton's face.

"OK man, OK. I tell you." Wynton held his hands up. "Thomas asked me if I wanted some cheap blow when we was at Rudi's on Christmas Eve. I told Mr. C cos he my usual man and he get mighty upset."

"So, hang on, what you're saying is your friend Thomas is involved in supplying cheap drugs and creating this war with the Jamaicans? Is that what you're telling me?" Ray was suddenly stone-cold sober.

"Listen man, I don't want to get no one in trouble. Thomas is my brother in music. We play great together, but him and Alex, they got some bad shit goin' on. That's all I know." He picked up his guitar case. "Now I got to go home to my girlfriend."

Ray looked across at Mr. C, who was packing his records away and said, "We need to talk. My office tomorrow, Charles," and the detective walked back over to the bar and picking up a full glass of what he hoped was champagne, drank it back in one. "Happy new fuckin' year!"

New Year's Day and DCI Law was in his office nursing a hangover. He remembered breaking up the argument between Mr. C and Thomas Wilson Jr, and what Wynton Brown had told him; after that he wasn't sure. His phone rang, further fuelling his headache, and the voice at the other end told him he had a visitor called Charles. He thought for a moment before realising it was Mr. C the DJ. "Ahh! Send him up."

"OK so let me get this straight; you threatened Thomas that your guys would sort out the Rota Bocan, is that right?"

Charles was sitting opposite Ray at his desk.

"They tryin' to take over the city, man! We not gonna let it happen. I speak to Errol and he say they gonna be sorted." Charles was quietly menacing in the way he was talking.

Ray wanted more. "So exactly what are we talking about here? Who is this Rota Bocan?"

"They're based in Miami; run by a guy called Benny Mulligan. He send two guys over here and want to steal our business. They use that drummer boy as their mouthpiece, but he in deep shit if he carries on the way he is."

"So, where do these two guys hang out?"

"They keep movin' around. No one knows where they are." Charles stood up. "But I tell you, Errol will sort it. Just you wait and see." He walked out of Ray's office leaving him none the wiser.

CHAPTER FOURTEEN

THE FOUR members of the Association were sitting in the back room of St Mary's Irish Club drinking their Guinness. They'd wished each other a Happy New Year and also toasted their guest.

Joe finally spoke. "Now! We have your money here Frank. One thousand pounds but we'd be obliged if you would go through your plan one more time."

Frank took the pile of notes and counted them slowly. "Thank you for that, gentlemen. Ok, Molly will take the device with her on Wednesday morning. Once she's in the club, she will set the timer for eleven o'clock the following morning, when the shipment arrives. As you have already shown Joe, it is always on time, so the bomb will detonate while it's being delivered. I've taught Molly exactly what to do and how to set the timer correctly. Then when she leaves the club, she will take the train to Holyhead and catch the ferry over to Dublin, where she'll quietly disappear.

"I will spend another two weeks here working as usual, and then hand in my notice and drive up to Stranraer, where I'll catch a ferry back to Dublin and disappear down South. I suggest you all make sure you have cast iron alibis, just in case the police have any reason to suspect it has something to do with us, although I doubt they will. Especially with the distraction of the notes linking the threats to the Americans and the Jamaicans. Just sit tight and don't do anything stupid. Oh and Joe, you should get rid of all those photographs you've taken. Any questions?"

Michael leaned forward. "What if she sets the timer wrong?"

"She won't. I've shown her what to do. All she has to do is set the time to eleven o'clock and slide a switch to the right."

Niall looked up. "Why to the right?"

Frank stood up. "It works in twelve-hour phases. To the left is twelve hours; to the right is twenty-four hours. But don't worry she's practised hundreds of times. It will be fine."

Molly Gallagher was up early on Wednesday morning. She'd made love with Frank the previous night and promised to meet up once he was back in the Emerald Isle. He'd given her the device wrapped in a towel, which was now safely in her duffel bag. She'd gone over what she had to do one final time, and Frank had left for work, leaving her to finish her breakfast. She got herself ready and put the case she'd already packed by the front door. She'd bought her advance train ticket to Holyhead so all she'd have to do was come home, get changed and catch a bus to the station.

As usual, the club was empty when she arrived, and she let herself in making sure to turn off the alarm. It was ten thirty and she knew there would be no one in until at least midday, by which time she'd be gone.

There was a note for her explaining there was a show that night, and asking her to make sure the toilets were cleaned. This was unusual as the club was usually closed on Wednesdays. She took her duffel bag with its lethal package inside and turned on the lights in the main room. It always felt eerie when it was empty, and she felt a shiver down her spine. Making her way to the back of the stage she took out Frank's device and opened one of the cases under the stage. She'd just put it into the case when she heard the front door open and close. She froze as footsteps approached and came into the room.

"Hello? Hello?" It was one of the musicians who played with Alex Mitchell, the American one. She recognised his voice.

She was panic-stricken. What should she do? If she called out, he'd come round and see the case open with the device in it. She stood still holding her breath. Then the door banged again. He must have gone outside. She had to move quickly; he could come back at any minute. She remembered what Frank had told her; first set the timer. She was shaking as she held it, moving the hands to eleven.

The door opened again and she heard two voices. Suddenly, everything Frank told her became a blur. She knew she had to click the switch, but was it to the right or the left? She couldn't remember. The voices were coming nearer the stage and she had to make a quick decision before they saw her. She pushed the switch and closed the case lid, twisting the catches to lock it.

Just as she stood up, Wynton walked round the back of the stage to switch on the power.

"Hey, we thought you'd be 'ere," he said. "We got a rehearsal for tonight's show. You OK? You look like you seen a ghost."

She was still shaking. "No, no I'm fine. You surprised me. I didn't think there'd be anyone in until later. You'll have to excuse me; I have to clean the toilets before I go."

"No worries," he carried on setting up as she made her way over to the toilets.

She broke into a cold sweat. Had she pushed the switch to the left or right? She couldn't remember – and it was locked in the case under the stage so she couldn't go back to check. And what had she done with her duffel bag? She must have locked it in the case with the device.

Well, it was too late now. She just knew she wanted to get out of the club as fast as possible.

At the same moment as Molly Gallagher was in Holyhead, boarding the seven thirty Sealink ferry to Dublin, the opening band at Rudi's were playing their first tune of the night.

It had been Alex Mitchell's idea to open on a Wednesday for a new jazz night. An up-and-coming band would play the first half of the show, followed by his trio. Jazz was becoming popular in the city, and he had a good crowd in for the first night.

Gerry and Janine had come down to show their support although neither were big fans of the music, and they had left at the interval before Alex's trio had started their set.

Ray Law had also shown his face, but in a professional capacity. He had promised George Williams he'd keep an eye on things, even though the team had stood down and the case was now regarded with less urgency since the Christmas Eve gig. He wasn't a big fan of jazz either, and didn't intend hanging around once the show was underway.

He'd noticed Richard Kennedy sitting at one of the tables at the front with an attractive blonde. He'd beckoned Ray over but the DCI pointed at his watch with an apologetic look, and took the opportunity to leave before the music started.

Niall Fitzgerald had seen the advert in the evening news and taken his wife to see the Alex Mitchell Trio as a special anniversary treat. He was a big jazz fan but, although she'd never tell him, his wife found it boring and sometimes struggled to follow the tune. In all fairness she preferred a night at the Irish Club with her girlfriends dancing to a Ceilidh band.

But it was a lovely night out, and Niall had treated her to a meal in the Grand Hotel earlier, so she couldn't complain.

The first band was an exciting new five-piece line-up of piano, double bass, electric guitar, drums and tenor saxophone, who had played an interesting selection of well-known jazz classics, as well as some of their own material. Their particularly inventive version of Herbie Hancock's 'Watermelon Man' had finished the set, and the audience gave them a warm reception.

Mr. C had complemented the night with a fine selection of jazz and soul records, making sure everything flowed. By the time Alex Mitchell and his two fellow musicians were ready to take the stage, the audience was raring to go.

Alex started the first tune on his own, working on a simple melody then gradually building the chords and the rhythm, showing off his technique. Then Wynton Brown picked up on the bassline with his left hand and took the tune to the next level. Just when it seemed they couldn't go any further, Thomas Wilson Jr powered in with a mesmerisingly rhythmic pattern. The three then locked together with an astonishing intensity, rising to a blistering crescendo with Alex reverting back to his original melody before the three finished in perfect unison with a dead stop. There was a moment's silence before the audience erupted.

As the ferry docked at Dun Laoghaire, Molly thought back to the moment she had pushed the switch before locking the case. Then, looking out over the heads of people waiting on the quay, she saw her brother waving. Case in hand, she rushed down the gangplank.

It was ten forty-five and the trio had just finished their last number, their version of the Miles Davis tune 'So What' featuring a brilliant bass solo from Wynton. The audience had given them a standing ovation, and finally Mr. C had put on the first of a collection of slow tunes to wind down the evening.

It had been a successful night and Alex was already planning for next week's show. He came off stage and headed back to his office to dry himself off and count the evening's takings. It was approaching eleven o'clock as he walked outside to pay the first band, who were loading equipment into their cars.

Thomas and Wynton were on stage packing up and talking to a few of the audience who had gone over to congratulate them. Thomas's brother James was helping him with the drums.

Richard Kennedy was finishing the bottle of champagne he had shared with the blonde woman he'd met earlier, and with whom he was planning on spending the night in the penthouse apartment just around the corner.

After a great evening, Niall Fitzgerald was on a promise and was getting ready to leave with his wife.

In their top floor apartment overlooking the club, Gerry and Janine had just finished watching a film. Janine had drunk the best part of a bottle of champagne and was contemplating going to bed. The door to the balcony was open, and she was about to close it, when there was a blinding white flash from one of the buildings below them followed by a deafening roar. The apartment shook with the force of the blast, and Gerry jumped off the sofa and ran out onto the balcony.

"Oh shit! It's Rudi's," he screamed. "They've fuckin' blown up Rudi's!"

Janine had dropped her glass in shock and was standing motionless. Gerry rushed back in and took hold of her shoulders. "Come on, babe. We need to get there as fast as we can." He grabbed his coat and ran out of the door to the lift.

In the ensuing chaos, Ray Law had appeared as if from nowhere, and had instantly taken control. He'd been in a bar round the corner having a drink with one of his team, and on hearing the blast, they'd immediately sprung into action. The fire brigade arrived within minutes, at the same time as the first of the ambulances and police cars. Two young police constables were already cordoning off the street as Gerry ran up. One of them tried to tell him he couldn't go past the tape, but Ray spotted him and called out to let him through. Together they stood and surveyed the devastation. People were staggering out coughing, quite a few covered in blood.

Gerry started to go into the club through the wreckage that had been the entrance, but Ray held him back. "There's no way anyone can go in there until the fire brigade say it's safe."

"But there might be more survivors. We can't just stand here." Gerry was shaking. "I'm going in there." He shrugged off Ray's grip and climbed across the remains of the front doors, disappearing into the billowing smoke.

Inside, chairs and tables had been blown across the room, along with the people who were sitting at them. There was a huge hole in the middle where the stage used to be, and straight away Gerry could see the two bodies of Alex's musicians. It was obvious they had taken the full force of the blast and had suffered horrendous injuries. He fought back the urge to throw up at the sight of their mutilated limbs but forced himself to go on. It was difficult to see clearly as most of the lighting had been damaged, and only a few safety lights were working. He heard moaning from one side of the stage and saw the DJ podium lying on its side. Mr. C was pinned underneath, crying out in pain.

Gerry pulled debris away but the podium itself was too heavy and he couldn't lift it. He could hear other rescuers now in the room and he called out for help. With two fire officers Gerry was able to get the heavy structure lifted but Mr. C appeared to be in a really bad way. It took the fire officers and two ambulancemen working together to lift Charles gently onto a stretcher, and then carefully to pick their way over the debris and out of the room.

There were cries coming from all directions, Gerry didn't know who to help next. The smoke and fumes were overpowering and he was finding it hard to breathe. He thought what he could smell was roast pork but realised with horror it was the smell of burnt human flesh.

He stumbled over two bodies in the semi-darkness, a man and a woman, who he remembered seeing at the beginning of the night. He recalled her lilting Irish accent as they shared a joke coming into the club, and of how it reminded him of Janine.

In the half-light he could see people climbing over the broken remains of tables and chairs, clambering to safety. His head was spinning and he began to feel faint, grasping hold of part of what was once the bar. The decorative mirrors on the wall at the back had all shattered, and a couple of the bar staff were lying lifeless across the top. He forced himself to go on looking for more casualties but felt himself beginning to lose consciousness. Luckily one of the fire officers grabbed his arm and gave him an oxygen mask, before leading him slowly back out of the wreckage.

Ray Law was shouting orders to the rescuers as Gerry emerged into the fresh air. Janine had arrived and was passing blankets to the walking wounded. The street outside was full of rescue vehicles with flashing lights, and a full emergency had been declared. The Chief Constable had arrived and, standing alongside Ray Law, was now directing operations.

Across the street Alex Mitchell watched from a shop doorway. He had been outside paying the bass player from the opening act when the bomb went off, and apart from a few cuts from flying glass, he was all right, although everything sounded muffled due to the explosion. He knew he should get up and help but he couldn't – because in his mind this was all his fault. He'd allowed the drugs shipments to be delivered to the club, and when he tried to quit, Thomas had said it would end badly. He would have to think fast. He'd be one of the first suspects the police would want to talk to. His mind was racing; how would he get out of this situation? And what had happened to Thomas and Wynton? They were on the stage packing up when he left them. And where was James? His sweet, adorable James.

Suddenly, there was a deafening noise. Part of the roof collapsed and rescuers came rushing out of the building just in time. The local press photographer had arrived and was taking dramatic pictures of survivors being cared for on the pavement. Alex thought he recognised the photographer but was too confused to remember from where. An outside broadcast van was already parked further down the street with a reporter talking to a cameraman in front of a bank of blinding lights. The police were doing their best to hold back the ever-growing crowd of onlookers, but it was becoming chaotic.

One of the policemen had noticed Alex and came over to see if he was injured. Alex was trying to tell the policeman he was all right when Gerry spotted them and made his way across the tangle of fire hoses.

"What the hell happened?" He needed to shout to make himself heard over the fire engines.

Alex stood up unsteadily and leaned against the shop front. "I don't know. We'd finished playing and I went into the office to check the door takings. Then I came outside to pay the other band and there was this huge flash and an explosion, and I was thrown across the street."

The conversation was cut short by the police officer's insistence that Alex should go to hospital, and Alex was not unwilling to allow himself to be helped over to one of the waiting ambulances.

Gerry was making his way back to Ray Law and George Williams when he passed a stretcher on the floor. He recognised the man lying on it as Richard Kennedy, and was about to ask how he was, when the attending doctor crossed himself and gently pulled a blanket over Richard's head.

Gerry stood clenching his fists. His hands bled from where he'd pushed his nails into his palms. *Somebody will pay for this!* he promised himself, as he looked across at the remains of his club.

Further down the street with his press pass clearly visible, Joe Burke systematically captured every harrowing image. He knew his pictures would make the front pages of all the papers, and he was doing his best to remain professional, but inside he was in turmoil. *What had gone wrong? It wasn't supposed to go off until tomorrow. Frank had assured them there wouldn't be any problems.* He'd have to get in touch with the others. They needed to talk as soon as possible. Joe, at least, had a strong alibi; he had been working in the office all day, and went out on a story before hearing about the explosion and heading straight to the scene. He hoped the others could also vouch for their movements. Even though they'd sent the letters making it look like the Americans were behind this, there was always the possibility their past would catch up with them.

As he stood there, he saw Janine outside the club. He hadn't spoken to her for a while and was annoyed at her for not getting in touch. He called out her name. She looked up, ran down the street towards him and threw her arms round him.

"Oh Da! It's terrible, I can't believe it," she sobbed into Joe's shoulder. "Who would do such a thing? Gerry says it's all about drugs."

"I don't know for sure. There're some evil bastards about," Joe said, holding her at arms length to inspect her. "Are you all right my girl? I've been worried about you. I always said that husband of yours would be trouble, and now look at this terrible mess."

"It's not Gerry's fault. He hates drugs. For God's sake he doesn't even drink," she shouted at her dad. "I can't talk to you now. I've got to get back and help," and she rushed away to where the injured were being attended.

Joe took a few more shots of the remains of the building, now brightly floodlit by the rescue services, and packed his camera away. It would be a long night in the dark room when he got home.

Errol had been told about the explosion, and was sitting in his armchair watching a portable TV trying to find out more information but the news was patchy. There was a special report just starting from outside the club, but the reporter just repeated what had been said earlier.

Errol was expecting to hear from Charles or the men he'd spoken to about the problem, but so far no one had been in touch. Charles was a good man and Errol was sure he'd come round as soon as he could. He was probably helping at the club; he was that kind of guy. Errol prayed he was all right.

Frank had been at home in Molly's house listening to the radio, when news had come through about the bomb at a club in the city centre. He'd smiled to himself, *Job done! That should teach the feckin' yanks a lesson, tryin' to muscle in where they aren't wanted.*

Thankfully, Molly was safe over in Dublin, because the first thing the police would do would be to speak to anyone connected to the club. Frank felt sure he'd be all right, as long as none of the others did anything stupid. He'd been working all day on the site and then spent most of the night at a club with his friend, Sean, playing darts, making sure they were very visible. Now they just had to keep their heads down and stick to the plan.

The following morning, the nightclub disaster was headline news on national television and radio. The police held a press conference. A tired-looking DCI Law read out a statement confirming that a bomb had exploded at Rudi's nightclub at twenty-three hundred hours on Wednesday, 7th January.

"As of this moment," he said, "there are ten confirmed dead. They are Thomas Wilson Jr aged twenty-five, James Wilson aged twenty-three, Wynton Brown aged twenty-four, Richard Kennedy aged thirty, Niall and Niamh Fitzgerald – ages unknown, John Preston aged twenty-two, Ann Hewitt, nineteen, Michael Burton, twenty-four, and Audrey Green aged twenty-eight. There are currently five casualties in intensive care, including the DJ from the club. Our thoughts are with the families and friends of the victims, and I can assure you that every effort is being made to find the perpetrators of this terrible atrocity."

George Williams and Ray Law had been up all night, contacting all the members of the special force who were now assembled in the briefing room at police headquarters. No one had slept, but at the moment, sleep was the furthest thing from their minds.

George stood up and addressed the crowded room. "All right everyone. Now we all know how terrible this is, the pictures on the news leave nothing to the imagination. DCI Ray Law is leading this investigation and will report directly to me. Over to you Ray."

Ray put down his coffee and looked at the team. "I feel partly responsible for this because we were given warnings, and when we thought we'd beaten them at Christmas, we relaxed. But they conned us. They knew all along they weren't going to do anything on Christmas Eve. Instead, they were waiting for us to drop our guard. Now I want these bastards, and I don't care what it takes. As soon as that building is safe, I want forensics in there, going over it with a fine-tooth comb. I want a team to bring in the Jamaicans. Errol must know something. I believe Mr. C the DJ is in intensive care – as soon as he's well enough to speak we need to talk to him. We need witness statements. Get a team on the survivors from the club, and let's check if there was anyone in the area who might be suspicious."

Ray paused and wrote something down on his notepad. "Right, you all know what to do. Seamus will assign the duties. Let's go!"

As the assembled team began to split into various groups, Ray called out to one of them as he was leaving the room. It was Matt Burgess. He'd been drinking with him in a bar around the corner from the club when the bomb went off. He was a stocky, six-foot, blond-haired, Black Countryman, who played rugby in his spare time, and had become a good friend since Ray had been down in the Midlands.

"Matt, it's just a hunch, but you remember the two well-built black guys in the bar last night?"

"Yeah; the two Yanks. I remember them well. Really big guys. Looked like they played American football. They left just before the explosion. Shit! You don't think they had anything to do with it?"

112

"Right now I'm clutching at straws, but the rumours are that the Rota Bocan is two Americans from Miami, and that no one has seen them because they're always on the move. Their contact was Alex Mitchell's drummer, and he was one of the victims. I need that DJ to pull through – he was the one who told me. Let's put out an APB just in case we get lucky."

After all the teams had left on their various assignments, Seamus took the opportunity to slip out of the office and was in a telephone box calling Michael Brennan. "Jesus Michael, what the fuck happened? You said that friend of Sean's promised it would go off today. It's like a feckin' madhouse down here."

"I'm as in the dark as you are mate. And Niall and his wife were there. The poor bastards." Michael choked as he spoke. "Yer man Frank said it couldn't be traced back to us. I just hope to God he's right."

"I'll do me best to let you know what's happening, but I have to watch my back yer know. They're lookin' to speak to the old Jamaican guy Errol to see if he knows anything." Seamus said. "Look I have to go now. Take care of yourself Michael." Seamus put the phone down and opened the door. Ray's friend Matt was having a coffee in the cafe across the road and noticed Seamus looking around suspiciously. He watched as Seamus walked back to the office and wondered if he should mention it to Ray.

Janine was in the apartment, sitting on the sofa with her legs tucked under her. She was in her dressing gown watching the TV reports on last night's tragedy. She'd been shocked when Gerry told her about Richard Kennedy, and hearing his name again today in the list of victims had really upset her. He had been great fun, and even though she had decided to move on, she felt devastated by his death. She pictured him standing in his penthouse apartment holding a bottle of champagne wearing just his socks. Tears flowed down her face.

She stood up, walked out onto the balcony to look down at the remains of Rudi's. Most of the roof had collapsed, and the fire brigade was still there making sure the scene was safe. Ray Law and a team of forensic officers had been allowed into the site, and were painstakingly searching for clues as to who the culprits might be. The TV news were already speculating that it might be linked to a drugs war between the Jamaicans and a group of Americans called the Rota Bocan.

She thought back to the FAM party when Ray Law had first told Gerry about the situation, and how he'd asked her about Alex Mitchell. Could Alex have been involved? Gerry had said his drummer was linked in some way, and she remembered the argument on New Year's Eve with Mr. C.

She'd had a phone call that morning from Pete Peterson saying he'd just heard the news, and that he'd been worried in case she'd been involved. It had been good to hear his voice, and she remembered the last time she'd seen him. He'd said he was coming up to start rehearsals with the band for the tour, which was due to kick off soon.

Gerry had managed a couple of hours sleep before getting back down to the club. In reality there was nothing he could do, because the police were treating it as a murder scene, so no one was allowed in.

He'd reluctantly taken Ray Law's advice and gone over to his offices above The Hideout. In an attempt to take his mind off Rudi's he'd started to organise the tour for The Flames. His first task was to speak to Bobby McGregor and convince him to become Pete Peterson's tour manager. All of the UK dates had been confirmed before the Christmas holidays, and now the middle three weeks of the European section was the only problem, but Gerry was confident they would be filled by the time the tour began.

Gerry knew Bobby should have probably fought his last fight and must be considering his future, but he needed to be subtle in his approach; not to seem as if he was encouraging Bobby to give up boxing, even though he knew it was the correct choice. Pete Peterson liked Bobby which was a good start, although it was more important that Pete respected him, because if Bobby were to accept the job there would be times when he would need to tell Pete and the other members of the band what to do and they would have to obey him.

Gerry's secretary Judy Watson had become indispensable, and he knew that anything he asked her to do would be taken care of without any fuss. She was becoming an asset to the business and had a keen eye for new talent; she reminded Gerry of himself. Judy had already spotted a couple of bands that she'd suggested Gerry consider for management once The Flames were settled and now that he'd sorted Janine's involvement in the businesses, he would have to start considering improving Judy's contract. In the tough world of the music industry, players such as Judy were rare, and he'd sooner have her on his side than against him.

Bobby McGregor arrived while Gerry was still deep in thought. Judy showed him up and made them both a drink, but Bobby was more concerned about what had happened at Rudi's.

"Bad news, Gerry. Really sorry. Do the police have any clues yet?"

"Ray Law is in charge and he's down there with a forensic team at the moment, but he's playing his cards close to his chest. He told me they were talking to someone called Errol. Do you know him?"

Bobby smiled. "Old Errol? I've known him for years. Used to spar with him once upon a time. That is until he got into the ganja. Ruined his fitness. All he wanted to do was sit around all day listening to his music. Makes good money from it though."

"Is he a supplier then?" Gerry asked.

"Nah, he's just the middleman; he never really said where he gets the stuff from. I heard a whisper it was something to do with the Irish, but that was a long time ago – haven't seen him for years. Shame about his nephew, Charles."

Gerry sat up, his attention piqued. "Charles! You mean Mr. C is Errol's nephew?"

"Yeah he's a good guy. I hope he pulls through." Bobby couldn't help noticing that Gerry had suddenly become rattled.

"Wait a minute. What the fuck have the Irish got to do with drugs?"

Gerry was very agitated as Judy came in carrying a tray with two steaming mugs of coffee. "Steady on Mr. F; you'll give yourself a heart attack," she said, passing him and Bobby their drinks.

Gerry put his mug straight down on the desk. "Judy can you get me Ray Law on the phone."

Judy went downstairs and moments later the phone buzzed. It was Ray Law. "Gerry; what is it? I'm up to my eyes, man!"

"Ray, I'm sorry to bother you. I'm sitting here with Bobby McGregor and he's just told me that Jamaican Errol is Charles's uncle."

"Yes, I knew that. He told me when he came in to see me last week."

Ray tried not to sound annoyed.

"But did he tell you that his uncle's drugs suppliers are the Irish?"

There was sudden silence at the end of the phone.

"Gerry, are you sure?" Ray suddenly became business-like.

"According to Bobby, years ago when Errol first got into drugs, his suppliers were the Irish."

"So what you're telling me is there's possibly Irish involvement in this?" Ray thought for a moment. "But we spoke to Errol earlier and he never mentioned any Irish link." He paused again as someone spoke to him in the background. "Gerry I'm sorry, I've got to go. I'll talk to you later."

Ray had been passed a message to say that the two American suspects he and Matt had seen in the bar the previous night, had been picked up at Heathrow Airport. An eagle-eyed policeman had spotted two men answering their descriptions as they attempted to buy two tickets to Miami and they were currently being driven back to Birmingham by the flying squad for questioning.

He sat with his feet up on his desk, hands clasped behind his head, staring at the ceiling trying to make sense of all the information he had so far. His biggest frustration, as always, was waiting for forensics. Behind the wreckage of the stage, they'd found the remains of a yellow plastic duffel bag in reasonably good condition, and they were hoping to be able to lift prints off it. He knew it was a long shot, but he kept his fingers crossed.

In the excitement of the phone call to Ray Law, Gerry had momentarily forgotten the reason why he'd asked Bobby to come down to the office. Finally, he managed to put the idea to Bobby and now sat studying his friend's face for a clue as to what he was thinking. Gerry had made him a very lucrative offer, much more than he was making at the moment, but he knew his decision would be as much about pride as money.

Gerry's offer had taken Bobby by surprise. He had never considered a job like the one Gerry was offering, but he couldn't think of a reason why he shouldn't do it. In all fairness to Gerry, he hadn't mentioned his boxing career, but Bobby knew in his heart that he would never now reach the heights he had aimed for. His last bout had been a disaster and it would be a long way back. So, the question was, would he be happy being known as the great underachiever, or could he see himself travelling the country, and possibly further, with a famous rock 'n' roll band?

He liked Pete Peterson and he felt that Pete liked him too, but as Gerry had said, 'on the road is a completely different thing', and Bobby would have to gain the band's respect.

In the end it hadn't really been a difficult decision for him to make, but he kept Gerry waiting all the same. "I'll do it," he said eventually, with a big smile. "When do I start?"

"Brilliant; that's great news," Gerry jumped up and shook his hand. "To be honest you can start as soon as you want. There's plenty to do, and the sooner you get to know the guys the better. You can also help with booking the hotels and transport because you'll be in charge of all that once you're on the road. I'm really happy, Bobby, and I know I can trust you to do a good job."

Alex Mitchell had woken up in hospital. He had been admitted as a precaution, suffering from a mild concussion. He had been dozing when the television in the ward had shown footage taken the previous night outside the club, and then cut to the police statement being read out by Ray Law.

The sound was turned down low, but Alex read the names of the victims on the screen. Suddenly, his life was turned upside down. Not only did he hold himself responsible for what had happened, but his musicians and his lover were all dead. He lay there wondering what he would do now. What could he do? Surely it would only be a matter of time before the police would want to speak to him. As long as he was here in hospital they wouldn't be able to put too much pressure on him. He had to use the time to think. At least his agency scam would be safe. He'd just close it down for now.

The artists he'd booked to appear would understand, and if they complained he'd use the act of terrorism clause in their contract.

Alex's main concern was the link to the Rota Bocan, and how he was going to get out of that. In one sense, Thomas dying meant there was no one who could prove he had anything to do with it, and in actual fact he'd never had contact with anyone else other than Thomas. If they were to testify in court and try to implicate him, he would deny all knowledge of it and blame the whole thing on his drummer, it would be their word against his.

A nurse had come over to his bed to check his temperature, but he was so deep in thought he hadn't noticed her. He jumped when she said his name. "Mr. Mitchell; time to take your temperature and blood pressure." She wrapped the pressure sleeve around his arm and began pumping it up.

"Is there any news about the others in intensive care?" Alex asked, as she released the pressure on his arm.

"Well one of my friends was up there earlier and she said the club's DJ is in a bad way. He may lose his legs – it's touch and go. Terrible, really terrible." She shook her head. "Did you know him?"

Alex blinked back tears. "Yes. He's a really cool guy. I hope he's gonna be OK." He looked down the ward as the doors opened and two men came in; one he immediately recognised as DCI Ray Law.

They spoke to the matron who turned and pointed at Alex. As the two men walked towards his bed he slid down under the sheets, wishing he could make himself disappear.

CHAPTER FIFTEEN

MICHAEL BRENNAN was nursing a monumental hangover after drinking the best part of a bottle of Jameson Whisky he'd been given for Christmas. Since talking to Seamus on the phone he'd been trying to contact Joe Burke, but Joe's wife had said he'd spent most of the previous night in his darkroom then gone straight to the office, and she had no idea when he'd be back.

Sean Whelan wasn't answering his phone either, and as a result Michael had tried to calm his nerves with a few drinks. Unfortunately, the more he drank the more nervous he became, and he had woken up in his armchair in front of a television which was showing the test card.

Joe Burke had spent the previous night developing and printing the photos of the horrific scenes down at the club. It had been good to see Janine, but he wished it had been under different circumstances, and he felt they'd parted on a strained note. He'd have to speak to her sister and get them all together once this had all died down.

The following day, after just a couple of hours sleep, he'd gone into the office to send his images to all the major press agencies. He was just finishing up when his wife called to say Michael had been trying to contact him. Joe was immediately on his guard, thinking back to the last meeting when Frank had told everyone to sit tight and not to do anything stupid. Michael needed to keep his head down and not panic. It was terrible that Niall and his wife had been involved, but there was nothing any of them could do to change it now. As Frank had said at the last meeting, the letters they had sent had focussed the blame on the Americans, and as long as everything went to plan they would all be fine.

Sean Whelan had stayed in and ignored the phone all day. Since spending the night playing darts with Frank, making sure everyone would notice them, he'd sat watching the reports on the news. The images were horrendous and he was privately horrified at what had happened, but he would never let his true feelings show to the others. He was concerned that Michael might be panicking and wanting to talk to Joe, but Frank had said to sit tight whatever happened and that's what he would do.

Over on the construction site at the edge of the city, Frank was eating his lunch in the canteen caravan, listening to the conversations of his workmates. The news bulletins had reported on the arrest of two Americans at Heathrow airport, and the general consensus of opinion was that they were to blame, which was good news. The plan with the letters was working, at least for now. But as soon as the police questioned the Americans, he wondered how long it would be before they figured out there were other forces involved. Hopefully by that time, he'd be safely back in Cork.

The two Americans had been separated as soon as they arrived at police headquarters, and had spent the night in individual cells waiting to be interviewed.

Early the next morning Ray Law, accompanied by Matt Burgess, had walked into Interview Room One, and immediately sensed an atmosphere. The first of the Americans was relaxing with a cigarette – his feet stretched out in front of him. He hardly reacted to their entrance.

Larry Carmichael was at least six foot four, and built like an American footballer, although the excess weight he carried around his waist indicated his preference for burgers over sport. He had an air of confidence that Ray had picked up on as soon as they walked in. Carmichael had used his phone call to enlist the services of a high-powered solicitor, far superior to the class of brief Ray was used to dealing with, and he was sitting with his client waiting for Ray and Matt to sit down at the table.

The officers introduced themselves for the record and the solicitor identified himself as Angelo Silvoni. Ray suddenly realised the implications of his being there. The Silvoni name was linked with the Miami Mafia, and his company had represented clients in high-profile cases of money laundering, extortion and more recently, drugs. The case had now taken a completely new turn and Ray decided he should speak to his boss before proceeding any further.

"What the hell is a high-profile lawyer from New York doing sitting in my interview room?" George Williams demanded. "I was led to believe this would be an open and shut case. We've got the letters implicating the Rota Bocan, and they were there the night it all went off. So what went wrong?"

Ray was standing in front of George's desk, equally bewildered. "I'm as much in the dark as you. Matt and I saw them in the bar and sent out the description. It was almost as if they wanted us to catch them."

"Angelo Silvoni doesn't waste his time on crappy little cases. He probably earns more on one case than you and I put together earn in a year. No, there's something fishy going on here and I want to know what."

Ray went back and resumed the interview.

"I assume you're aware of the reason why you're here? You and your associate were seen in the Apollo bar just around the corner from Rudi's on the night of the explosion. My colleague and I saw you leave immediately before the incident, and the following morning you were attempting to leave the country. Rather suspicious don't you think?"

Larry Carmichael looked straight at Ray. "No Comment."

"I can inform you that we have evidence currently under forensic investigation that will reveal the person or persons responsible for planting the bomb."

Again Larry Carmichael replied to Ray, "I have no objection to providing proof of my innocence."

Ray smiled. "What about your associate next door, Mr. Swann? Will he do the same?"

This time Angelo Silvoni answered before his client could speak. "I object. Only Mr. Swann can answer that."

Back in the Chief Constable's office, Ray said, "He's so cocksure of himself. I don't get it. When I mentioned forensics he didn't even blink."

"Where are we with all that?" George asked. "Have you spoken to forensics? We need to put a rocket underneath them."

"They're going as fast as they can. The good news is, they've managed to lift a couple of good prints and a partial from the piece of duffel bag that was found at the back of the stage, and they think they've got something on one of the letters they missed the first time. The explosive was definitely Semtex – we're checking suppliers to see if anyone is using it in the region. From the force and direction of the blast, it would appear the device was planted with a manual timer, in a stack of cases under the stage. I remember mentioning the cases to Alex Mitchell when Gerry Fortuna and I met with him before Christmas. I asked him to get them moved. The last I heard he was still in hospital. I think I'll pay him a visit for a chat."

Ray Law and Matt Burgess sat on chairs drawn up on either side of Alex Mitchell's hospital bed. He was looking a lot better than the last time Ray had seen him as he was being helped into an ambulance outside the club. Now they needed some answers to their questions.

"If you remember, when we had a meeting at the club with Mr. Fortuna and Mr. C, I suggested you move the pile of cases that were at the back of the stage, but according to our forensics, that's where the explosion occurred. What can you tell me about them, Mr. Mitchell?" Ray felt amply justified in being so abrupt.

Alex looked at the policemen and tried to remain calm. "I'm sorry about that, I did ask the cleaner if she would move them, but obviously she didn't."

Matt looked up from his notebook. "Who was the cleaner, Mr. Mitchell?"

"Molly - she was there since we opened. Pleasant Irish lady; she'd always have a chat. Used to bring me homemade cakes in her yellow duffel bag every week."

Ray sat up straight and looked at Matt.

"Molly who?" Matt asked, trying to remain calm so as not to fluster Alex.

"Erm...I never knew her other name, but it will be in the staff register," Alex said.

"We can get that from Mr. Fortuna. Thanks for your help," Ray said, and nodding to Matt they both stood up to leave, just as the lady with the tea trolley made her appearance.

"They found the remains of a yellow duffel bag at the back of the stage." Ray said as they walked out of the ward. "Could be she just left it there by mistake, but we need to find her and fast. I'll call Gerry Fortuna and see if he can get her details for us."

Gerry and Bobby McGregor were in the office sorting out travel schedules for The Flames tour when Ray called.

"Unfortunately, I don't have the staff register for Rudi's here," said Gerry. "It'll be in the office down there in one of the filing cabinets. I haven't been allowed in since your guys did their search, but if it's all clear now I'll come down and help find it. I can meet you down there."

Ray and Matt set out from their office and met Gerry and Bobby in front of the club, which was still closed off with police incident tape.

"You're in luck," said Gerry, as he walked into the office. "It's not too bad in here. I think this should be the one." He opened a drawer in the filing cabinet over in the back corner of the room. "Here you go - staff register. What did you say her first name was?"

"Molly," Ray answered.

"Molly…Molly…let me see. Ah, here she is, Molly Gallagher."

"Is there an address?" Ray asked.

"Yes - 15 Bennetts Road, Western Green."

"Thanks Gerry, that's perfect. We'll get over there and have a chat with her - maybe she saw something."

As they arrived back in the office, Ray called the number Gerry had given them but there was no reply. "Come on Matt, let's take a trip over there to check it out," Ray said, picking up his car keys and heading downstairs.

They fastened their full racing harness seatbelts in Ray's treasured white 1.6L Lotus Twin Cam Escort, and pulled out of the underground car park. It was his pride and joy and he loved to show off his driving skills. Matt had heard that Ray was a bit of a boy racer, but wasn't prepared for the white-knuckle ride that took them through the outskirts of the city to Molly Gallagher's address. He breathed a sigh of relief when they finally arrived at her house.

There was a light on in the hallway as they rang the doorbell, and they were greeted by a thickset, dark-haired, man with a distinctive walrus moustache.

Ray produced his warrant card. "Good evening, sir. My name is DCI Ray Law and this is DS Matt Burgess. We're looking to speak to a Mrs. Molly Gallagher. Does she live here?"

The man answered in a broad Irish accent. "Aye she does, but she's not in right now."

"Do you have any idea when she'll be back?" Ray asked.

"I'm sorry, I'm afraid I don't," the man replied. "But I can give her a message when she does."

Ray gave him one of his cards. "If you can ask her to call me as soon as possible, thanks. Oh, I didn't catch your name…"

"Kelly - Frank Kelly. I'm only the lodger here, but I'll make sure she gets the message." He closed the door.

As they walked back to the car, Matt stopped and thought for a moment. "I'm sure I've seen him somewhere before," he said. "It'll come to me."

The drive back was slightly slower due to local football match traffic, when Matt suddenly exclaimed, "Got him! I knew I recognised his face. He was at an Irish social club where we played rugby. We were all in the bar having a drink after the game, and there was this side room with four guys having a private meeting. The reason I remembered, was when the door opened they were all sitting around a table and one of them stood up, escorted him in, and then a bit later escorted him out again. Then he stood on his own waiting at the bar. Just seemed a bit strange at the time. Formal, you know, like he was in front of a committee. Oh, and another thing, one of the guys sitting at the table was the photographer who was outside the club the other night."

"Are you sure?" Ray asked, putting the Escort into gear as they moved off.

"Yeah, definitely. I saw him taking the pictures of the casualties. They were in the paper the next day."

Ray drummed his hands on the steering wheel. "Hmm, there's something not right about this whole case. We've got two American suspects with a heavyweight lawyer, sitting in the cells willing to prove their innocence. The Jamaicans openly admit they control the drugs in the city, but claim they've got nothing to do with the bomb, and then Gerry calls me to say his man Bobby vaguely remembers Errol having some kind of historical connection to the Irish. And now we have an Irish cleaner, with a lodger you saw with the photographer who was outside the club."

"Could just be a coincidence," Matt said.

"I don't like coincidences, Matt." Ray slipped the clutch and they shot through an opening in the queue of traffic in front of them, missing a lorry by inches.

Back at police headquarters, George Williams poured Ray a cup of coffee, and sat down behind his desk. "So let's go through this again Ray. What have we got so far?"

"We have two American suspects in our holding cells represented by a high-powered lawyer willing to prove their innocence in connection with the bomb. I think they're working for the Rota Bocan although I can't prove it; and the only person who I think could was Alex Mitchell's drummer, and he's dead. Then we have the Jamaicans who we know are the main suppliers in the city, but Errol denies all links to them, and in fact I witnessed his nephew Mr. C, arguing with the drummer on New Year's Eve. I heard him say that they were going to sort them out once and for all." Ray stopped and took a sip of his coffee. "Then - and this is where it starts to get confusing - we have a possible Irish connection."

"How so?" George asked, looking quizzical.

"A couple of days ago, Gerry Fortuna called me to say his friend Bobby McGregor knew Errol years ago when they used to spar together at his boxing club – and according to Bobby, Errol had lost his way and got into drugs. But more interesting was that his suppliers were rumoured to be a group of Irishmen, using him as the middleman. That was all he could remember, and at the time it was only a whisper. All the same, we now have an Irish cleaner working at Rudi's, and her lodger, who Matt Burgess recognized from a club he was at recently, meeting with the photographer who was taking photos outside Rudi's on the night of the explosion."

"Wait a minute," George sat up. "You don't mean Joe Burke do you? He was there that night."

"I believe that's his name. Why?" Ray asked.

"Joe Burke is Janine Fortuna's father! We've had him on a secret watch list for years. He was originally a high-ranking member of an IRA splinter group over in Ireland before he and his family turned up here. But we've never had cause to be concerned about him. He works for the local paper and has never been in any trouble. In fact the last time I saw him was at Janine and Gerry's wedding, when he was drunk as a skunk, dancing in just his braces and trousers with his other daughter." George reflected. "So, do we know anything about the lodger?"

"He said his name is Frank Kelly, but we were looking for his landlady

Molly Gallagher, so we never paid him much attention until Matt remembered where he'd seen him."

"What about forensics? Have we heard back from them yet?"

"I was going to pay them a visit after I finish here."

"Right, well you best get on that right away. And keep me informed."

There was a note waiting on Ray's desk to call forensics straight away. With his heart in his mouth, he dialled their number and was put through to the chief examiner, 'Ginger' Thompson, a talented forensics officer well regarded for his skill and his bright red hair.

"Ginger, what do you have for me?" Ray asked, trying to remain calm.

"Right, well the bad news is, the piece of duffel bag we found was pretty badly burnt," he said in his slow methodical way.

"So, give me the good news," Ray prompted him anxiously.

"Ah, yes. Well we have analysed the traces of explosive we found on the material and it's definitely Semtex."

"Semtex? Where would you get that?"

"It's commonly used in the construction industry for demolition and rock blasting when they're building roads. Ah, but more interesting is that we have what looks like a large piece of the timer used – and there's a perfect thumbprint on it. We're checking our records now."

"Ginger, you're the best. I owe you a drink for that."

"All part of the service," said Ginger.

Ray and Matt Burgess were sitting in the meeting room surrounded by members of the team, hastily assembled after the news from forensics.

Ray stood up. "As I see it we have a few promising leads that need to be followed up. The cleaner Molly Gallagher, her lodger Frank Kelly, the photographer Joe Burke and the Irish club where Matt saw the meeting."

A voice from the back of the group asked, "What about the two Americans?"

"They're clean," answered Ray. "We checked their fingerprints against the one found on the piece of timer and it's no match. We could probably try to get them for importing drugs, but unfortunately we have no proof – and with a lawyer like theirs we'd be wasting our time. We need to get them on a plane as soon as possible."

"Aren't the Jamaicans involved in some way?" The question came from one of the WPCs who had been at the Christmas Eve gig.

"That's a good question," Ray said. "We know they were the main suppliers, and unless things got out of hand we were quite happy to let them get on with it. However, a few facts have come to light recently, which complicate things. As I already mentioned, we have a few Irish persons of interest. There is also some as yet unfounded information, that the Jamaicans, in particular Errol, could be the middlemen for drugs supplied by a group of Irishmen. We should talk to these people urgently. Seamus will assign you your specific tasks, so thanks for your time and let's get on with it."

Two hours later, Seamus Byrne was finally able to slip out of police headquarters to the public telephone box across from a café. Putting the coins into the box, he connected to Michael's home number.

Michael answered immediately, sounding nervous. "What's happening Seamus? I've just heard on the news they've let those two Yanks go. I thought those letters would make sure you lot would think it was them."

Seamus tried to sound reassuring. "Look, Michael, you have to stay calm. They're looking to speak to Molly and Frank, so there's no problem there. Molly's in Ireland and Frank knows what to do. Just keep your head down for now, and don't worry. If they start asking around at the club no one'll say anything."

"Why are they interested in the club?" Michael asked.

"One of the team was at the club when you met with Frank, and our guy recognised him. It's nothing to worry about; they're just guessing. Look, I have to go. I'll speak to you soon."

Seamus replaced the receiver and cautiously left the phone box looking around him as he crossed the road heading back to the headquarters.

Unluckily for Seamus, Matt Burgess was once again enjoying a coffee in his favourite café directly opposite the phone box – and Seamus had been spotted. Matt hadn't said anything to Ray the first time, but, his suspicions now thoroughly aroused, he figured this time, he should.

CHAPTER SIXTEEN

JANINE HAD decided, at the last minute, to attend Richard Kennedy's funeral. It was a bitterly cold day and she'd worn a long, black, fur-trimmed coat with black boots. With the addition of large black sunglasses, she looked every bit the successful businesswoman she now was.

She didn't recognise anyone at the ceremony, until just as the proceedings were about to start, Ray Law walked in and sat at the back. He acknowledged her and motioned that he'd speak to her later. It was a touching service, and Janine couldn't help shedding a few tears when she thought back to the times she and Richard had spent together.

Afterwards, as the guests were standing outside, Ray Law came over and suggested they go for a coffee. She'd come in a taxi, so Janine accepted a lift in Ray's car, although he made an effort not to go too fast for once. As they approached the city centre, Janine suggested he come up to the apartment where she could have a proper drink. What Gerry had said the last time he'd been there went through his mind, but Ray felt he had a genuine reason, as he wanted to ask Janine about her father.

She slipped out of her coat and kicked off her boots. She had a tight-fitting black roll-neck sweater on, which accentuated her figure – Ray couldn't help noticing. She smiled as she brought him his coffee, sat down opposite him, and lit a cigarette. He refused the offer of one, as he didn't smoke. In fact, women smoking had always turned him off, but for some reason he was willing to make an exception for Janine.

He took out his notebook and pen in an attempt to get things on a professional level. "If you don't mind, I'd like to ask you a few questions about your father," he said.

She looked surprised. "My Da? Sure, but why do you want to know about him?"

"Well it's probably nothing, but he was seen with a man who we're looking to talk to about the recent bombing at Rudi's. I saw you talking to him there on the night."

"Yes he called me over. He was taking pictures for the paper; that's what he does. He's a professional photographer."

"Do you remember much about when you lived in Ireland? Ballykobh wasn't it?" Ray asked tentatively.

"To be honest, not really, I was only ten when we moved over here. I remember being upset to be leaving my best friend and not knowing where we were going." She looked reflectively out of the window and across the rooftops towards the skeletal remains of Rudi's.

Ray tried pressing her, but he knew he had to tread carefully. "What about your father? Did you ever see him with groups of men at the house?"

She thought back. "There were a few friends he had who used to come round and they'd all sit in a room together talking and drinking, but that was a long time ago. Why are you asking?"

He was about to reply, when the door opened and Gerry walked in. He knew straight away from the look on Gerry's face that coming back to the apartment had been a mistake.

Gerry took off his coat and threw it across the back of a chair. "I thought I asked you to conduct any future police business with my wife at your headquarters," he said with an aggressive tone. "Unless of course it's not police business, in which case what the fuck are you doing here, DCI Law?"

Janine jumped up. "Calm down Ger, it's my fault, I asked him to come here. I didn't fancy going to the Cop Shop. Anyway he was just finished, weren't you DCI Law?" She flashed him a wink that Gerry didn't see.

Ray stood up and put his notebook and pen in his pocket. "Yes, and thanks for the coffee Mrs. Fortuna, you've been very helpful."

Janine opened the door for him and he made his way over to the lift. Before he had chance to turn round, she closed the door. Ray breathed a sigh of relief. *I really must be more careful with that woman. She is definitely dangerous to be around.* Although something inside him wanted to ignore the warnings.

"I told him not to come here again. So what did he want this time?" Gerry asked, as Janine closed the door.

"He wanted to ask a few questions about my dad and our life back in Ireland. And I told you, it was my idea to come back here. He was at Richard Kennedy's funeral and drove me back. Why weren't you there anyway? You said you would be?"

"Couldn't make it in the end. Bobby wanted a meeting with me and Pete about the tour."

"How's all that going? I must come down and check them out. Pete was saying it's all sounding great now the keyboard player's there."

"Yeah, Bobby wanted a chat about money, and to make sure Pete was happy with things. There was a bit of friction with one of the band yesterday, but according to Pete it's all sorted now. One thing Bobby mentioned after Pete left worried me though. Seems he has a way of disappearing into the gents' loo and moments later he comes bouncing out full of energy. Bobby reckons his drug habit is getting worse, and if we don't watch out it could cause us problems later on. You've seen him and spoken to him, what do you think, babe?"

Janine thought for a moment. "I know what Bobby means. The last time I was down in London with him he did take some stuff. When I pulled him up on it he got shirty and said he was fine and knew what he was doing. Maybe now I've got the time, I should get involved. He does talk to me. What d'you think?"

"This is gonna be a big year for The Flames and we don't want the main man fuckin' it up do we? So, whatever it takes, babe." Gerry gave her a passionate kiss and she found herself responding. It was ages since he'd made any kind of advance, and she liked the way he held her. It was almost like the first time; except they weren't in his car.

She pushed him down backwards on the chair behind him and straddled his legs as she opened his bulging zip. This time she didn't need to use her mouth, as they both came to a shuddering climax together and she lay forward holding his head as she kissed him.

Ray Law arrived back in his office just as DS Matt Burgess turned up to see him. The teams were still out looking for Frank Kelly and Molly Gallagher, but Matt wanted to speak to him about something else.

"You know the rule we have, where even though it might be nothing, say it anyway just in case?"

Ray looked at him questioningly. "Go on."

"Well it didn't bother me the first time, but the second time I thought it might be worth a mention."

"Yes. Go on. Go on!" Ray said impatiently.

"OK. So I was in the little café around the corner and there's a telephone box across the road. And who should walk over to use it but Seamus."

"Sergeant Byrne?"

"Yes. The first time he did it I thought no more about it, but when he did it again yesterday I thought I'd say something to you. It's just the way he looks around him all the time, as if he's nervous – and why would you use a phone box when you could just pick up the phone on your desk?"

Ray frowned. "Could be something or nothing as you say. Matt, can you have a discreet look into his family background?"

Alex Mitchell was back in his flat. He'd finally been released from hospital and was feeling much better apart from a few remaining bruises. The bodies of Thomas and his brother James had been flown back to Chicago by their parents, where they would be buried together. Alex was devastated by the death of James, but there was no way he could afford to fly over to attend the ceremonies. He also thought there might be some friction with James' parents, as he'd always got the impression from Thomas that they didn't understand their youngest son's sexuality. Wynton Brown's funeral was also taking place that week, and he had made arrangements to go to the service. He'd contacted Wynton's girlfriend and said he'd like to play a special piece on piano, as a tribute to his friend.

Thankfully he'd had no further visits from the police, and according to the newspapers the Americans had been released from custody and flown back to the States. With them out of the way he was beginning to feel more relaxed, especially as so far there was no mention of the drugs connection with the club, but he knew he had to be on his guard, particularly where Gerry Fortuna and DCI Law were concerned.

It was a bright crisp winter's day for Wynton's funeral, and the small church was packed with family and friends. Alex noticed a few members of the press crammed into the back pews, along with DCI Law and the other police officer who'd visited him in hospital.

The touching tributes and heart-lifting gospel singing made what could have been a desperately sad occasion into a joyous one – and finally it was Alex's turn. Desperately holding in his emotions, he walked to the piano that had been set up at the front and began to play.

He'd decided to incorporate some of Wynton's favourite tunes into a medley, and soon the congregation, sensing what he was doing, started to clap along to the rhythm. As he finished, the whole church stood and cheered, and Alex with tears streaming down his face, looked up and smiled, knowing his friend was now playing with his idols.

Standing at the back, Ray Law found himself clapping along with everyone else, and at one point singing to one of the songs he remembered from his days back in Liverpool when he had dreams of becoming a soul star. As they filed out of the church, Ray noticed Errol leaning on his walking stick talking to a few of Wynton's relations. Ray waited until he'd moved away on his own and seized the opportunity to have a word.

"Always sad affairs, funerals," he said, standing next to Errol. "Did you know Wynton well?"

"He was a good friend of my nephew, Charles," he said with a sigh. "And such a gifted musician. He first started playing with the gospel choir when he was a boy. I heard you singing before; you have a good voice – maybe you should come to one of our services."

"Ah, thank you," Ray replied. "But sadly I don't have time to do that anymore,"

"We should all make time for the Lord."

"How is Charles?" Ray asked, changing the subject.

"Not good. Still in intensive care. The doctors have managed to save one of his legs, but they're still concerned. Thank you for asking."

Errol turned to go and Ray caught his arm. "Before you go, when we spoke last time, you never mentioned you had links with the Irish. Why was that?"

Errol was slightly taken aback by the question. He paused, considering his answer. "I didn't feel it necessary. That was a long time ago. What makes you ask?"

"I heard that you were a middleman for them where the supply of drugs was concerned." Ray stared him straight in the eyes.

Errol avoided his gaze, and on the pretence of spotting someone in a nearby gathering, made a show of acknowledging them before turning to Ray. "I'm sorry, I have to go now. It was nice to see you again, Detective Chief Inspector."

"That surprised him," DS Matt Burgess commented, as Errol walked away leaning heavily on his gnarled, wooden walking stick.

"Yes, I think there's more to this Irish thing than we first thought," said Ray, as they walked back to his car.

Frank Kelly had just arrived back at Molly Gallagher's house after a double shift at work, when the phone rang. His first impulse was to ignore it and let it ring, but for some reason he picked up the receiver. The female voice at the other end was crying. He knew straight away it was Molly.

"What the hell are you doing ringing here?" Frank said, trying to remain calm.

"Oh God, Frank what have I done? What have I done?" she cried. "I have to come back. I can't live with myself for what I did."

"You'll do no such thing, Molly Gallagher!" Frank replied. "What good do you think you'll do coming back here? For everyone's sake you need to stay where you are. It wasn't your fault. Now promise me you'll go back to your brother's and wait 'til I come to fetch you."

"But it was my fault. I panicked when the musicians came in and couldn't remember which way to push the switch. If I'd tried to reset it they would have seen what I was doing."

Just then the doorbell rang. "Molly listen to me," Frank said. "I have to go. There's someone at the door. Stay there and I'll be over soon, but don't ring here again." He put the phone down.

The doorbell rang again and he opened it. There were two uniformed police officers standing there who showed him their warrant cards and introduced themselves as PC Tony Carter and WPC Jackie Rose.

"Sorry to bother you, sir. We're enquiring as to the whereabouts of Mrs. Molly Gallagher. Is she in?" Carter asked.

"No I'm afraid not, can I give her a message?"

"And who are you, sir?"

"I'm her brother over from Ireland here for a holiday," Frank said. "She's away down the bingo, but I'll tell her you called as soon as she gets back."

Tony Carter gave him a card. "If you'd be kind enough to ask her to get in touch as soon as possible. Oh, and your name, sir?"

"Arlow, Arlow Gallagher," Frank replied.

The following day during their morning briefing, PC Carter and WPC Rose were reporting on their visit to Molly Gallagher's house, when Matt Burgess interrupted. "Hang on. You said her brother answered the door. What did he look like?"

Tony Carter looked at Jackie Rose for support. "Well-built, dark hair and a strong Irish accent," he said.

"Did he have a thick moustache?" Ray asked.

"No, but he might have done," Jackie replied. "I thought at the time it looked a bit strange; like he could have shaved one off recently. The rest of his face was tanned as if he worked outside a lot and he had this pale patch over his top lip."

Ray and Matt looked at each other. "That sounds like the lodger we met," said Ray. "Something's definitely not right here. OK! This now becomes priority. We need to speak to this Frank Kelly – or Arlow whatever he calls himself – urgently, and let's get a nationwide APB out for Molly Gallagher. Tony and Jackie can you check with airlines and Irish ferry companies around the tenth."

As the meeting broke up, Ray and Matt stayed behind to talk. They'd already decided to tail Seamus if he left the building.

True to form, a couple of hours after the team meeting, Seamus slipped out of the side door and made his way to the phone box. Matt was already sitting inside the café nursing a cold cup of coffee watching out for the Irish sergeant. Once inside the call box, Seamus dialled Michael's number and inserted the coins. As soon as Michael answered he didn't wait for him to speak. "They're looking for Frank; they're onto him."

"Jesus, what'll we do?" Michael was alarmed.

"You need to tell the others. Tell Joe, he'll know what to do," said Seamus. "I've got to go. Take care." He finished the call.

Back at the telephone exchange, the engineer clicked off the recorder and called Ray Law. "I have it, sir. What would you like me to do now?"

"Just hang on to it. My DS, Matt Burgess, will be along to pick it up, and thanks for your cooperation." Ray put down his receiver. "Got you!"

Another member of Ray's team had been making enquiries about the membership of the Irish club, where Matt Burgess had seen the meeting between Frank Kelly, Joe Burke and three other men. By cross-checking the list of names and addresses, he'd made an interesting discovery. One of the members of the club was Michael Brennan, who it turned out, was Seamus Byrne's brother-in-law. Also in the list of members, was Niall Fitzgerald. The same Niall Fitzgerald who had perished along with his wife, in the attack on Rudi's.

Ray was in his office when Matt Burgess returned with the recording of Seamus's phone call. He also had the list of members from the Irish club on his desk, and a confirmation that Molly Gallagher had travelled from Holyhead to Dun Laoghaire on the seven-thirty Sealink ferry on Wednesday, 7th January. He'd underlined the names of Joe Burke, Niall Fitzgerald and Michael Brennan on the list. Now all they needed was the fourth member from the meeting and Frank Kelly. Ray's phone rang, interrupting them.

"George Williams wants to see me in his office pronto," Ray said, jumping up from his chair.

George was frowning as Ray entered his office. "Sit down Ray," he said. "I've just got off the phone with Special Branch. You're to back off investigating Joe Burke and his team immediately."

Ray's look of amazement turned to anger. "What the hell? Are you kidding me?" he spluttered. "We've almost got everything in place. Sir, what's going on? I mean…"

George cut him off. "I'm sorry Ray, but this is well over my head too. It seems Special Branch have been watching a splinter cell of ex-IRA activists who moved to the mainland years ago. They'd been quiet for a long time, when all of a sudden they popped up on the radar again. I think I mentioned Joe Burke, Janine Fortuna's father, to you before as a person of interest? Well it seems he's been setting up meetings with the other original members at an innocent little Irish club out in the suburbs. There's been an undercover officer working there for a while now and he began to notice an increase in activity from Joe and his team. He spotted your DS Burgess there, but for obvious reasons couldn't reveal himself. He reported the same incident that Matt saw, back to his superiors and as a consequence all four members have been under surveillance. Of course when your team became involved, the alarm bells started to ring – hence the phone call today."

Ray was shaking his head. "But if they've been aware of them, why didn't they stop the bomb?"

"Ah, that's where it gets complicated. According to Special Branch they were unaware of the bomb threat. Their remit was to follow the drugs supply and catch them delivering the goods. Errol's been involved in this for ages, but couldn't say anything to you when you spoke to him at the funeral the other day."

Ray was still shocked and shaking his head. "Why weren't we told? I mean we now have evidence that links one of our sergeants to the group. This is crazy!" He slammed his fist down on George's desk.

"Take it easy! Look if it's any consolation I know exactly how you feel. I've been in this situation before – when I was a DCI the same as you. Working on a murder case, all the parts lined up to take the suspect down, when we had word from above that he was on a special watch list and we had to back off. He walked free and we had to sit on our hands. It's shit I know, but that's how it works sometimes. There're two of the team on their way up for a briefing later today. I'll call you when they arrive."

Ray left George's office, kicking the door to the stairs on his way out.

CHAPTER SEVENTEEN

THE TWO officers from Special Branch were already sitting in George Williams' office drinking coffee when Ray Law walked in. George introduced them as DCIs Jack Morton and Robbie Simpson, and they both stood to shake hands. Ray was impressed at how well dressed they were; both wearing smart suits and ties. They could have been mistaken for high-profile businessmen.

George got the meeting underway. "Pleasantries over chaps, let's get down to business. As I'm led to believe, Special Branch has had the four members of this group under surveillance. Is that correct?" He looked at the two men sitting opposite him.

DCI Jack Morton – a six-foot, dark-haired, well-built cockney – nodded his head. "That's correct. They'd been off our radar for quite some time but then we picked up a lead that they'd got themselves into the drugs game here in the Midlands."

DCI Robbie Simpson took over at that point. He was slightly shorter with prematurely greying hair and a hint of a Geordie accent. "Joe Burke would appear to be the leader. He was pretty high up in the ranks when he was in Ballykobh and managed to get himself and his family over here. They all met at the Irish club that you know about, where luckily for us we managed to get one of our Irish lads in there as a barman. He's been keeping an eye on them, and got wind of their involvement with a Jamaican guy who was acting as their middleman supplying drugs. He'd seen him turn up regularly for a meeting in their little office."

"To be honest," Jack Morton carried on, "we were quite happy with the situation. We knew you guys were aware of the Jamaicans, and we could leave things as they were providing nothing got out of hand – better the devil you know sort of thing. That's when it all started to get messy though – when those Yanks came on the scene. They were moving around so much we couldn't keep track of them. We got a tip-off that they were using that club, Rudi's, to bring the stuff in, and that the manager and one of his musicians were part of the deal, although we never had proof. Of course when it all went up, that was that."

Ray had been listening intently. "So, why stop my investigation? I have evidence that your group were somehow involved in the bombing, and we're a long way down the line piecing the case together."

"Look mate," Jack Morton answered; "We're not here to stop you; we're here to help. Our superiors want this little Irish group eradicated by any means, so we're all ears. Let's have what you got."

George looked at Ray with a relieved smile. "Gentlemen, more coffee?"

An hour later they'd gone through Ray's notes, Ginger's evidence and listened to the telephone recording of Seamus Byrne.

Robbie Simpson said, "Well for one thing, we know who the fourth member is. He's called Sean Whelan. Our source has regularly seen him with the others, and he was the one who introduced Frank Kelly to them. They seemed like good mates our man said."

Ray was thoughtful. "Who is this Frank Kelly character? I think he holds the key to all this. We need to get him in for questioning, and quick before he has chance to make a run for it. I'll organise an APB and get it out straight away."

Robbie nodded.

"Can't we use this Sergeant Byrne of yours in some way?" Jack Morton was drumming his fingers on the table. "What if we make him believe we have this Gallagher woman in custody over in Ireland, and we're flying over to speak to her."

"I could let it out at tomorrow's briefing," Ray added. "Then if Seamus – Sergeant Byrne – contacts his brother-in-law, hopefully he'll panic and contact the others. We could do with getting a tap on this Michael Brennan's phone."

"I can authorise that," George Williams said.

Seamus took the bait and phoned Michael Brennan as soon as the briefing was over. Michael was worried. He tried to speak to Joe Burke, but his wife said he was out on a story for the paper and wouldn't be back until late. He then called Sean Whelan's number but he wasn't in either.

Frank had specifically said they should stay calm, but Seamus had said that they had the Irish cleaner in custody over in Ireland and two Special Branch officers were on their way to interview her. That meant it was only a matter of time before she gave them all away. He was sure she would.

Frank Kelly had left Molly Gallagher's house as soon as the two police officers had driven away. He'd cursed himself for not leaving after the previous police visit, but there were things he'd had to do. He'd handed in his notice at the site, collected his pay packet and then gone home to shave off his moustache. He'd packed a bag with his few belongings and would have left sooner had it not been for Molly ringing. If he hadn't answered the phone he would have been gone before they arrived. Now he was on his way to meet his friend Sean Whelan in their local pub, The Royal Oak. Sean was a good friend and Frank knew he could rely on him.

Sean gave Frank the address of a place that had rooms to rent. "It's pretty basic y'know, but no one'll bother you. The girls are friendly like, but they just get on with their business."

Frank looked at Sean. "It's not a feckin' whore house you're sending me to is it?"

Sean laughed. "No, no nothin' like that. By the way, do you like Indian food?"

Frank screwed up his face. "I feckin' hate Indian food!"

"Ah that's a shame." Sean replied. "It's above one of the best Indian restaurants in the Midlands. Second to none."

"Jesus! Look, did you manage to get me the little extra I asked you for?"

"I did, but I'm tellin' you, be careful Frank. You're treading on dangerous ground there." Sean handed over a small brown paper parcel.

"Don't worry, it's only a bit of insurance, just in case," Frank said, putting it in his bag.

They went back to drinking their pints as the six o'clock news came on the television which was high up on a shelf behind the bar. The headline story was the continuing coverage of the club bombing. The sound was turned down but loud enough for them to hear the newsreader say that police were looking to question a man known as Frank Kelly, and there on the screen was a Photofit of Frank. Not a brilliant likeness, but close enough. They quickly finished their pints and without saying another word left the pub.

Outside, they shook hands and Frank made his way to the bus stop across the road, while Sean walked to his house just around the corner.

140

He wondered if he'd done the right thing getting Frank his little extra.

Back at police headquarters Ray, Jack Morton and Robbie Simpson, had decided the time was right to arrest Joe Burke, Michael Brennan and Sean Whelan on suspicion of involvement in the bombing. They didn't have any solid evidence, only the recording of Seamus telling Michael what was going on during the briefings, and the report from the undercover barman at the Irish club saying he'd seen them all together with Frank Kelly, so Ray knew that with a good lawyer, none of it would stand up in court. However, he was hoping it might be enough for one of them to panic.

The three suspects had all been picked up at the same time early the next morning, by pairs of officers from Ray's team. None of them had offered any resistance, and they were now in separate interview rooms at police headquarters.

Joe Burke had been sitting down to eat his breakfast when the officers knocked on his door. He'd calmly reassured his wife everything would be fine and climbed in the back of the panda car. On arrival he'd made a phone call to the solicitor he knew from St Mary's Irish Club, and he was now waiting for him to arrive. The same solicitor had recommended two of his colleagues to represent Sean and Michael, and they too were on their way. Seamus had been cautioned by Matt Burgess and was waiting to be interviewed by him and Ray.

Joe Burke's solicitor finally arrived, and the Special Branch DCIs entered the interview room. Unlike some, this one had recently been redecorated and smelt strongly of new paint. They sat down opposite Joe Burke and his solicitor Patrick Bloom, a short, curly-haired Irishman in a well-worn suit that had seen better days, and all identified themselves for the record.

Robbie Simpson spoke first. "Mr. Burke. Are you aware of the reason why we've brought you here?"

Joe glanced at his solicitor then turned to Robbie. "I'm happy to help your enquiry in whatever way I can."

"That's good to know. So would you mind explaining the purpose of the meetings which you attended at St Mary's Irish Club over the last month, in the company of Michael Brennan, Sean Whelan, the late Niall Fitzgerald and a man we are led to believe is called Frank Kelly?"

Joe looked at Patrick Bloom and said, "Yes, no problem. We were discussing the St Patrick's Day parade which the club will be taking part in."

"And why did that include Frank Kelly? He's not a member of the club, is he?" Jack Morton asked.

"That's true, but he volunteered to help with making the float for the parade," Joe replied.

Robbie looked at his notes. "Where were you on the night of Wednesday, 7th January, between the hours of seven and midnight?"

"I was out working on a job for the newspaper in the early part of the evening, and then once I received news of the explosion I was outside the club taking photographs until the early hours of Thursday morning."

"Do you know the whereabouts of Frank Kelly, Mr. Burke?" Robbie asked.

"I don't see what that has got to do with my client," the solicitor answered before Joe had time to reply.

Joe again calmly replied. "I'm afraid I'm not a personal friend of Mr. Kelly, so I couldn't tell you, Officer."

Robbie looked at Jack and they both stood up. "That will be all for now, Mr. Burke."

Ray and Matt were in the observation room when the others came in. "What do you think? That excuse about the St Patrick's Day parade is a bit too obvious don't you think?"

Robbie shook his head. "I wonder if the others'll be quite as confident as him. OK, who's next?"

"I'd say Sean Whelan," Ray said. "I think we should leave Michael Brennan to sweat. He sounded rattled on the tape to Seamus."

"Good thinking. Right, Sean Whelan it is. Lead on Robbie." Jack opened the door to leave the room.

"From what I saw when I was at the club, he seemed pretty friendly with Frank Kelly," Matt said.

"Alright, I'll bear that in mind, thanks," Jack said as they left.

Interview Room Two smelt strongly of sweat and stale cigarette smoke.

Sean Whelan was sitting with his solicitor, a younger associate from Patrick Bloom's firm who, judging by his new suit, had just recently qualified.

Jack Morton sat down and spoke first. "Good morning, for the record my name is DCI Jack Morton."

"And I'm DCI Robbie Simpson. Would you state your names please?"

"Sean Whelan."

The young solicitor went red and nervously coughed. "I'm, err, Philip Sutton and on behalf of my client I would like to protest at the amount of time he has been kept waiting."

Jack smiled at the young solicitor who was obviously trying hard to make his presence felt. "Yes Mr, err, Sutton – your comment has been noted. Now Mr. Whelan, am I correct in saying you are a friend of a Mr. Frank Kelly?"

Sean Whelan looked at his young solicitor and then at Jack. "No comment."

Jack tried another question. "Mr. Whelan, were you at a meeting the week before Christmas at St Mary's Irish Club with a Mr. Frank Kelly?"

Sean leaned back staring at the ceiling. "No comment."

"Well Mr. Whelan, your friend Mr. Burke has admitted that he was with you and Mr. Kelly at St Mary's. What have you to say to that?"

Sean sat forward and stared at Jack. "No comment."

Jack returned the stare, then stood and motioned for Robbie to follow. "Thank you, Mr. Whelan, that will be all for now."

Ray was pacing about at the back of the observation room as they entered. "Clever bastard! He needs knocking down a peg or two."

"Don't worry there's plenty of time. But he did react to being told that Joe Burke had admitted being with Frank Kelly. Let's see what the next one has to say."

Ray stepped forward. "If it's alright with you guys, I'd like to have a crack at Michael Brennan."

"Sure be our guest," Robbie said. "This is Sergeant Byrne's brother-in-law, right?"

Ray nodded. "Yeah and he might just be the one to crack under a bit of pressure. Matt, you coming?"

They entered the interview room to find Michael Brennan sitting with an attractive woman. She was wearing an expensively tailored, grey pin-striped business suit, stylish glasses and black patent leather high heels. Her long, chestnut-brown hair was fashioned into a French plait. Ray noticed her perfume was almost overpowering but at the same time intoxicating. She crushed her cigarette in the ashtray on the table in front of her and straightened her skirt as Ray and Matt sat down.

"Good morning," they said, and introduced themselves.

The solicitor looked pointedly at Ray. "Oh, it's still morning? We've been here so long I'm surprised it's still daylight outside! For the record my name is Julia Davies.

Ray ignored her barb and addressed Michael. "Would you state your name for the record please?"

Michael Brennan identified himself.

Ray continued; "Mr. Brennan, we have evidence that you know a man called Frank Kelly – with whom you, Joe Burke, Sean Whelan and Niall Fitzgerald met before Christmas. Can you tell us the reason for these meetings?"

Michael glanced at Julia Davies, who was writing a note on her leather-bound pad. She looked up as Michael answered Ray. "No comment."

"Mr. Brennan, what were you doing in the company of Joe Burke, Sean Whelan, Niall Fitzgerald and Frank Kelly at St Mary's Irish Club before Christmas?"

"I don't remember any such meeting," Michael replied.

"Well now, that's very strange," said Ray. "Because earlier today one of your friends, Mr. Joe Burke, told us how you and he met with Messrs. Whelan, Fitzgerald, and Kelly, at St Mary's on at least two occasions to discuss the St Patrick's Day parade. So how about we cut the bullshit and start telling the truth!"

Julia Davies looked at Michael with a frown and turning back to Ray said, "I'd like a moment or two with my client, if you don't mind, DCI Law."

The two detectives left the room and Julia swung round sharply to face Michael Brennan. "OK before we go any further, you have some explaining to do Mr. Brennan," she hissed. "Were you, or were you not, in that club with the others?"

Michael sat quietly for a few moments before speaking.

"Yes, yes I was, but we didn't want it to happen like this," he said, choking back a sob. "It was meant to be a message to the Americans, to back off. We never meant for anyone to get killed."

"So the truth is that you, Whelan, Burke, Fitzgerald and Kelly planned this attack on the club, but you didn't think anyone would be injured?" Julia dropped her pen down on the table. "You must think I'm stupid, never mind the police!"

"No, it wasn't like that. It was supposed to go off at eleven o'clock the next morning, when the manager and drummer were there picking up the drugs. Frank assured us that's how it would be. We'd never have agreed otherwise."

"So who is this Frank Kelly, and how does he fit in to what happened?"

"He was a friend of Sean's, over here working on the new roads. He said he could get some explosive, and that he would take care of everything."

"So how did he plant the bomb?"

"He didn't. He got Sean's cousin Molly to do it – she was a cleaner at the club. He said he'd show her how to set it to go off twenty-four hours after she planted it under the stage."

"So what was your involvement?" she asked, writing more notes on her pad.

"I was part of the Association, a group of sympathisers from the old country," Michael explained. "We would meet once a week, in the back room at St Mary's to talk about the old times."

"Michael, I need you to tell me everything, and I mean everything, if I'm to help you here. So tell me about the drugs."

Michael nodded and carried on. "We supplied the old man Errol with stuff we brought in from Ireland. Just a case of supply and demand really."

"So why did the Americans cause you problems?"

"Well, it was Errol who brought it to our attention. His nephew Mr. C was the DJ at Rudi's, and he'd been approached by Alex Mitchell's drummer Thomas who was going round trying to sell stuff much cheaper than Errol, and he asked us to help."

"And the stuff you refer to…is drugs being sold by the Americans?"

"That's right."

"And this Alex Mitchell, he's the manager at Rudi's?"

"Yeah, a real gobshite if you ask me."

Julia ignored his comment. "Did he know what was going on?"

"Course he did. A package was delivered to the club and picked up by the drummer, same time every week. Then the next day the streets would be flooded with cheaper stuff than we could supply Errol with. It was pretty obvious."

"OK, I've been writing everything down. I'm going to give them a statement from you in return for a deal."

"Do you think they'll go for that?"

"Just leave it to me," she replied. The door to the interview room opened, and DCI Law and DS Burgess came back in.

"I think you've had enough time to consult with your client," Ray said to Julia.

"Thank you for your patience DCI Law," Julia replied. Michael was looking apprehensive, but she calmed him with a reassuring look. "I think my client is ready to answer any questions you may have. However there are certain stipulations."

Ray Law gave an exaggerated sigh. "And what might they be Miss Davies?"

"For the record DCI Law, it's Ms.," Julia snapped back.

Ray tilted his head slightly and smiled.

She went on. "My client is happy to answer your questions in return for immunity from prosecution."

"That's a bit of a tall order," Ray said. "I'll have to consult with my superiors about any deals. But why don't we see what Mr. Brennan has to say first."

Julia nodded. "I have a statement from Mr. Brennan which you might care to read before we continue." She passed over a sheet of paper.

Ray read it, raised his eyebrows, and passed it to Matt Burgess.

"So Michael, you don't mind me calling you Michael?" Michael nodded. "Thanks. What's your connection to Sergeant Seamus Byrne?"

Michael sat upright and looked at Julia Davies. "Is this relevant?" she asked.

"Just answer the question Michael," Ray carried on, undaunted.

Julia nodded.

"He's my brother-in-law," Michael said.

"He seems to have been making lots of phone calls to you recently," Ray continued. "Just about family and things," Michael stuttered.

"Well it's strange that each time you've talked about family and things, it happens to have coincided with one of our case briefings. He wouldn't have been passing on information to you Michael, would he?"

Ray leaned back in his chair watching Brennan squirm.

"No, no. I said it was just about family things. He's a member of St. Mary's. We meet up there sometimes." Michael was starting to sweat.

"So, if I told you we have a recording of the last phone conversation between you and Seamus Byrne, in which he tells you, and I quote, 'They're looking for Frank, they're onto him. You need to tell the others. Tell Joe, he'll know what to do.' What's your reply Michael?" Ray paused. "You seem confused." He pushed more. "You may also be interested to know we have Sergeant Byrne in custody, and he is currently making a full confession as to his part in the events at Rudi's nightclub. What're your thoughts now Michael?" Michael looked stunned. "What's the matter, cat got your tongue?"

Julia leaned over and touched Michael's arm. "My client has nothing more to say for the time being."

"I bet he doesn't," said Ray. "Interview suspended. Come on DS Burgess, I think Ms. Davies and her client, have some serious thinking to do."

Meanwhile, back in Interview Room Two, DCIs Morton and Simpson were back with Sean Whelan and his solicitor Philip Sutton.

Jack Morton was first to speak. "Good morning again Mr. Whelan, and er, Mr. Sutton."

The sarcasm was not lost on Sean, who snatched an anxious look at his solicitor.

"So, any more thoughts on the situation Sean? You don't mind me calling you Sean?"

Sean nodded his head.

"You've had the statements of both Mr. Burke and Mr. Brennan and I assume you've read them carefully."

Sean nodded again. His attitude seemed to have changed from their earlier meeting. "It's Frank Kelly we're after and it seems you know where he is, Sean. Come on, be sensible and give us an address before things get worse."

Sean leaned back in his chair, and then suddenly sat forward. "So, what's in it for me?" he asked. "It wasn't me who planted the bomb. I didn't want anyone hurt."

"We know that, Sean, but we need to speak to Frank," Jack said.

"He was your friend. Tell us where he is before things get a lot worse." Robbie added.

Sean sat thinking. He'd read the two statements from Joe Burke and Michael Brennan, both naming him as one of the conspirators – but he was still nervous about shopping Frank. Frank was a hard man, and if he found out that Sean had given him away, he'd come looking for him. Even if Sean was inside, Frank would find a way.

Jack Morton knew he would tell them eventually, but the secret was not to rush him. If they panicked him he might just clam up and revert to No comment.

On the next floor up – at the same time as Sean Whelan was considering his future safety, Seamus Byrne was sitting opposite DCI Ray Law and DS Matt Burgess, who had run up the stairs from Interview Room Three. In front of Byrne was a transcript of the telephone conversation he'd had with his brother-in-law, Michael Brennan.

"Tell us why, Seamus," said Ray. "Your career's finished you must know that, but you might as well do the right thing while you have the chance."

Seamus was close to tears. He looked at Ray. "He's family. While I didn't agree with the drug thing, I had to try and help him."

"Did you ever meet Frank Kelly?"

"No. I knew about him, and what they were planning, but it was never meant to happen like it did. They weren't like that."

"Try telling that to the innocent Irish victims they killed back in the troubles," Ray snapped back.

"But they had changed. The drug thing was a good sideline, and it was under control until the Americans tried to muscle in and take over. You know yourself how it works. Old Errol ran his side of the business and everyone was happy, including us."

"So who's the leader?"

"Joe Burke. He's the main guy. Everything goes through him."

"Janine Fortuna's father!" Ray exclaimed. "Shit, this could get messy, especially if Gerry finds out. We're gonna have to be very careful how we handle this. Matt, make sure this conversation stays between us, and George Williams. Nobody else sees the notes besides us." Ray thought for a moment. "We need to talk to Jack and Robbie. Matt can you find out where they're up to."

Matt Burgess stood up, leaving Ray and Seamus Byrne together.

"Look Seamus, I'll see what I can do, but I can't make any promises. The fact you're helping us will go in your favour, but we need to find Frank Kelly and quick."

Matt Burgess went downstairs and found Jack Morton and Robbie Simpson outside Interview Room Two having a cigarette.

"How's it going guys?" he asked. "Ray was wondering if you've managed to get anything out of Whelan. The other two have given us quite a lot, but we're still no nearer to tracking down this Frank Kelly guy."

"Give us half an hour and he'll give us something, I'm sure," said Jack Morton. "He's breaking, especially after he saw his pals' statements."

"What about you and Ray, what did our friendly sergeant have to say?" Robbie asked.

"Pretty much the same as the others, and we've found out the leader happens to be the father of the club owner's wife. But keep that to yourselves. There could be major ructions if it gets out."

Matt left them to it and Jack and Robbie finished their cigarettes and went back in to continue pressuring Sean Whelan.

"I want to know what's in it for me if I give you Frank Kelly?" Sean said as soon as they sat down. "I'm gonna need some kind of protection. He's a tough bastard and he's got a gun."

"What?" Jack sat up straight. "How do you know that?"

"Because I got it for him. He said it was just an insurance policy in case there were any problems, but no one expected things to turn out like this."

CHAPTER EIGHTEEN

A COUPLE of miles away, Frank Kelly was lying in bed in a room above the Simla Tandoori Restaurant on the Stortford Road; one of the main routes out of Birmingham. It was small but comfortable, with a sink in the corner, a wardrobe against one wall and lurid purple wallpaper. It would have been fine, apart from the mauve Brentford Nylons sheets on the bed, and the constant smell of curry.

"I can't stand nylon sheets," he said, crushing out his cigarette butt in a metal ashtray on the small bedside cabinet. "And I hate the smell of curry!" He turned over and smiled at the girl lying beside him. He had a charming smile and he knew it.

Nina was twenty-five years old and of African descent; she also lived above the restaurant.

"Don't worry, you'll get used to it," she said as she cuddled up to Frank, reaching down between his legs.

"I could get used to you though, girl," Frank said as he responded to her touch.

"You don't mind that I'm black?" Nina asked coyly.

Frank looked at her. "Everyone's the same colour inside," he said.

"You know I shouldn't really be doing this for free, Raj would kill me if he found out."

"Don't worry about Raj. I can deal with him. Now how about finishing what you started," he said, lying back and pulling her head down to his rapidly growing manhood.

At police headquarters, Ray Law, Jack Morton, Robbie Simpson and Matt Burgess were having a meeting in Ray's cramped office.

"According to Sean Whelan, Frank's got a room above the Simla Tandoori on the Stortford Road," Jack said.

"I know that place. Isn't it a bit of a knocking shop?" Matt asked, pouring coffees for them.

"It's rumoured to be," Ray replied.

151

Jack carried on. "The only problem is, we've just found out he's got a gun."

"Shit, are you sure?" said Ray.

"Positive," replied Jack. "Because Sean told us he got it for him. Frank said he wanted it for insurance purposes evidently."

"Well that makes it a whole new ball game," Ray stood up and paced around his desk. "I'd better get George Williams in on this."

Janine was with Gerry in the office above The Hideout. She turned to him, holding a copy of the day's newspaper. "The Evening Post says three suspects are currently being held on suspicion of causing the explosion at Rudi's. Jackie rang to say Mum called her first thing in a terrible panic. The police came to their house early this morning and arrested my dad. Gerry, you know George Williams; can't you have a word? Dad wouldn't be involved in something like this. I'm sure it's all a big mistake, but I need to see him."

Gerry was reading a contract and put it down on top of a pile of papers on his desk. "I'll do what I can. But I've got to ask you this Janine; did you ever know your old man was into terrorist stuff? I mean why would he want to blow the club up? Surely he knows you're involved? You could have been there when it went off."

Janine was thoughtful. "That's the weird thing. DCI Law asked me the same thing about him. I can remember when I was young living in Ireland. Some nights my mum would take my sister and I out while Dad and his friends had meetings in our house. I never knew what they were doing, and nothing was ever said, but thinking about it now sends shivers down my spine. Are you thinking he could be behind this?"

"Look, I don't know what's going on," Gerry picked up the phone on his desk and dialled a number. "I'll give George a call and see if I can find out anything, although it might be difficult – especially if your dad is involved. Let's not get too worked up about it until we know more."

Ray Law knocked on George Williams' door and walked in just as George was finishing a call. He motioned for Ray to sit down in one of the two leather armchairs over in the corner.

"I'm sorry, I can't promise anything until I have all the details. Yes, I'll call you as soon as I know more." He put the phone down. "Coffee?"

Ray was already buzzing from the amount of caffeine he'd had earlier, but couldn't resist George's special roast. Nodding he said, "We've got a major problem, sir."

The Chief Constable stood up and walked over to the filing cabinet. He poured two mugs of coffee from his personal percolator, which was bubbling away on top. He passed Ray a mug of steaming coffee and sat down opposite him.

"We've all got problems Ray. That was Gerry Fortuna on the phone. Janine Fortuna wants to speak to her dad. Don't suppose you know how she could have found out so soon?"

Ray shook his head slowly. "Matt and I made sure that our notes from his interview were kept strictly secret. I thought there might be a problem as soon as we found out who he was. His wife was there when they picked him up – maybe she called Janine. Damn! We need to keep a lid on this. What did you tell Gerry?"

"Well I stalled him for now, saying I couldn't allow Janine access to Joe until we'd finished questioning all the suspects. But he's a persistent character, as you know only too well. So what was the major problem you came to see me about?"

"Ah yes. We've got an address for Frank Kelly, but according to Sean Whelan, he's armed with a revolver."

"That's all we bloody need!" exclaimed George. "Right, I'll need to get on to the MDP. We'll have to make sure we risk as few members of the public as possible. Where is he?"

"That's the problem. He's in a room above an Indian restaurant on the Stortford Road. We've had it on the radar for a while now."

"Not the Simla Tandoori?" George laughed. "I know the owner, Raj Hussain. Bit of a shady character, but he serves the best Chicken Bhuna in the city. So he's staying there is he? From memory there's about six rooms upstairs. We've never been able to pin Raj down to anything strong enough to raid the place, but by all accounts he has some very attractive young women staying there, if you know what I mean. Hmm, I'll give him a call. Maybe we should book a table and check out the place while we're there. I've not had a good curry for ages."

As George was dialling the number, it occurred to Ray that things were becoming quite surreal. A suspected bomber armed with a pistol – and they were going for a curry.

Later that evening, the Chief Constable, DCI Ray Law, and the two Special Branch DCIs, drove down the Stortford Road to the Simla Tandoori. It was impossible to miss the large ostentatious establishment, situated in the middle of a row of rundown shops. Inside it was decorated with maroon flock wallpaper, large mirrors on the walls and a dark-blue ceiling with luminous stars to resemble the night sky. Slowly rotating fans were suspended from above.

The policemen were shown to their table, which had comfortable high-backed chairs upholstered to match the wallpaper, and a colour coordinated tablecloth and napkins. The owner, Raj Hussain, had welcomed George Williams like a long-lost friend, fussing over him, eager to recommend the specialities of the house. In a matter of seconds, a huge pile of poppadoms and condiments had arrived – and disappeared just as quickly. Now one of the waiters brought out the main courses on a large serving trolley. The aroma of the different dishes was fantastic, and as the waiter was serving them, Jack Morton noticed a man enter the restaurant from a door at the back.

He sat down at a table and another one of the waiters approached him. "Good evening, sir. What would you like tonight?"

"Chicken and chips," the man said. "And no curry sauce! Just plain chicken and chips."

The waiter bowed and headed off to the kitchen.

Reaching for a bowl of pilau rice, Jack leaned forward to Ray, "Don't look round, but the man who just came in, looks like Frank Kelly. He's behind you at a table on his own."

Glancing sideways, Ray could see the man through one of the mirrors on the wall. "He certainly looks like the man Matt and I met. Just be calm and don't make any sudden moves."

Jack whispered to Ray. "Listen. In a minute I'll go to the toilet at the back and block his escape."

George Williams was suddenly aware of what was happening, and attracted Raj's attention, on the pretext of a problem with the food. This created enough of a diversion, that Jack Morton's passage to the toilets past Frank Kelly's table seemed to go unnoticed.

It was as well that the restaurant wasn't too crowded because as Ray slowly stood to make his way towards Frank Kelly, the latter's survival instincts kicked in and the chair went over as Kelly pulled a revolver from his jacket pocket and pointed it at Ray. "Don't come any closer. I'll shoot!"

Ray stopped and spread his arms showing he was unarmed. "Don't be foolish Frank. There's no need for anything like that. Look, I'm unarmed. We just want to talk to you."

Jack Morton had come out of the toilets and was directly behind Frank, moving slowly so he wouldn't be noticed but Frank spotted Jack's reflection in the mirror on the wall. ..Turning his head slightly the Irishman said, "Don't try anything copper!"

Ray couldn't help seizing the opening to make a move forward, but as Frank turned his head back, catching the slight motion out of the corner of his eye, he reflexively pulled the trigger.

The bullet fired at close range hit Ray in the stomach and he collapsed instantly to the floor. In the ensuing chaos, Jack Morton made a grab for Frank from behind while Robbie Simpson hurled himself across the restaurant and brought both Jack and Frank down, sending plates, glasses and furniture scattering everywhere. The gun, knocked from Frank's grasp, landed in front of George Williams, who calmly picked it up and shouted to Raj to call an ambulance immediately.

The two Special Branch detectives had Frank Kelly pinned down on the floor, and George Williams turned his attention to Ray Law who was motionless and bleeding profusely. Getting him swiftly to hospital was clearly vital.

The ambulance arrived within minutes but George was worried about the amount of blood Ray had lost. He wanted to accompany his young DCI, but the two ambulancemen assured him Ray was in good hands; seconds later they were speeding off to the nearby emergency department with their lights flashing and siren wailing.

George turned to where Frank by now was standing, held securely by Jack Morton and Robbie Simpson. He pointed the gun at Frank's head and walked slowly towards him. "God help you if he dies," he said, through gritted teeth. "You bastard! I'll kill you myself!"

He turned away as the sound of police sirens filled the air.

CHAPTER NINETEEN

FRANK KELLY sat in an interrogation room deep in the bowels of police headquarters. Unlike the ones that the members of the Association had been in, this one was rough and intimidating. It too stank of stale cigarettes and sweat, the two fluorescent light tubes buzzed over his head with one flickering intermittently, and the table in front of him was scarred with cigarette burns. On it was a polystyrene cup, half full of cold tea. He was still dressed in the shabby suit he had been wearing in the restaurant; with one of the pockets ripped and a bloodstain on the collar. He was handcuffed and flanked by two officers when DCIs Jack Morton and Robbie Simpson came into the room. On the other side of the two-way mirror, George Williams had just joined DS Matt Burgess to watch the proceedings.

"What the hell happened to him? He looks like he's just done ten rounds with Marvin Hagler," George Williams said.

Matt Burgess smiled. "I think he bumped into a door frame on his way here."

"More than one I'd say," said George.

The two Special Branch officers took their seats opposite Frank.

"So how about we go through your evidence one more time, Frank?" Jack Morton threw the sheaf of papers he had onto the table.

"It's just as I said. I was in the club with my friend Sean Whelan playing darts, having a few beers. There's plenty of folks who were there who'll vouch for me." Frank was confident and leaned back in his chair, a trace of a smile on his face through the bruises. The chair creaked loudly as he tipped backwards on the two back legs.

"Take it easy," said Robbie Simpson. "We wouldn't want you hurting yourself, would we!"

Frank eased himself upright, his eyes fixed on Robbie.

Jack continued. "Do you normally carry a revolver in your pocket when you go for a meal?"

"Look I told you; I didn't know it was loaded. What would you do in my position? I'm sitting in a restaurant minding my own business, waiting for my chicken and chips, when suddenly two complete strangers come at me. I thought if I bluffed with it you'd leave me alone. He shouldn't have come at me like that."

Jack said. "You're full of shit, Frank and you know it. We've got a signed confession from your pal Sean, saying how he got the gun for you, 'For insurance purposes', you said. Did they include shooting a cop? Oh, and you might like to know, we have a certain Molly Gallagher in custody in Dublin – she's rather upset with you. She's told us the whole story. How you tricked her into planting the bomb and setting the timer wrong."

Frank scowled and gripped his fists into balls. "Stupid fuckin' bitch," he spat out. "They're all fuckin' stupid! Setting the timer wrong! Did they really think I was gonna set it to twenty-four hours? Them Yanks needed teaching a lesson, and that gobshite of a club manager."

"Hang on, hang on, slow down," Jack sat up. "You're saying you knew that bomb would explode at eleven o'clock that night, and not the next morning?"

"Course I did! There never was a twenty-four-hour timer! If you're gonna do something, then do it right!" Frank was starting to sound cocky.

Jack encouraged him to tell them more. "So the four members of the club didn't know it was going to go off when it did?"

"They're all pussies. They wanted the Yanks getting rid of. So I did. Now they're all crying cos someone got hurt. They should have thought of that before asking me to sort it out."

"But you killed one of your own members – Niall Fitzgerald – and his wife. Doesn't that bother you?" Jack asked.

"Collateral damage! You win some, you lose some!" Frank's smile carried a sinister edge.

Behind the two-way mirror, a jubilant George Williams patted Matt Burgess on the back and started to leave the observation room. "Well that just about wraps it up, don't you think?"

Instead of joining in the celebration though, Matt Burgess held up his hand. "Hang on a minute sir. Did I just hear him right? Did Frank just say, 'that gobshite of a club manager'? Is he referring to Alex Mitchell?

Ray had suspicions but could never pin anything on him. Could we get a message to Jack to push him a bit more, sir?"

"If you think it'd be useful," George Williams said.

As Matt was about to leave, the phone rang and George picked it up. His previous euphoria faded as he listened to the voice on the other end.

"Shit!" he exclaimed, as he slammed the phone down. "That was the Head of Special Branch. Evidently, something big's happened involving the PM and the security forces, and we've to suspend everything until further notice. There's a Home Office minister already on his way. You better get Jack Morton and Robbie Simpson in here pronto, DS Burgess!"

Ray Law woke up in a hospital bed two days after being shot. He had tubes coming from what seemed like every part of his body, and horrendous pain in his stomach. He was still feeling sleepy when a nurse came into his room to check up on him.

"Hey, good to see you back in the land of the living. We were a bit worried about you for a while." She walked round the bed and checked the drip at his side. "Looking good. The doctor's on his way to see you. He'll be pleased you're awake." She wrote down a couple of notes on the clipboard hanging on the end of the bed.

Ray smiled and tried to move, but the sharp pain in his stomach made him gasp.

"It's OK, you shouldn't try to move too much; you've had a major operation and your stitches need to heal. I'll see you later."

Moments later the doctor walked in, flanked by two more nurses.

"Ah, the patient awakes," he said brightly. "Good to see you back with us, young man. That was a lucky escape you had. Another half inch to the right and you'd have been a goner. As it was, the bullet just missed your most vital organs. You lost a lot of blood though. Good job that ambulance driver put his foot down!"

Ray's mouth was dry and his tongue stuck to the roof of his mouth. He croaked a reply as they were leaving. "Thanks for that, doctor. Have you any idea how long I'll be in here?"

"Well, that depends on how fit you are, but you look in pretty good shape, so let's see how things go."

The doctor turned to walk away only to be stopped in his tracks by another utterance from his patient. "I need to get back to finish off the case I was working on."

"Yes, I heard about that," the doctor said. "I'm not making any promises. You have to understand you were in a pretty bad way when you came in." At the door he remembered something else. Looking back over his shoulder he said, "Oh, and you'll be interested to know there's been someone keeping a regular check on you over the last couple of days. Seemed pretty concerned about you. She's phoned constantly but wouldn't leave her name."

Ray closed his eyes as the doctor left. *She wouldn't leave her name? That's strange,* he thought, as he drifted off to sleep.

In another room further down the ward, Errol was visiting his nephew Charles. He was sitting in a chair at the side of the bed, watching the machines connected to Charles beep as they kept him alive. A group of doctors at the end of the bed were in deep conversation.

The DJ was still in a bad way, almost a week after the explosion at the club. He'd lost one of his legs caused by his podium falling on top of him. The surgeons had worked miracles and managed to save his other leg, but they were still concerned about his condition. He wasn't responding to treatment as fast as they'd like, and they were currently discussing whether to operate again. The problem was whether he was strong enough in his present state to survive more major surgery.

Errol was devastated. He blamed himself for what had happened that night at Rudi's. He'd contacted the Irishmen who were his suppliers, and demanded they sort out the problem with the Americans. Never in his wildest dreams did he think they would do something as drastic as blowing up Rudi's. But then what did he expect them to do? It was their problem as much as his. They stood to lose control of the drugs trade if they didn't do something about it. But why did it have to involve Charles? Errol had promised his late sister he'd keep an eye on her son, and for the best part he'd kept his promise, but now sitting there looking at Charles, he didn't know what to do for the best. It was all down to the doctors now, and he prayed they would succeed. Maybe he should put his faith in God and pray for Charles. It was something he'd stopped doing a long time ago. Perhaps now was a good time to start again.

While he was deep in thought, the doctors had left the room and Errol was once more alone with his nephew. He leaned over and held his hand. "This is not the end," he said quietly. "The Lord will be your salvation."

Errol stood, and gripping his cane walked off the ward.

Janine Fortuna had called the hospital again to enquire about DCI Ray Law. She'd seen the newsflash about the shooting of a police officer at the Simla Tandoori restaurant and had known instinctively it was Ray. Initial reports had been sketchy, but then it had been confirmed that DCI Ray Law had been injured in the process of arresting an Irishman, Frank Kelly, the man wanted for questioning in connection with the bombing of Rudi's nightclub. At first his condition was reported as being critical, but it had improved over the last twenty-four hours and he had been taken off the danger list. Now, according to the latest reports, he was stable.

Janine had been surprised at how concerned she'd found herself, and she certainly wasn't going to let Gerry see her so upset, but deep down she knew why she felt this way. She remembered the first time Ray had walked into The Hideout with his boss George Williams, to meet Gerry about the trouble with Jimmy Walsh. He was a great-looking guy, immaculately dressed, and he hadn't been able to take his eyes off Janine. She was loath to admit it, but the feeling had been mutual. Then there had been the couple of times when Ray came to the apartment. It would have been easier for her to go to the police headquarters, but he had insisted on coming round, even though he knew Gerry wouldn't be happy. There was definitely something about DCI Ray Law that she found completely intriguing.

Her flings with Pete Peterson, and to a lesser degree Richard Kennedy, had been fun – but Ray was different. Maybe it was because for once, she couldn't get what she wanted, even though she felt certain there was a spark between them. In the back of her mind, she questioned herself. Why should she jeopardise her marriage to Gerry? True, Gerry would give her whatever she wanted; he'd recently made her a very rich woman on paper, by appointing her a director of FAM, but was that enough? He constantly frustrated her with his single-minded approach to running the business. Even though she was now a shareholder, it was always Gerry who made the final decisions. Indeed, she'd recently started to have suspicions he was formulating plans for a new music club, even though the wreckage of Rudi's was still smouldering. Sure, it was the sign of a successful businessman that he didn't let a tragedy like Rudi's affect him, but she was tiring at the lack of attention he paid to her when he became engrossed in his latest project which was why she had started allowing herself to be side-tracked with other interests, mainly the opposite sex. She loved the excitement of the chase, and she certainly loved the sex that came with the conquest.

And then there was something that had piqued her interest; a word on the grapevine that Ray Law was extremely well endowed. With a smile, she thought it might be worth the risk to find out if the rumour was true.

There was also the troubling situation with her father. She still hadn't been able to speak to him even though Gerry had pestered his friend, the Chief Constable. She wanted to ask him why he was still involved with something that stretched back to when she was a child, and more importantly, was he part of the reason Gerry's club - and her's come to think of it! - had been targeted? Since the original report in the press, there had been a sudden clampdown on details connected with the bombing, and Janine had been unable to find out anything further regarding her father. The only piece of interesting news, was that the man suspected of making the bomb, Frank Kelly, was in police custody. She'd called Jackie, who was presently looking after their mother, to see if she knew anything, but she was in the dark just like Janine.

Their mother had always been a quiet woman and was overshadowed by their father, who could be a domineering character at times. Janine couldn't remember too much of her early childhood in the green countryside of Southern Ireland, only that she and her sister never wanted for anything. It had been a shock when one day they were suddenly uprooted and moved to Birmingham. It was so sudden she hadn't had time to say goodbye to her friends, and she often thought she'd like to go back and find them again.

Now Janine was sitting with her mother in her sister's front room, with a cup of tea and a slice of cake; traditional Irish hospitality which she missed so much. Jackie had given her two children something to do to keep them busy while the three adults talked.

"I can vaguely remember being taken out for a walk while dad and his friends were talking together in the house," Janine said.

"It wasn't something we mentioned back then," her mother spoke quietly. She pulled her cardigan tightly around her. "Your father had his group of friends, who regularly got together to discuss what was happening with the government and how it affected them. They were concerned about the North and what could be done, but I was never allowed to hear what they talked about; and neither were any of the other wives. Joe said it was better that way."

"So what happened, for us to leave so suddenly?" Jackie asked.

"To this day I still don't know," her mother had tears in her eyes. "Joe came home one night and said we were leaving, and the next day some of his friends came around to help us pack. The following day we were on the boat. Someone who your father knew met us when we docked in Liverpool and brought us down here to Birmingham. We stayed with him for a few weeks at first; then your dad got a job as a photographer on the local paper, and we moved to the house where we live now."

"And he never gave a reason why we left so quickly?" Janine asked.

"No, it was never mentioned. I left behind some really old friends who I never saw again."

Janine had another pertinent question. "So what's this Association thing dad's involved with, that meets at St Mary's?"

Her mother took a sip of tea and a mouthful of cake before she answered. "To be honest, I thought it was a group of boys from the old country getting together for a few beers. Your dad said he did some photography for a few of the members - birthdays and weddings; that kind of thing. He would spend ages in his darkroom at home, and I was always on at him about making sure he got paid for what he did."

The Chief Constable was in his office with the two Special Branch DCIs where they had been joined by a tall, elegantly dressed man, the Home Office Minister, William Greene. He had shaken their hands as he was introduced but then, without speaking, had placed his leather attaché case on George Williams' desk, opened the two locks with a key on a chain attached to his wrist and removed from it a file which had Top Secret written in large letters on the front.

Finally he spoke. "Gentlemen, please accept my apologies for interrupting your good work, but unfortunately something rather urgent has happened, which directly concerns you and your ongoing case. I have been instructed by the Prime Minister, to meet with you today and explain the situation."

George Williams was the first to speak. "You do realise, our main suspect in the nightclub bombing has just admitted his guilt. The whole team involved in the supply and distribution of drugs in Birmingham, are currently under arrest. I fail to see what can be more important than that."

"Ah yes," the minister replied. "Most commendable. And we at the Home Office want to be the first to congratulate you and your team, Chief Constable."

"So why do I get the feeling you're about to piss on our bonfire?" George asked.

"Hmm, an interesting metaphor, Chief Constable, and unfortunately correct in a way. You may or may not know, that secret negotiations have been taking place over the last few weeks between our government, led by the prime minister, and representatives of the Southern Irish government. Late last night an agreement was made, which will guarantee the disarmament of the Irish Republican Army, ending all hostilities with immediate effect. Sadly, one of the conditions of this agreement is the release of all Irish prisoners currently serving time or about to be convicted."

"What?" Jack Morton couldn't contain his anger. "You're saying that some bunch of pricks, who have no concept of the real world and who make decisions on our behalf, are considering allowing some of the most evil bastards to walk free?"

William Greene was remarkably calm. "They're not considering anything. They have made the decision and the agreement is signed."

Jack Morton was livid. "I don't fucking believe this. You mean to say we've just got that shit to admit he killed and maimed all those innocent people in cold blood, and now you want to let him walk free?"

"Well it's not quite like that," the minister said, trying to calm Jack down. "It's not a case of letting him walk free, as you say. He'll be deported back to Southern Ireland."

"What about the other three? What happens to them?" Robbie Simpson asked.

"Well that's a bit more tricky," Greene replied. "Because they've got British citizenship they can't be deported as such, so they will be released on conditional bail. Officially they will be free, but they will be taken back to Ireland where they will be given new identities and will have to report to the police on a regular basis. Most importantly, they will never be allowed to contact their relatives again."

George Williams had been quietly listening to everything the minister had to say. "This isn't going to sit well with my DCI who is currently in hospital. He nearly died after being shot by the suspect, Frank Kelly."

"Or the relatives of the ten victims who died!" added Robbie Simpson.

"Yes, we know all about DCI Law" replied Greene. "In fact the PM is considering a recommendation for the Queen's Gallantry Medal, in recognition of his bravery."

"Or maybe using it as a cover-up for what's really going on!" Jack Morton said as he stood up and walked out of the room, slamming the door.

William Greene looked anxiously at George Williams, but the latter raised his hands. "Don't worry about Jack. He's a good copper and a professional. So what happens next?" He was trying to ease the tension in the room.

William Greene opened the file he'd removed from his case.

"The official statement will say that Frank Kelly will be moved from here to a secure unit, and then transferred to a prison in Dublin where he'll be tried by an Irish court of law. The others will be released without charge due to lack of evidence. Both you and I know that not to be the case, but unfortunately that is the way it has to be."

"The papers are going to have a field day with this," said George.

"Hopefully, as DCI Morton pointed out, the bravery award to DCI Law will keep them occupied for the moment. Anyway gentlemen, if there are no more questions I have to be getting back."

William Greene fastened his attaché case, and after shaking hands with all involved again, he left.

The three officers sat quietly, hardly able to take in what had just happened.

CHAPTER TWENTY

JANINE HAD been right about Gerry's plans for a new music club. Instead of letting what happened to Rudi's dent his ambition, he'd started work on a new project, which was going to be bigger and better than anything he'd done before.

The city was alive with music; bars and pubs were all clamouring to put on music in any space they could create, but Gerry wanted to top the lot. He had the first-hand experience of working at The Cave, he knew all about the Coliseum Ballroom run by Harry Castle, and his own venue The Hideout, but the time was right for something special. The city deserved it, and Gerry was going to build it. It was a massive undertaking that was going to cost a lot of money, but Gerry had never resisted a challenge before, and he wasn't about to start now.

As if that wasn't enough, Pete Peterson and The Flames were about to go out on the biggest tour of their career so far, and Gerry was masterminding it through FAM. But there was a problem: Pete was fast becoming a liability. His drug taking was getting out of control, and although Gerry had made the shrewd move of employing Bobby McGregor as tour manager, he hoped his friend would be strong enough to cope with Pete and his inevitable tantrums. Only time would tell.

Pete Peterson and The Flames were rehearsing downstairs in The Hideout. There was only a month until the start of the UK and European tour, and things were getting a little strained.

Pete had insisted on bringing a keyboard player called Dave Sanchez into the band, which meant that a lot of the original musical arrangements had to be changed to accommodate the extra instrument. Although he was a good player, Dave was taking time to fit in, and the bass player Tony Waters was losing patience. Pete had suggested they have a coffee break and had called Tony over. "What's the problem, man? You need to chill out. It's not helping Dave having you on his back all the time. I know it's taking longer, but when it does come together it sounds great."

Tony was impatient, as usual. "Yeah, well I'm used to coming in ready to play, but it seems like he's having to learn the song every time, and it's taking ages. When it was just the four of us we'd have had this well sorted by now."

"Look, I'm trying to take us to the next level, and it's gonna be tough, but I know it'll be worth it. I used keyboards on the album, and to make it sound the same on stage, we need Dave there."

"You might want to tell him to stop playing with his left hand so much then, it's clashing with my bass parts."

"Why don't you tell him yourself?" Pete replied. "Maybe you'll get to know him better and spend less time whingeing!"

Pete wandered off to the toilet. Once inside, he took out the silver foil wrap from his jacket pocket, tapping some of the white powder on the top of the toilet cistern. Rolling up a ten-pound note, he snorted the powder up his nostril, rubbing the remains onto his gum. The euphoric feeling quickly spread through his body, and he bounced back into the room, ready to play again.

Bobby McGregor had been sitting at the back, quietly watching what was going on. He wondered what had happened to Pete in the toilet to cause such a noticeable transformation. He'd need to keep an eye on him over the coming weeks, he thought, especially as he would be working closely with him on the tour. He also noticed how Pete appeared to have become the absolute band leader, dictating how everything should be done. He remembered Gerry saying that it was a cooperative in terms of money, and that they were on equal shares, but Pete certainly seemed to be in charge. Bobby wondered how Pete would take to being told what he could and couldn't have. Something else he'd need to watch.

The following day, Janine went to The Hideout to listen to Pete and The Flames. She'd worn a pair of tight hipster jeans and a brown suede jacket with tassels across the back and down the sleeves. In her high-heeled, leather cowgirl boots she felt she had the perfect image for management of a rock 'n' roll band. The Flames were in full flow as she walked into the club. They sounded fantastic. As the guys noticed her, the song became disjointed, until Pete, who had his back to her, turned round to see what the distraction was.

"Wow! Don't you look the rock chick, Janine?" Pete looked her up and down appreciatively. "Guys let's take a break. That was sounding great."

"Sorry to interrupt you. It was really sounding amazing," said Janine.

Pete took his guitar off and leapt from the stage to give her a hug. "Back in a sec," he said, and disappeared into the gents' toilet.

Janine watched him go, then turned back to the others in the band. "How's it all going guys? Any problems? I got to say the new songs are sounding so cool." The other musicians nodded and smiled at her.

Pete reappeared and came bounding over – almost too energetically, like someone had wound him up like a spring and let him go. "What d'ya say, guys? How about we run the set again from the top?" He was speaking so fast his words were almost running into one another.

Janine noticed the looks between the others and took hold of Pete's arm. "Before you do that, can we have a quick chat up in the office? There's a few things we need to sort out for Bobby. Guys you can go grab a coffee. We'll see you back here in half an hour, yeah?"

The band took off their instruments and left the club, while Janine guided Pete up the stairs to the offices and past Judy Watson, the secretary.

Janine slammed the door behind them and faced up to Pete, her green eyes blazing. "What the fuck do you think you're doing?" she yelled at him, poking her finger in his chest. "How much of that stuff are you planning on shoving up your nose? Do you think you're so clever that no one's noticed?"

Pete looked shocked by her rant. "Hey be cool. It's not a problem. I know what I'm doing. You don't have to worry."

She looked at him and shook her head. "I'll tell you now, if you fuck this tour up you won't only have Gerry to deal with. If you think he can be a bastard, don't even think about screwing with me. I'm part of this company now and I expect the same level of professionalism from everyone; from Judy right up to you. Do I make myself clear?"

Judy had in fact discreetly disappeared down the stairs. She didn't want to be party to whatever was happening between Pete and Janine.

Pete had a wry smile on his face. "I love you when you're angry. I often think about us screwing, babe."

Janine slapped him hard across the face.

"That was then. Now it's business, and just you remember that."

169

It was mere luck that as Pete reached out to touch Janine, she slapped his hand away a fraction of a second before Gerry pulled open the door.

"Hey guys, Bobby and I have just done a mega deal on the transport for the tour. Got a really cool minibus Pete, for you and the band; all mod cons." Only then did he notice the tension in the air. "How's it going down there?"

"Uh. Great man, yeah great." Pete made his way past Janine to the door without looking at her. "The guys are really getting it together. I'd better get back down so we can have another run through."

Gerry looked at Janine as Pete went down the stairs. "He OK? Not a problem is there?"

Janine gave Bobby a knowing look, then smiled at Gerry. "No problem Ger. No problem at all."

DCI Ray Law was going stir crazy in his hospital bed. He was making good progress according to the doctor, mainly because he was so fit. All the drips and machines had gone and he'd been moved out of intensive care to a private ward. He was desperate to get back to work, but the doctor was refusing to be rushed.

"Look, I know how important your job is, but until I'm satisfied you're completely recovered, you're staying right here where we can keep an eye on you." He wrote a note on the clipboard hanging on the end of Ray's bed just as the door opened and George Williams walked in with Matt Burgess. "Looks like you have a couple of important visitors, so I'll be back later. Don't go getting him excited gentlemen," he said as he left the room.

"Brought you some fruit," said Matt putting a large bag of apples, pears, grapes and oranges on Ray's bedside table.

Ray gave them a warm smile as they both sat down. "Sir, Matt, thanks for coming, I'm going mad in here. What's the latest? It all seems to have gone quiet on the news."

"It's good to see you looking better, Ray," George Williams said, putting a grape in his own mouth. "We've had a couple of major problems while you've been away, and I thought I'd better come down to explain the situation before you heard it from someone else."

Ray noticed Matt shift uneasily in his chair. "So tell me the news," he said sitting up.

"We had a visit from a Home Office minister last week whilst we were interrogating Frank Kelly. In fact, Jack Morton and Robbie Simpson did a great job on him, and he'd confessed to everything, including giving us the three from the Irish Club as well."

"So why don't I get the impression that's good news?" Ray looked confused.

"Well that's where things get complicated," George continued, eating another grape. "As I said, the Home Office minister, William Greene arrived with a directive from the Prime Minister's office to shut down all cases concerning Irish criminals. Including current ones. Apparently, the PM has done a deal with the Irish government guaranteeing the disarmament of the Republican Army, in exchange for the release of Irish prisoners held over here."

"Wait a minute! Are you saying that those bastards are going to walk free?" Ray started to get out of bed.

"Now calm down, Ray, and listen to what I'm telling you," George managed to stop him and he sat back down. "It's not quite that. Frank Kelly will be deported back to Southern Ireland where he'll stand trial for murder. The three remaining members of the Association – the name they called themselves at the Irish Club – will be released without charge due to lack of evidence; although they will be returned to Ireland with new identities and have to report to the police over there. Oh, and one other thing: you're to be awarded the Queen's Gallantry Medal."

Ray looked shocked. "So I get a medal and a pat on the head? What about the ones who died and their loved ones – what do they get? Where's the justice? How can that be right?"

"Right now it's all there is," said George. "I know it's not what you want to hear, but I wanted to be the one to tell you. I'm sorry Ray, you must understand my hands are tied."

George stood up and made to leave the room.

"Apologies for my outburst, sir," said Ray. "And thanks for letting me know. That's a lot to think about – especially the medal."

George Williams left the room, but Matt Burgess hung back. He'd been quiet so far, but now with the Chief Constable out of the room, he spoke.

"Listen Ray, there's something that I need to talk to you about, and I think it's important. When Jack Morton and Robbie Simpson were questioning Frank Kelly, he said something that they didn't pick up on. I mentioned it to George Williams but before I had time to do anything about it, he got this phone call and everything was stopped."

"What are you talking about?"

"Well Frank Kelly was pretty riled and started slagging off the others involved: the cleaner, Molly Gallagher, who planted the bomb, and the Association lot from the Irish Club. Then he said, 'Them Yanks needed teaching a lesson, and that gobshite of a club manager'."

"Alex Mitchell, the club manager? Why would Kelly mention him unless he was involved somehow?"

"Exactly!" said Matt. "Trouble was, I didn't get chance to ask Jack Morton to press him more."

"Where is Alex Mitchell now?" said Ray. "What's he up to? I mean, he doesn't have a club to manage does he? We should make some enquiries."

"Wow; none of this 'we', mate." Matt stood up to leave. "You're still confined to bed remember. Don't worry; I'll keep you in the loop. I'll get Tony Carter and Jackie Rose on it."

Alex Mitchell had received many compliments about the piano piece he'd played at the funeral of his bassist Wynton. It hadn't really sunk in until now that he no longer had a band. He'd never played solo before, but with so many people telling him how much they enjoyed his playing that day, he'd decided that maybe he should learn some tunes. In actual fact he needed to start earning some money, since Rudi's no longer existed, so neither did his job…and more importantly, he'd lost his illicit extra income.

Gerry Fortuna had called him to set up a meeting to discuss his situation, but in the meantime Alex had contacted a small Italian restaurant in the city centre. The Santa Maria was owned by an old friend, who had readily agreed to let Alex play there at weekends. He'd also already received bookings from another bar in the Arts Quarter to play two nights a week, and suddenly found himself in demand.

On Friday night, as he was starting his second session at the Santa Maria, he noticed a couple being shown to a table near the small stage where he played. He thought he recognised them from somewhere, but couldn't place them. It was only as he was halfway through his set, that he remembered where he'd seen them before. They were two of the undercover cops at Rudi's on Christmas Eve. Strange that here they were again, but not in uniform. Maybe they were a couple having a meal on their night off. Or maybe they were keeping him under observation. His imagination started to run riot and he noticed he'd stopped playing. He'd need to be careful; little slips like that would draw attention to him. It was crazy to be thinking like that. What could they possibly have on him? His main threat, Thomas, was dead. The two Americans had gone home, and Gerry had never given him the impression he suspected him in any way. In fact he had a meeting with him tomorrow to talk about his future. He told himself he should calm down and concentrate on his playing. But at the back of his mind, he remembered the visit from DCI Law and his partner while he was in hospital.

PC Tony Carter and WPC Jackie Rose were in fact seeing each other outside of work, and had jumped at the chance of some paid overtime when Matt Burgess had mentioned the surveillance operation. The Santa Maria was one of their favourite restaurants, so it was a bonus that they could have a meal there on duty whilst observing Alex Mitchell. They'd been given explicit orders not to spend too much money as the budget was tight, but Tony had decided it was too good an opportunity to miss, and had ordered his favourite Fegato alla Veneziana - Venetian liver and onions - while Jackie was having Bistecca Pizzaiola – a braised steak covered in tomato sauce. They'd forgone starters in favour of a nice bottle of Chianti. It certainly was a rare treat, topped off by some great music.

By the time Alex had finished his third set, Tony and Jackie had polished off a second bottle of Chianti and two Irish coffees and were a little worse for wear. Slipping quietly out of the back door, Alex was in his car on the way home before either of them noticed he'd gone. Thankfully, nothing had happened during the evening, so there wasn't anything important to report back to Matt Burgess in the morning, although Jackie had wondered if Alex had recognised them at one point, and if so, it had certainly had an effect on his playing. Strange for such a competent musician, she thought. Maybe it was worth keeping up the pressure.

The police had issued a statement explaining that due to insufficient evidence, the three suspects who had been arrested in connection with the bombing of Rudi's club, were being released without charge. Patrick Bloom, Philip Sutton and Julia Davies had all been notified, and were at the police headquarters where Joe Burke, Michael Brennan and Sean Whelan were ready to leave. Patrick Bloom had been mystified by the circumstances of their release, and the paperwork that had been presented for each of them to sign.

He was taken up to the Chief Constable's office where George Williams was waiting for him.

"So what you're saying, in effect, is that my client and his two friends are being released without charge, but with a proviso that they are returned to Ireland with new identities and report to the police on a monthly basis. Is that correct?" Patrick Bloom held the official document in his hand.

"That's correct, Mr. Bloom, yes," George Williams replied. "Look let's get one thing straight shall we? You know, and I know, that they're guilty. Frank Kelly did them no favours by telling us everything. But thanks to the intervention of Her Majesty's government they are free to go, providing they adhere to the conditions laid down in that document you're holding."

Patrick Bloom was about to say something, but George cut him off.

"It is non-negotiable, Mr. Bloom. I suggest you go downstairs and consult with your colleagues. I expect three signed copies on my desk in, let's say, ten minutes."

Ten minutes later George Williams had the three documents in front of him; all signed and witnessed. Shaking his head, he put them into the official pouch addressed to the Home Office, which would be delivered to William Greene by the waiting dispatch rider.

There was one outstanding problem George had to deal with; Sergeant Seamus Byrne. Whilst Seamus had not been directly involved, the fact that he'd passed on highly sensitive information was a serious disciplinary matter, and George would have to decide the severity of the punishment. Taking into consideration the fact that Byrne had admitted his misdemeanour and provided information, George was inclined to be lenient, and decided that demotion to the rank of constable would be sufficient, considering the others had walked free. However, it would be kept quiet so as not to inflame the escalating public interest in the case.

George had already received a petition from the families of the victims demanding action, and he was consulting with the police lawyers as to what his next steps should be. He had a feeling that whatever was said, he had not heard the last of this situation.

Janine's mother had received a phone call from her husband to say he had been released from custody and was on his way home, so Jackie had called straight away, and they were all in Alderton waiting for Joe. He arrived home in the back of a police car, looking tired and slightly worse for wear. He slumped in his armchair in the lounge. Janine's mother fussed around making cups of tea for everyone and finally they all sat down.

Janine was the first to break the silence. "Dad, we've all been so worried. What's going on? Why were you arrested?"

Joe took a sip of his tea and put the china cup and saucer down on the coffee table. "I think the less you all know about what's been going on, the better," he said rubbing the back of his neck. "All I will say, is that I'm not allowed to discuss the events of the last few days with anyone, and that includes you all. I've had to sign a document regarding the Official Secrets Act and should I break the terms I'll be in serious trouble."

His wife came over and held his hand. "Well you're back safe and sound, and that's all there is too it!" she said, smiling at the others.

"Surely that can't be it though," said Janine. "What about all the families of the people who died? Don't they get any sort of explanation? Gerry's club was destroyed. What about him? There's something very strange about this."

"I'm sorry, Janine, as I said I'm not allowed to make any comments, not even to you. And now I'm really tired and I'm going for a lie down." Joe stood up, kissed his wife and went upstairs leaving them in the lounge, none the wiser.

CHAPTER TWENTY-ONE

RAY LAW had been released from hospital and was sitting in his apartment just outside the centre of Barlowe. He was glad to be home, but frustrated that he hadn't been allowed to return to work. The doctor had been pleased with the speed of his recovery but warned him not to push himself too much. "I don't want to see you back in here again, just because you won't do as you're told," he said, as Ray left in the company of Matt Burgess.

Fortunately, Matt lived just down the road in Stratton with his young wife and child and had volunteered to pick him up.

"Listen, there's a new pub opening on Saturday night," Matt said. "Why don't we go? There's a band on; it'll be a great night. Her indoors has given me a pass for the night. We can get a few beers and have a laugh."

Ray wasn't sure, but under pressure from Matt finally agreed it was a good idea.

"Great pick you up at eight o'clock," said Matt as he left.

On Saturday night, Ray and Matt had just arrived at The King's Head – a huge pub set back from the road on the way to Stratton. The car park was packed, and as they made their way through the doors, the sound of the band washed over them. It was a local rock band playing something from the Top Ten, not usually Ray's cup of tea, but they were very good. They pushed their way up to the bar, and Matt managed to shout over the noise of the music to order a couple of pints. As they turned round to find a seat, Ray bumped into a woman with a brown ponytail, wearing a short, brown leather jacket and tight jeans. He narrowly avoided spilling his pint and turned back to apologise.

"Well, hello DCI Law fancy meeting you here," said the woman.

Ray was momentarily at a loss, until suddenly he placed her. It was Julia Davies, the solicitor who had represented Michael Brennan.

"Ms. Davies," he said with a smile. "I didn't recognise you without the glasses. What brings you to Stratton on a Saturday night? I had you down as a city centre kind of lady."

"I've just bought a house down the road and was invited out by some of my neighbours. To be honest, they're lovely people but really boring," she said pulling a face. "Are you here with someone?"

Ray looked around. "Well I was with my friend Matt, a DS from work, but he seems to have disappeared with some friends over by the band."

"Come on then, follow me." Linking his arm, Julia dragged him off to the back of the room, where a booth had just become vacant. "Quick in here," she said, elbowing her way through the crowd. "That's better!" Plonking her glass of wine down she slid into the seat.

Ray sat down opposite her, realizing for the first time what a good-looking woman she was. Without her glasses, her hazel eyes were entrancing. He took a guess that she was mid-thirties; and there it was again – the perfume he remembered from the interrogation room. Definitely intoxicating.

"I was very upset when I heard what had happened to you," she said, lighting a cigarette. "Sorry, would you like one?" She offered the pack to Ray.

"No thanks, I don't smoke."

"Ah sorry, it's a bad habit of mine I know. I keep trying to quit." She stubbed it out in the ashtray.

"You didn't have to do that because of me," Ray said.

She waved her hand dismissively at him. "Anyway as I said, I was really worried when it was on the news about you. How are you now? You look like you've lost a bit of weight." A coy smile. "Suits you."

"I'm fine, thanks. In fact I'm desperate to get back to work, but the doctor says I just have to take it easy for a while." Ray picked up her glass. "Can I get you another drink?"

"Actually, I was thinking you might like to come back to my place? I've got a lovely bottle of champagne on ice and to be honest, this place is giving me a headache." She leaned over and gave him a kiss. "Nobody will notice if we slip out the back. My car's in the car park."

Ray was surprised by how forward she was. He knew he'd been told to take things easy, but he wasn't going to pass up an opportunity like this. Matt wouldn't mind. He'd disappeared off with some of his friends.

"Let's go," he said.

They left through the exit at the back, and grabbing hold of his hand

Julia led him over to a red Porsche 911. They climbed in and as Ray sat down she leaned over and grabbed his jacket collar, pulling him to her and kissing him hard.

"Mmm, I think we're going to have some fun," she said, as she started the engine and accelerated out of the car park in a shower of gravel.

Ray liked to drive fast, but he was quite unprepared for the speed Julia drove at on the way back to her place. Fortunately, it was only about a mile down the road – any further and Ray might have got really worried.

Julia swung the 911 into her drive and pulled on the handbrake. Jumping out she ran across and opened the front door. It was getting dark and Ray couldn't really get a good look at the house, but from what he could see it was large and newly built.

"Come on in," Julia called, as she headed for the stairs. "The champagne's in the chiller in the kitchen. Grab a couple of glasses. I won't be a minute. Go on through to the lounge and make yourself at home."

Ray closed the front door behind him and walked down the cream carpeted hall into the kitchen. Bright white units surrounded him and a slate-grey work surface stretched around three sides. He noticed there were no kitchen gadgets anywhere, apart from a large champagne chiller, which stood at the side of a huge fridge-freezer.

He found a couple of cut-glass flutes in one of the units, and opening the chiller door he chose a bottle of vintage Veuve Clicquot which he took through into the lounge.

The room was furnished with two huge three-seater sofas and had the same cream carpet as the hall. *My whole flat would probably fit in here – there must be some money in being a solicitor*, he thought to himself.

He turned round as Julia wafted into the room and nearly dropped the bottle. She was standing in front of him wearing a red kimono, which hung open over a white silk basque, with matching stockings and suspenders, and crimson stilettos. She had shaken her hair out and it looked incredible, hanging down to her shoulders in waves. It was the most seductive sight he'd ever seen.

Julia walked over to kiss him and reached down to stroke the rapidly growing bulge in his trousers. He managed to put the glasses down before she pushed him back on the sofa, and undid his belt, slowly pulling down the zip to release him.

"You know there's a rumour going round chambers that you're rather well endowed!" she said, bending down to take him in her mouth. Ray leaned back on the cushion with a groan. Julia sat up, smiling. "I'm beginning to think it's true."

Ray wanted to slow the proceedings down a little. "Hang on a minute. Don't you think there might be a conflict of interest, considering what we do and how we're both involved in the recent events?"

She carried on stroking him while she thought. "Well as far as I can see, I'm interested in fucking you, and I think you're interested in fucking me so, no M'lud, there's no conflict whatsoever!" She laughed as she lifted up her leg to climb across him, lowering herself slowly. She held him there for a second, then gradually started to ride him faster and faster, teasing him by stopping as he tried to thrust up into her. "Patience!" She slapped his chest. "Let me." She started riding him again. Ray was groaning in ecstasy and finally came as she plunged down on him and held him tight.

"Oh my God," he said breathlessly. "Julia, you are incredible. But you didn't come." She climbed off him. "The night is young. Now darling, where's that champagne?"

Taking the bottle and glasses, Julia led Ray upstairs to her bedroom. It was tastefully decorated with a king-size bed dominating the room and a huge mirror on the ceiling directly above it. She kicked off her stilettos and lay back on the black satin sheets.

"Open the bottle will you, darling, I need a drink."

Ray carefully popped the cork, remembering how he'd seen Gerry Fortuna do it at Georgie's. Julia clinked his glass and took a deep draught of the sparkling liquid. "That's better, I love champagne."

"This is a fantastic place," Ray said, looking around as he sipped his Veuve Clicquot. "Must have set you back a few bob."

"Actually, it was part of my divorce settlement. My ex was a successful property developer and it was one of his new acquisitions."

"How long have you been divorced?"

"Just over a year. Rich was a real charmer, always mixing business with pleasure. Last I heard, he was screwing some club owner's wife. It was a sad way to go though. I wouldn't have wished it on anyone – being blown up like that."

Ray suddenly realised who she was talking about. "Hang on a minute, do you mean Richard Kennedy? The guy who died in the bomb at Rudi's?"

"Yes, Richard was my ex-husband. I changed back to my maiden name after we divorced."

Richard Kennedy screwing Janine? Now that's interesting, Ray thought to himself.

"Now where were we?" Julia reached over and pulled Ray to her. "My turn!"

Ray arrived home the following morning feeling like he'd run a marathon. Julia was a demanding woman who liked to dominate, both in her job and in her bed. It had been an incredible night, but nonetheless he couldn't help having reservations about seeing her again. She was, after all, representing one of the suspects in the bombing of Rudi's – and it worried him. Finding out her ex-husband was Richard Kennedy who was, according to Julia, involved with Janine Fortuna, also rang alarm bells.

But hadn't he been with a different woman at Rudi's? Ray was sure he'd met her when he'd been helping survivors out of the club. She was lucky that she'd decided to freshen up her makeup and had been in the ladies' toilet at the front of the building when the bomb went off while, sadly, Richard had been waiting for her at their table by the stage and taken the full force of the explosion.

Still, for Ray the encounter with Julie Davis had proved something vital. Apart from a few twinges he'd proved he was both fit and raring to go.

CHAPTER TWENTY-TWO

THE PALACE Theatre in Manchester was rocking. Pete Peterson and The Flames were coming to the end of their set, and the fans were on their feet, dancing in the aisles.

Janine Fortuna had caught the train up from Birmingham to watch the show; the third in their UK tour. She was standing side-stage with tour manager Bobby McGregor watching as the band came running off for their 'false tab' - the quick break at the end of the set before they return for the encore. The guys had gone into the small green room and were refreshing themselves with beers. All except Pete, who was nowhere to be seen.

Janine had noticed he'd been last off stage and hadn't followed the others, so she went to look for him. There was a room just a little bigger than a cupboard, on the other side of the stage where the crew stored their bags, and Pete was crouched with his back to her, leaning over a case. He didn't hear her approach, and Janine watched as he snorted a long line of white powder up his nose using a rolled up ten-pound note.

"What the fuck are you doing?" Janine screamed at him. "You swore you were off that stuff before the tour started. Have you been doing this every night?"

"Be cool, babe. It's all under control," he said, reaching out to take her hand.

"Fuck you, Pete." Janine slapped away his hand. "Does Bobby know about this? I'll kill him."

"Calm down, Janine," Pete said. "No, Bobby doesn't know. I'm just having a boost before the encore. Everything's going great. Just listen to the crowd. Look, I've got to go back on. Let's have a drink after the gig. We've got some shampoo especially for you."

He ran off past her and followed the others back onstage to a deafening roar.

Janine went after him and shook her head as the band launched into their latest single. What the hell was she going to do? Her first impulse was to have it out with Pete, but she risked him going off in a mood, which could affect the next gig. Alternatively, she could let Bobby deal with it, but it seemed to her that he didn't know what was going on. She would have to sit down with him later and find out.

The show finished, and after playing another encore the band made their way up to their dressing room. Suddenly, there were raised voices, and Bobby ran up the stairs, pushing the door open to the sight of Pete holding Tony Waters by his neck against the wall.

"If you don't like it then you know what you can do." Pete was shouting in his face. "All you do is fuckin' moan!"

Tony's twin brother Billy was trying to separate them as Bobby burst in.

"All right, all right, that's enough. Pete – Out! Now! Go in the room next door and calm down."

"Man, it's like this every night," Billy said to Bobby. "He's like a volcano waiting to blow. And always when he comes off. If it's not the band, it's the sound."

"OK guys, leave it to me. Grab a beer and I'll see you on the bus."

Bobby found Pete next door with Janine. Before he had chance to speak, Janine started on Pete.

"What is the matter with you? Carry on like this and you're gonna blow the tour. Then you won't just have me to deal with. So far, Gerry has left it to Bobby and me, but if he gets involved, God help you. You've got a great band – the shows are sold out. What more do you want?"

"The band is shit; the bass player never stops moaning. I hate the sound. The bus is cold."

"Seems to me like these problems only appear after the encore, which is when you mysteriously disappear into your cupboard and stick that shit up your nose," Bobby said. Pete looked questioningly at him. "And if you think I don't know what you do every night, man, then you're dumber than I thought. Gerry employed me to make sure the tour runs smoothly, and that's what I'm doing. If you need to use that shit to finish the show, that's fine by me, but as soon as it starts to cause problems then I'll put a stop to it. The choice is yours, Pete. Don't fuck me around. You won't like me if I get fucked around. Now, are we cool?"

Pete had calmed down enough to take the message on board. "Yeah, we're cool," he said.

Bobby looked at Janine and raised his eyebrows as Pete stood up and left the room. "Bobby, you're a genius," she said, giving him a hug and kissing him on the cheek.

"Come on. There's a bottle of bubbly on the tour bus for you, let's get it opened." And he took her down to where the band's transport was parked.

Bobby knew that things weren't right. Trying to keep Pete under control was taking all of his time, and it felt like he was fighting a losing battle. Thankfully, the band were experienced enough to be able to take care of themselves, but he was concerned about the European dates. Pete was increasingly unpredictable, and there was a strong possibility of him really screwing things up. There were another fifteen dates in the UK, including London and their hometown, Birmingham. Both gigs were really important – especially London - because Gerry had lined up all the music press to be there. Bobby would just have to make sure he stayed on Pete's case.

Ray Law had finally been signed fit for work by his doctor and had returned to a warm welcome. All his colleagues made an effort to come and say hello, and he felt humbled by all the attention. Matt Burgess had dropped into his office during a quiet moment – he had a sly grin on his face. They hadn't spoken since the night with Julia Davies.

"What happened to you then? One minute we're at the bar, and the next you're slipping out the back with the Sex Queen of Stratton. You want to watch her mate; she's got a bit of a reputation."

"You don't have to worry about me, that's well gone," replied Ray. "Far too domineering for my liking. Although I have to say – what a body!"

"Yeah, well it might be a good idea to keep it quiet. If it got back to the boss I don't think he'd be too impressed – conflict of interest and all that."

Ray's phone rang on his desk. "Yes sir, on my way," he said jumping up. "Got to go. George Williams."

Ray knocked on the Chief Constable's door and walked in.

"Ah Ray, welcome back." George Williams motioned towards the corner where a man in a different uniform was already sitting. "Take a seat. This is Inspector Donal McGuiness from the Irish Garda. He's here to officially escort Frank Kelly back to Dublin."

Ray shook the inspector's hand.

"Sorry it's taken so long to sort out the paperwork, but it's done now and we'll be taking him back today. A nasty piece of work without a doubt. He's showed no remorse for what he did."

"He's downstairs in the cells," said George. "He'll be taken under armed guard to Liverpool, and then by ferry across to Dublin where he's due in court next week."

"I'd like to see him before he goes," Ray said thoughtfully.

"Come with me then," said Donal. "I'm on my way now to make the final preparations."

They went downstairs to the holding cells, where Frank Kelly was waiting to leave. One of the armed guards unlocked the cell door and led the way in followed by Donal. The other guard and Ray took up the rear.

The first guard told Frank to hold out his hands while he put on the handcuffs. After that it all kicked off in an instant. Frank standing with his hands out in front of him seemed to stumble, bumping into the guard, and whipping the revolver from his holster.

He held the gun to the guard's head. "Back off or I'll blow his feckin' brains out."

Donal held both hands out wide and stood his ground. "Don't be stupid Frank. There's nowhere you can go. Just give me the gun."

"No feckin' chance," Frank said. "Well, well! Look who's here." He had spotted Ray at the back of the cell. "Thought I'd done you already," he sneered.

"Frank, give it up. You've no chance."

"That's where you're wrong copper. I'm gettin' out of here, and you're gonna help me. We're gonna walk slowly through that exit to the car park. Don't try anything funny. I will shoot him." Frank jerked the guard. "Don't forget, I've done it before." He smiled at Ray.

They slowly made their way through the exit next to the cells, to the underground car park.

"You got a car?" Frank looked at Ray. He nodded. "Get it and don't try anything smart."

Ray walked over to his car. Unlocking the door, he climbed in and started the engine, fastening his three-point racing harness as he did so.

He drove over to where Frank was holding the guard at gunpoint.

"Open the door slowly," Frank shouted as Ray pulled up next to him. He slickly backed into the front seat, pushing the guard away and firing at him from point-blank range. As the guard's body hit the ground, Frank swivelled to point the gun at Ray. "Now you and I are going for a ride," he said, pulling the door closed. "Drive!"

Ray spun the wheels and raced out of the car park. Frank was still pointing the gun at Ray as they roared down the street. Ray was concentrating on driving, but at the same time thinking about his options as they approached some roadworks that had been there awhile. There was a large concrete barrier in the road to stop people driving into a hole, and Ray noticed that in all the confusion Frank hadn't used his seat belt. It was a risk – but he knew he had to do something drastic. He turned to Frank. "Where to then?" accelerating towards the block.

"Just keep driving, I'll let you know."

He never noticed Ray glance towards the object they were approaching at speed and they smashed head-on into it.

Ray had braced himself in the harness holding him securely in his seat, ready for the g-force of impact, but Frank flew straight through the windscreen, head-first into the block.

Ray slumped in his seat as the sound of sirens filled the air. He couldn't believe he'd wrecked his beloved Escort, but in choosing to do so he knew he'd almost certainly saved his own life while ridding the world of a heartless killer.

He passed out as they lifted him into the ambulance.

Ray had woken up unsure of where he was until déjà vu struck and he realised he was in a hospital bed with the same doctor as before shaking his head as he approached.

The man picked up the clipboard from the end of the bed. "Only three broken ribs. You are indeed a very lucky man DCI Law. How fast were you going?" He looked at Ray over his glasses.

"About forty I think. It was my three-point racing harness that took the full force. If I'd been wearing an ordinary one, things might have been different."

"Yes. Well let's not make a habit of meeting like this. Oh, and you have a visitor. She's been waiting quite a while."

When she was allowed in, Janine Fortuna came at Ray's bed in a rush carrying a huge bunch of flowers and a basket of fruit. "You have to stop scaring me like this," she said. "I'll have to ask a nurse for a vase. I wasn't sure what to get you." She put the fruit down on the table at the end of the bed. "How are you feeling?"

Ray was taken by surprise. Janine Fortuna, visiting him in hospital! *I wonder if Gerry knows,* he thought.

"Gerry sends his best," she said as if reading his mind. "He was rather concerned. But what you did was incredible."

"Thanks. It's nice of you to come. But I thought you were on tour with The Flames and Pete Peterson."

"No, God forbid. I only went up for one night to see if the show was running OK. I couldn't stand to be doing that night in, night out. And then I heard about the accident on the news and came straight over here."

"And Gerry really doesn't mind?" he asked, wincing as he sat up.

Janine came over and plumped his pillows. "Gerry's involved in his new project at the moment. To be honest, I don't think he'd notice if I was there or not."

Ray took a moment to look her up and down. She was wearing a tight-fitting pair of black leather trousers and a white blouse embroidered with multi-coloured birds, and her hair was pulled back behind her ears with a velvet bow.

"So tell me, was it you who kept calling the last time I was in here?"

"Well that would be telling," she said with a little smile. "Would you mind if it was?"

"Truthful? I was kind of hoping it was," Ray said, wondering if he was in danger of getting himself into more trouble than even he could handle.

She leaned over and kissed him gently on the mouth. "Well, you'd better start getting better then," she said as she left the room, passing a nurse on her way out.

"Time to take your temperature and blood pressure, Mr. Law," the nurse said.

Ray thought both might just be through the roof, as the nurse stuck a thermometer in his mouth.

Gerry had called Alex Mitchell, inviting him to the office for a meeting. It had been a while since the night of the explosion at Rudi's, and he felt bad that they hadn't spoken since. The buzzer went downstairs, and he heard Judy open the door. Moments later Alex walked into his office. He looked well and was dressed smartly in a suit and tie.

"Good to see you again, Mr. Fortuna," he said, shaking Gerry's hand.

"Sit down Alex." Gerry pointed to the chair opposite his desk. "How are you? It's been a while since we spoke."

"I'm fine, thanks."

Alex seemed a little nervous, Gerry noticed.

"I'm playing again; on my own now. I have a couple of regular gigs in town. Restaurants mainly. It pays the rent, but I miss the trio." Alex momentarily felt a lump in his throat. "I miss the guys."

"Yes, that whole thing was a terrible mess. Look, there's something I'm working on that might interest you," Gerry said, trying to change the subject. "I'm looking to build a new club in the city, and I'm currently on the look out for the right premises. Let me tell you Alex, between you and me, this is going to be the biggest and best venue ever. It'll make The Cave and The Coliseum look like 'Noddy goes to Toyland'."

"Sounds great. Have you got anywhere in mind?" He'd used a bit of pathos to steer Gerry away from talking about Rudi's – as a tactic it never failed.

"A friend of mine in the property business has suggested I go and look at a place." Gerry sounded excited. "It's a rundown factory that used to manufacture chains. Not the little ones you get on a bike, but the huge ones that hold the anchors on ships. The owner is retiring and wants to sell up, and I think it might be just what I'm looking for. I'm going to see it next week – maybe you should come along, see what you think. An extra pair of eyes is always useful."

Alex was thinking that there might be an opportunity he could exploit once more.

I'll be there," he said.

CHAPTER TWENTY-THREE

IT WAS the last night of The Flames' UK tour and they were at London's Dominion Theatre. The show was sold out and the crowd was buzzing. Janine had made the trip down and was in the green room talking with the band.

Pete came stumbling into the room obviously under the influence of something, so Janine went looking for Bobby whose job it was to keep Pete under control and out of trouble. Bobby burst through the stage door as she reached the bottom of the stairs. "Where the hell have you been?" she yelled at him. "Have you seen the state of Pete? He's completely out of it. You were supposed to be looking after him!"

"I was, until he gave me the slip in a bar in Soho." Bobby explained, out of breath. "Everything was fine until he met up with a couple of his mates and they did a runner. Left me to pay the bill and disappeared. Thirty bloody quid it cost me!"

"Fuck the money! What are we gonna do?" Janine was fuming. "If he screws this show up Gerry'll go mad. He's got every music paper here to review it."

"Don't worry, leave it to me, I know how to handle Pete," Bobby said, running up the stairs two at a time with Janine trailing behind him.

Pete was in the dressing room slowly getting ready when Bobby walked in and sat down opposite him.

"Good trick, Pete," he said. "You and your pals got one over on me there. Cost me thirty quid. Look at the state of you. Listen, I don't give a shit what you do to yourself." Bobby was talking right in Pete's face. "Do you hear what I'm saying? I don't care if you want to fuck yourself up, but I do care about those fans out there who've spent their hard-earned money to come and see you. They're the ones who go out and buy your records. So think about it. I'm not bothered – but they deserve better. Oh, and by the way, Anders Neckermann and his cronies are sitting on the balcony; they're dying to see the great Pete Peterson fuck up. So it's up to you."

Pete looked up with tears in his eyes. "Give me five minutes. I'll give you one of the best shows you've ever seen."

Bobby and Janine left him to get ready. "Jesus, Bobby, that was some heavy stuff you said in there," Janine exclaimed. "Is Anders Neckermann really here?"

"I've no idea. But one thing I do know, is we have to pull the European dates and get Pete some kind of help, before either I kill him or he kills himself!"

They were making their way to the side of the stage, when the intro to The Flames first number rang out through the sound system accompanied by a cacophony of screams. Right on cue, Pete strutted up to the microphone looking every inch the rock star. He powered into the opening chords on his guitar, and proceeded - just as he had promised Bobby - to give one of the most amazing performances of his career. Every song was a masterpiece of rock theatre, as he controlled the audience – sometimes with a gesture of his arm, and others with a shimmy of his hips. They loved every second of it; his army of young female admirers hanging on his every move.

Two encores later, the band made their way back to the dressing room, laughing and hugging each other. Janine and Bobby were following them along the corridor when there was a shout. It was Jess Peters in the doorway calling for help.

Bobby carved a path through the crowded corridor only to find that Pete had collapsed on the floor. He looked in a bad way, and Bobby grabbed the nearest telephone on the wall and immediately dialled 999 for an ambulance. As the others watched on, Janine knelt by Pete, feeling for his pulse which was erratic. She discreetly removed the rolled up twenty-pound note from his hand as she leaned over him, brushing the white powder from his nostril before anyone else could notice.

She looked up at Bobby. "We're gonna have to keep this quiet. Can you deal with the guys while I take care of it?"

Bobby nodded and calmly ushered the band into the next room. "C'mon guys, in here," he said. "Pete's gonna be fine."

Tony Waters turned to his brother Billy. "Fucked up if you ask me. That shit always gets you in the end. Better start looking for a new gig Bro!"

The rest of The Flames sat around in shock.

Janine had put Pete in the recovery position she'd learned on a first aid course, and was on the phone herself when Bobby came back in. She covered the mouthpiece and beckoned him over. "I've called a private clinic that Gerry took his sister to once; it's very discreet. I'll need to go with him in the ambulance, and make sure they don't take him to a hospital. The last thing we need is for it to be all over the papers. If anyone asks, he's collapsed due to exhaustion. And don't worry; I'll deal with Gerry. Just make sure the band are taken care of, and that they keep their mouths shut, especially the bass player."

The dressing room door burst open and two ambulancemen rushed in carrying a stretcher.

There was nothing else he could do for Pete so Bobby left Janine in charge and went back to the band in the other room.

The next morning Pete's collapse made all the headlines in the daily papers:

"ROCK STAR COLLAPSES AFTER SHOW,

EXHAUSTION BLAMED!"

"FLAMES SINGER IN DRAMATIC

AFTER-SHOW COLLAPSE!"

Janine was sitting with a cup of coffee, after spending the night at the clinic with Pete. Thankfully, they'd managed to keep his whereabouts secret, and he was asleep in the private room she'd arranged. She was on the phone to Gerry.

"Everything's cool Ger. Thankfully I was there. If the press had got wind of what really caused it, God knows what would've happened." She listened to Gerry ranting on about drugs and the trouble Pete was going to cause him. "Look Ger, calm down; what's done is done. Bobby warned me yesterday there was a problem, and suggested we consider pulling the European gigs. Well, now that decision is out of our hands. But you were moaning last week that ticket sales weren't great, so maybe it's a blessing in disguise. I'm gonna jump on a train later. I think it might be an idea to have Judy come down and keep an eye on things. She's a good kid and knows what she's doing – give her a bit of responsibility for once. She likes Pete and I trust her."

Janine stood and looked down at the wreck of a person she'd once had amazing sex with. She shook her head as she closed the door behind her. What was it he'd said? It's all under control!

A week later, Janine was in FAM's office on her own. Judy was away looking after Pete in the clinic, so Janine was attending to the mundane daily tasks, one of which was opening the post. There were the usual bills, demo tapes from hopeful new bands, and forms from the council regarding license applications and building regulations. But one letter in particular caught her attention. It was an invitation from George Williams for her and Gerry to attend the presentation of the Queen's Gallantry Medal to DCI Ray Law. The ceremony was taking place the following week and Janine accepted without a second thought. She knew Gerry wasn't a fan of DCI Law, but she would definitely be there, even if she had to go on her own.

It said on the richly embossed card that it was a black-tie do, and she immediately started to make her plans. She would go out later and buy something special to wear. Something that would really blow Ray Law's mind.

While Janine was formulating her plans for Ray Law's event, Gerry was covered in dust, standing in the middle of an enormous old chain factory, with Alex Mitchell and the friend who had recommended he take a look round it. The place was perfectly situated in an old industrial part of the city which, according to a councillor he knew, was earmarked for redevelopment. He'd fallen in love with the building the moment he walked through the huge double entrance doors. It had a unique vibe that he'd picked up on immediately, and he was already imagining what it was going to look like. The great thing was it was all on one level, with a high roof spanned by steel girders, and just the right size to fulfil the ambitious plans for his new, live music, night-club.

In the plans he'd been working on, there would be two main areas - a large room to accommodate the latest up-and-coming bands, and a smaller lounge-style bar, featuring mainly jazz for his more mature clientele, most of whom were either friends or business associates. Alex stood in the middle of the site brushing the dust off his suit. Closing his eyes he could imagine himself playing the grand piano Gerry had promised him, in his own purpose-built room.

It was dark inside, with the only light coming from the glass skylights in the roof, but they could make out huge piles of old chains scattered across the floor. Industrious as always, Gerry could see them as part of the decor. The original offices at one end would be easily dismantled, opening out the whole space. There would be a large reception area from which a central corridor would lead to both rooms. He knew it was going to take a monumental effort to make this happen, but Gerry had never been afraid of hard work. He had lots of friends in the building trade, and with his contacts in the planning department he was confident it could be done. Money wasn't a problem as long as he was careful, and the insurance payout from Rudi's would cover most of the cost. All he had to do now, was convince the retiring owner to sell at the right price, and negotiating had always been one of Gerry's strengths.

Janine and Gerry were getting ready for Ray Law's presentation, and as usual Gerry was having trouble with his bow tie. "I'm not too excited about this do, you know," he said. "This Law character is a nuisance, and if I catch him round here once more there'll be trouble."

"Calm down, Ger." Janine came over and finished his bow tie. "There, you look perfect. And remember, it was Ray who got rid of that piece of shit who blew up Rudi's. Anyway, it'll be a good opportunity to have a chat with George Williams about your new licence. You could do with him being on your side."

Gerry wandered into the lounge mumbling under his breath.

Janine sprayed herself with Chanel No.5 and turned to look in the mirror. She was pleased with what she saw. Her full-length, black Dior evening gown was stunning. With the diamanté-trimmed, plunging neckline, it fitted her perfectly, and although it had cost her more than she originally planned, she knew it was the right choice. After all, she was a well-known face in the city now, and she had an image to maintain.

They'd arrived in Rollie, the 1966 Rolls-Royce Silver Shadow Gerry had bought to celebrate opening Georgie's. It was getting on a bit now, and as they parked in the underground police car park, he thought he'd need to consider replacing it soon.

A uniformed officer met them at the entrance and took their invitation. They were escorted to the lift, which took them up to the large assembly room being used for the occasion. Janine was impressed by the officers in their immaculate dress-uniforms, especially the Chief Constable's with its fine array of medals.

There were about a hundred guests waiting for the ceremony to begin, when Janine noticed Ray. He was looking pensive, and as she tried to catch his eye, a fanfare of trumpets blared out from the back of the room. She hadn't realised the proceedings were going to be this formal but then she recognised the person walking through the crowd as the Princess Royal, here as the Queen's representative to present Ray with his medal. No wonder he looked nervous.

The presentation went without a hitch though, and with the royal guest safely on her way back to London, everyone was finally relaxing. The bar was packed and Janine spotted Ray on his own for once. She'd tried to catch him before, but the stream of people congratulating him had been endless. Grabbing the opportunity, she squeezed her way through the crowd and Ray, seeing her coming, smiled. She kissed his cheek and asked if she could see his medal, conscious all the time that Gerry might be watching, although the last time she'd seen him he was deep in conversation with George Williams.

Her stomach flipped when she touched Ray's hand as he showed her his award. She leaned in close to whisper to him. "So when do we have our own party to celebrate this?"

Ray had never noticed her fragrance before; it was subtle and expensive.

"That would be nice," he replied. "What do you suggest?" He was scanning the crowd keeping a look out for Gerry.

Janine was smiling; still pretending to admire the medal. "How about I come round to your place?" she said. "Tomorrow night?"

Ray was trying not to appear excited but couldn't help smiling. "That would be very…nice."

"Good that's settled then," she said, giving him back his medal. "Why don't I call you in the morning and you can give me your address."

Gerry suddenly appeared through the crowd. "Congratulations DCI Law," he said with his hand outstretched so Ray shook it. "I've just been talking to George Williams, and he's been singing your praises. Keep up the good work."

"I will Mr. Fortuna, and thanks."

"Gerry, son. Call me Gerry. You ready, babe? I've a busy day tomorrow." He turned away and Janine gave Ray a knowing smile and followed her husband.

Ray stood on his own, his heart beating out of his chest. *You've done it now*, he thought to himself. He spotted George Williams and some of his other colleagues at the bar and went over to join them.

In a private clinic on the outskirts of Woking, Pete Peterson was responding positively to the treatment he was receiving. It was a tough daily regime being administered by a no-nonsense team of specialist doctors and nurses. But the one thing that was helping him the most was the constant presence of Judy Watson, the petite blonde secretary from the FAM office, who Janine had sent down to stay with him.

Janine had noticed there was chemistry between Judy and Pete on a few occasions, so she'd taken a chance that he might just respond quicker to treatment with Judy around. It had certainly worked, and when Bobby McGregor had arrived unannounced, he had found them sitting in the lounge together holding hands. He had stood unseen, watching them through the glass panel in the door, eventually making a noise to make them aware someone was coming. They'd disentangled before he was in the room and seemed pleased to see him. Pete even jumped up to give him a hug.

"You're looking good, Pete my man." Bobby stepped back to take in the view of a much healthier-looking musician. "We were pretty worried for a while you know."

Pete looked embarrassed for once. "Yeah, I can't thank you enough – you and Janine – for what you did. How you managed that I'll never know."

"Listen, don't thank me. Janine was the one in charge. I just did as she told me." Bobby said. "Oh, and the guys in the band all send their regards. They said take your time and they're ready whenever you are. Pretty cool eh?"

"Man, those guys are the best," Pete said, shaking his head. "I put them through some shit on that tour. I owe them!" He wandered over to pour himself a glass of fruit juice.

Bobby looked at Judy. "Janine said to pass on her thanks to you too. Both her and Gerry really appreciate what you've done." He moved close and whispered in her ear. "Best keep the situation between you and Pete under wraps for now though. Wouldn't want Gerry finding out just yet. You know what he's like." He gave her a wink.

A nurse wandered in, carrying a glass full of liquid. "Time for your afternoon treatment Mr. Peterson," she said, handing Pete the glass. He pulled a face as he drank it down.

"What's that?" Bobby asked.

"Nutrients and vitamins," the nurse answered. "It helps build up his system and replace all the bad enzymes with good ones. He's doing well – a model patient." She smiled at Pete.

Janine had also charged Judy with the unenviable task of trying to persuade Pete to move back to Birmingham. Both she and Gerry recognised the value of Pete to FAM, and Gerry had been working on an American release of The Flames' last album. It made sense for him to be back where they could keep him under control. A few of his friends had been worried that since he'd moved to London, he'd got in with a dangerous group of musicians who spent all their time experimenting with drugs. It had only been a matter of time for the reckless lifestyle to catch up with him. His collapse in London was a warning, and they had to make sure it didn't happen again.

Ray Law's phone rang at exactly ten o'clock, and a sexy Irish voice wished him good morning. "How're you today? You looked fabulous last night in your posh uniform."

"So did you. That dress was sensational," Ray replied, remembering how fantastic she had looked.

"Well thank you, kind sir," she joked. "So are you going to give me your address or what?"

"Are you sure this is a good idea?"

"Ah you're not getting cold feet on me, DCI Law, are you now?" She sounded disappointed.

"No, course not," he picked up on her change of mood. "Just wanted to make sure you were still up for it."

"Just wait and see," she said.

"Flat 2, 47 Oaks Road then"

"Grand! I'll be there for eight o'clock and I'll bring us a picnic."

She rang off.

The rest of the day was a blur, and Ray managed to get home in time to tidy round and have a shower. He'd just finished when his buzzer went. He looked at his watch; it was only seven forty-five. Surely she wasn't early? He decided to wait. He knew she was a stickler for time so it couldn't be her. He held his breath as the buzzer went again.

Creeping into the bedroom, he peeped out through the curtain, as Matt Burgess walked down the footpath. That could have been embarrassing, he thought.

He'd just calmed down when at exactly eight o'clock the buzzer went again. He picked up the intercom.

"Hi, quick let me in!" said Janine and Ray's heart jumped.

Janine came into the apartment carrying a large box of food and champagne. It clinked as she put it on the table.

She looked amazing with her hair tossed by the wind, and as he took her in his arms and kissed her, he'd never felt so excited.

Finally untangling themselves, Janine rooted through the box for a bottle of her favourite Bollinger and Ray expressed his embarrassment at only having ordinary wine glasses.

Janine said she didn't care as the bottle was uncorked with a gentle hiss – he was getting good at this.

They sat drinking the luscious, biscuity-flavoured liquid until Ray took Janine's hand and led her through into the bedroom. The only illumination came from the candles he'd lit earlier, and in their flickering light he laid her down on the bed, kissing her gently.

She reached up, opened his trousers, pulled them down and gasped.

"Jaysus, that's one hell of a lad!" she exclaimed. "What the feck d'ya feed it on?" She burst out laughing. "Ah, babe I'm sorry, but that is incredible. You're gonna have to be careful with me."

Ray was already lowering himself between her legs.

"Oh God, I've been waiting for this for so long," he said.

Later, sitting on the bed surrounded by food, Janine and Ray were halfway through another bottle of champagne when Ray's phone rang. He sat up looking suspicious.

"I think I'm going to have to answer that," he said. "It could be important. Only work knows this number."

He picked up the receiver. "Hello. Yes it is. Wait a minute, how did you get this number. I see." He listened while the voice at the other end carried on. "Shit that's not good. Look I'll call you tomorrow. No, it's not convenient right now. No, I'll call you tomorrow first thing, and thanks for letting me know. Yes, you too." He put the phone down.

"Mr. C has just died. They tried to operate but he had a seizure on the operating table. This is not good."

Janine looked over at him. "Who was that who called? It sounded like a woman's voice."

"Yeah it was Julia Davies. She's a solicitor from Bloom's – the company who represented your dad. She was Richard Kennedy's ex-wife." He suddenly realised what he'd just said and Janine put her glass down suddenly.

"You sound like you know her quite well." Janine got up from the bed.

"Purely professionally," Ray replied, a little too quickly.

"How come she's got your number here?"

"Yeah, I don't know. Maybe someone from the office gave it to her. She's quite a forceful character. Gets what she wants." He sounded uneasy.

"Including you?" Janine looked him straight in the eyes.

"Look, do we have to talk business?" He poured her another glass of champagne. "Next time, I'll have some crystal glasses."

"Will there be a next time?" She still seemed edgy.

"I really hope so. Don't you want to do that again?"

She put her glass down and pulled him on the bed. "Yes I do, and I want to do it now, but carefully. Jaysus that's big!"

CHAPTER TWENTY-FOUR

THE FOLLOWING morning, the papers were full of the news about Mr. C. Somehow, information had leaked about the involvement of the four Irishmen in the bombing, and questions were being asked. There were already representatives of the grieving families contacting the authorities demanding information, and Ray's euphoria from last night soon evaporated as he walked into George Williams' office and saw the look on his boss's face.

"How the hell did that happen?" George said, waving one of the newspapers from the pile on his desk.

"Something tells me that a certain solicitor from Bloom's is behind this," Ray said, picking up one of the papers. "I received a phone call late last night from Julia Davies, the ex-Mrs. Richard Kennedy, informing me of Mr. C's death. If you remember, she's representing Michael Brennan."

"Well if she is, she's breached the terms of the undertaking which she and her boss signed when their clients were released." George was fuming, pacing up and down. "We need to speak to Patrick Bloom, pronto. Wait a minute, Richard Kennedy? The property developer, wasn't he one of the victims?"

"That's right. And having met Ms. Davies, she has her own agenda. Strong woman."

"Well if she's responsible, she could be sitting behind bars. The Home Office doesn't mess around," George said. "On second thoughts you'd better get them both in here."

Within ten minutes of Ray's phone call, Patrick Bloom and Julia Davies were in George Williams' office. Ray joined them. He noticed Julia's perfume the minute he walked in the door. She was wearing an expensively tailored navy-blue business suit, with a cream silk shirt and blue high-heeled shoes; a sharp contrast to Bloom's well-worn attire.

George looked up at the two solicitors. He addressed Julia. "Ms. Davies, I'm informed by my DCI that you contacted him last night with news of the death of the DJ from Rudi's nightclub. May I ask how you came by this information? And how you obtained DCI Law's private number, known only by the police?"

"I have my sources," Julia replied glancing at Ray.

"And are you also aware of the terms of the contract that you and Mr. Bloom signed here in this building, regarding the release of certain individuals?" George passed copies of the contract to Julia and Patrick Bloom.

"Of course I am. Why do you ask?" Julia replied tersely.

"Because someone has given details to the press of certain Irish individuals who were helping us with our enquiries. We are currently questioning the reporter who wrote the story." George held her gaze and she reddened slightly. "You are aware of course, that were we to discover the identity of the person responsible, they could be subject to a custodial sentence of not less than ten years?"

Julia stood up. "Hey, now wait a minute," she shouted. "Are you accusing me of leaking this information?"

"Of course not Ms. Davies. I was simply stating the facts which are clearly stated on the bottom of the agreement, which you and Mr. Bloom signed along with your other associate, Mr. Sutton I believe." George Williams motioned to Ray. "I think we're done here DCI Law. If you'd be kind enough to show Ms. Davies and Mr. Bloom out."

Ray stood up and opened the door. Patrick Bloom strode out, but Julia held back slightly, and waited until her boss had gone down the stairs. "I think we need to have a chat Ray," she said giving him a knowing look.

"I don't think so, Ms. Davies," said Ray in an official manner.

She stared at him. "You're going to regret this, DCI Law," she hissed through gritted teeth and she marched off, her high heels clacking on the stairs.

"A minute, Ray," George Williams called from his office. Ray returned and stood by the door. "Should I be concerned about that little conversation?" he asked.

Ray smiled. "No, sir. Nothing I can't handle," he said, heading back to his office.

Ray closed the door and sat with his feet up on the desk, staring at the ceiling and reflecting on his current predicament. He'd just spent the most incredible evening with Janine, and definitely felt there was something between them. Trouble was, she was the wife of Gerry

Fortuna, who, as he knew from past experience, was dangerous.

But just thinking about her made his stomach flip, and he couldn't wait to see her again. He would have to be on his guard constantly; one wrong word and he could be in deep trouble. So did he want to take the risk?

Then there was Julia Davies. He knew last week had been a mistake, but at the time it was sensational. She was a sexual dynamo, although he'd never been dominated like that before, and he wasn't sure he liked it. But more importantly, there was the massive conflict of interest that had just reared its ugly head. He was sure it was Julia who'd leaked the information, but to pursue her would only cause more grief, and he had enough on his plate already. He'd have to tread very carefully where Ms. Davies was concerned.

DS Matt Burgess knocked on the door, interrupting Ray's reverie.

"Come in, Matt. I was just thinking we should attend Mr. C's funeral," Ray lied. "I'd like to speak to the old man Errol again. I know he'll be pretty involved on the day, but there might be an opportunity to have a word."

"Good idea, boss, I hear that Alex Mitchell is going to play another piece like he did at Wynton's funeral. Remember? It was amazing."

"Yes, Alex Mitchell." Ray thought for a moment. "How are we doing with the surveillance team? Any leads?"

Matt shook his head. "That's just it. They've drawn an absolute blank. He just turns up at the restaurants where he plays, doesn't have much to do with anyone, plays and goes home. They've been to a couple of his gigs. Nothing. But they did say that he'd been to an old factory with Gerry Fortuna and another guy, who Tony Carter reckons is an estate agent."

"Ah yes, Janine mentioned Gerry was planning to build a new club and is looking for premises."

Matt raised his eyebrows.

"What? I was talking to her at the presentation the other night." Ray's answer sounded a little too quick.

Matt suddenly remembered he had to be somewhere. That was one situation he didn't want any part of.

Ray's phone rang and he picked it up on the second ring. It was George Williams. "On my way," Ray said, replacing the handset.

George was waiting in his office looking agitated. "I've just had the Home Office on the phone. Character by the name of William Greene who came up while you were in hospital. They're not happy about the reports in the papers about the Irish suspects who were released. You need to speak to Julia Davies."

"I'll call her and arrange a meeting," Ray answered.

"Well get on to it straight away. We don't want the Home Office lot breathing down our necks. Get her to contact that reporter who broke the story and play down the Irish connection."

"I'll see what I can do," Ray said.

Julia Davies had just arrived back in her office when her secretary rang her. "There's a DCI Law on the line for you Julia," she said.

Julia kicked off her high-heeled shoes and lit a cigarette. "Put him through," she replied, blowing the smoke out with a slow hiss. "DCI Law, how nice to speak to you again, and so soon. What can I do for you?"

"Julia, we need to talk."

She paused a moment. "Well I'm rather tied up at the moment, how about we meet at the King's Head later, say seven? We can talk over a drink."

It wasn't the ideal situation, but Ray decided it couldn't hurt. "All right, I'll see you at seven."

The King's Head was crowded when Ray arrived, full of people having a drink on their way home from work. He spotted Julia amidst a group of men wearing suits and approached her. She saw him coming and, taking his arm, introduced him to the group. "This is DCI Ray Law everyone. Ray these are some of my colleagues from Bloom's. Would you like a drink?"

"Just a beer please," he said smiling. "Julia, can we have a word, in private?"

Julia passed him his pint. "Of course, darling," she gushed, turning to the others. "I'll see you all tomorrow." She grabbed Ray's hand and led him over to a booth in the corner. "Now then, what can I do for you, DCI Law?"

Ray took a draught of his beer and sat back, looking at her. She'd freshened up her makeup – and there was that perfume again. He couldn't help thinking back to last weekend, but he had to stay focussed. This was business.

"Actually, I think it's more a case of what I can do for you, Julia," he said.

She stared at him. "Go on."

"After our meeting this morning, the Chief Constable received a phone call from the Home Office expressing their concern about the recent leak of information. In no uncertain terms, they are demanding the retraction of any reference to Irish suspects by the reporter who wrote the story. Now, both you and I know who gave him that information, so I'm suggesting he drops the story immediately and avoids a shitload of trouble. Do I make myself clear?"

Julia reached for her cigarettes and lit one, drawing deeply on it. She looked at Ray stubbed it out. "Sorry," she said, blowing the smoke away from him. "If you put it like that, I guess I'll just go and make a quick phone call. Will you wait here a minute?"

She stood up and walked over to the public phone, which was in an alcove across the room.

Ray sat drinking his beer, watching her gesticulate while she talked. Finally, she put the phone down and returned to the booth.

"You'll be pleased to know, I don't think we'll be hearing any more about Irish suspects," she said with an apologetic smile. "Listen, I didn't mean to cause any trouble, and I do still like you. How about we open a bottle of champagne back at my place to make up for it?"

Ray was just about to decline the offer, when she leaned across the table and kissed him. His stomach flipped. "OK, I'll follow you in my car," he found himself saying.

Ten minutes later he was lying naked between Julia's legs, as she pulled him into her. She lay back and looked up at the mirror on the ceiling, watching the slow, deliberate movement of Ray's athletic body. The champagne bottle stood unopened on the bedside table.

The following morning, a colossal crowd attended Mr. C's funeral. There were so many people crammed into the church that mourners had spilled outside. Ray had managed to get home from Julia's at a reasonable hour, and now he and Matt were squeezed into a pew at the back of the congregation, where they could watch as people arrived.

Mr. C had been a very popular DJ, with a reputation as a 'ladies' man' – and judging from the number of attractive young women who were there, it would appear to have been true. There had been a constant turnover of new go-go dancers at Rudi's, and they all seemed to have turned up to pay their respects.

In the same way as Wynton's funeral had been a celebration, Mr. C's (or Charles as he was referred to during the service) was a lively affair, interspersed with uplifting gospel singing.

The highlight, once again, had been when Alex Mitchell walked forward to the front of the altar, sat down at the piano and started to play. He'd known Mr. C long enough to understand his taste in music and had chosen a collection of his favourite soul songs, arranged into an instrumental medley.

At least that's how it started, but as soon as the people recognised what Alex was playing, they started to sing, including Ray; he'd forgotten how much he enjoyed singing. He belted out the melodies of one classic song after another, completely unaware of the admiration he was receiving from the people standing around him.

Alex finished to a standing ovation. He acknowledged the applause and walked back to his seat. He spotted Ray and Matt, and on his way past, slowly inclined his head towards them. It was almost condescending; once again Ray felt there was something about Alex Mitchell that bothered him. He had to find out what it was.

The service came to an end, and the congregation was filing out past Errol, who was standing in the doorway shaking hands with everyone. It came to Ray and Matt's turn, and Errol thanked them for coming, gripping Ray's hand strongly. "You have an amazing voice DCI Law; I've told you this before. I want you in our congregation; you can sing like no one else I know. The Lord would welcome you," he said.

Ray was flattered, and realised that people who had been sitting near him were patting his back and smiling as they walked by. He was momentarily lost for words. Then remembering the reason why he and Matt were there, he thanked Errol, asking if they might have a quick word with him before they left. Errol frowned, but said he would meet them outside in a few minutes if they could wait.

Ten minutes later, Errol appeared looking tired and weary. "I'm sorry, there are so many people here wanting to offer condolences."

Ray tried his best to be respectful. "Errol, I'm sorry to bother you on such a sad occasion, but we need to ask you a question. At Gerry Fortuna's New Year party, Charles had a row with Thomas Wilson about the supply of drugs, which he later told me were linked to an American cartel called Rota Bocan. We are led to believe that Thomas was using Rudi's to receive the drugs, and that Alex Mitchell was using his position as club manager to facilitate this. Can you confirm or deny that - off the record?"

Errol studied Ray's expression. "Off the record you say?"

"Off the record," Ray confirmed.

"I like you a lot, DCI Law. You have a wonderful voice, a gift from the Lord. So I will tell you what Charles told me." He leaned heavily on his walking stick. "Charles hated Thomas Wilson. He said he was trying to take away our business. He said there would be trouble and sadly he was right, but he never mentioned anyone else. I'm sorry I can't help you any more. Now if you'll excuse me, I have to go and mourn my nephew."

Ray and Matt watched as Errol slowly make his way back to the crowd of people outside the church.

"Shit!" Ray said. "Oh no, I shouldn't say that outside church should I?"

Matt laughed. "You said it; I thought it! So what now?"

"I'm not giving up on Alex Mitchell," Ray said. "He's involved in some way and I'm going to have him."

While they were having breakfast that morning, Gerry had told Janine they were going on a trip to see a businessman he wanted her to meet. He had declined the invitation to Mr. C's funeral saying things like that depressed him. Now, as they drove through the Warwickshire countryside in Rollie, Janine sat back in its luxurious comfort, watching the fields flash by bathed in the warm sunshine.

She'd often mentioned her love of trees and fields, and how much she'd like to live outside the city one day but when they eventually turned into a long drive, flanked on either side by tall trees leading to an old Georgian mansion, she was completely unaware of the surprise Gerry was about to spring on her.

Rollie's tyres crunched on the gravel as they stopped outside the front entrance. The old oak door creaked, as it was opened by Gerry's friendly estate agent. While they were viewing the old chain factory Gerry had mentioned in passing the possibility of a move out of the city. The result was the agent calling Gerry to tell him about a property that had recently come onto their books which he thought might be just what Gerry was looking for.

They walked through the oak-panelled hallway, past the imposing suit of armour at the bottom of the curved staircase, as the estate agent recounted the building's history. The previous owner had been an American singer from the flower power generation, who had had some success in the UK during the sixties and spent his royalties on a trendy 'Olde English Pyle'. Unfortunately, he'd neglected the place, spending most of his time on psychedelic trips, and smoking pot with a host of devoted followers. When his popularity waned and his money ran out, everyone deserted him. He'd eventually packed up what was left of his belongings and moved back to America, leaving the listed mansion empty and in a sorry state.

It had eight bedrooms, four bathrooms, a huge lounge with an inglenook fireplace, a heated swimming pool, stables and twenty acres of land. Gerry could see a lot of work would be needed to restore it to its former glory; some of the mullioned windows were in a bad state, there were damp patches on some of the bedroom walls where the roof was leaking, and the outside pool was completely overgrown. But overall, nothing a team of builders couldn't put right.

"It's a steal Gerry; daylight bloody robbery," the estate agent had enthused, as they finished the tour back in the hallway again.

Janine couldn't believe it. It was a fantastic property, and though they both loved it and knew it was perfect, Gerry said he was going to put in a substantially lower offer than the asking price.

"Bloody hell mate, I'm not sure the owner'll go for that," his friend said.

"Listen, he's broke and he needs the money," replied Gerry. "He'll accept the offer. And tell him I want the suit of armour as well!"

In the car on the way back, Janine was so excited she hardly drew breath. She had so many ideas for the decor and what they could do to the kitchen. Gerry just let her talk. She was happy, and when she was happy, so was he. The deal for the factory had been accepted and the estate agent was on his way back to his office to make Gerry's offer.

With Gerry's experience of buying properties over the years, he instinctively knew how far he could afford to go and was confident he would win. And after a couple of transatlantic calls, haggling with the ex-singer who was now growing soya beans on a commune somewhere in the depths of Iowa, Gerry's offer was accepted. He and Janine had their dream home, complete with an authentic suit of medieval armour in the hallway.

CHAPTER TWENTY-FIVE

PETE PETERSON had finally checked out of the clinic. He and Judy had grown close in the time they'd spent together, and she'd convinced him that leaving London and moving back home again was the right thing to do.

Resourceful as always, Gerry had spoken to his estate agent friend and found Pete a one-bedroom apartment. It was a comfortable space, in a great location overlooking the old canal basin. It suited him perfectly. It was simply decorated with off-white walls throughout, and furnished in the latest designer style. According to Gerry, plans he'd seen recently suggested the area was earmarked to become an entertainment hub in the city, with new bars, restaurants and clubs. Gerry had advised Pete to buy it, because one day it would be worth a lot of money. That was one of the benefits of having someone like Gerry Fortuna as your manager; he made it his business to know what was happening in the city, using his network of local business and council connections. It was one of his friends on the planning committee who'd shown him the recently submitted plans.

Pete and Judy had managed to keep their relationship quiet so far. Bobby had assured them their secret was safe with him, and although Janine knew, she had never mentioned it to either of them. Fortunately, Gerry was so tied up with the purchase and renovation of the mansion, and building his new club, he didn't have time to think about anything else.

Pete had organised a meeting with The Flames; they hadn't spoken since the last night of the tour. They'd all sent him messages of support, but this was the first time they'd all been together. They were all waiting in The Hideout when Pete walked in, and they immediately jumped up to shake hands and hug him.

Even Tony Waters gave him a warm embrace, noticing how much Pete had changed in appearance. "Wow Pete, man. You look great. It's good to have you back," he said.

Pete had put on weight and had a healthy glow. He was wearing a denim jacket and jeans, with brown leather cowboy boots and a cream Stetson; he had the old swagger back again.

"Thanks, I feel good. I'm sorry for putting you guys through so much shit during the tour. But I'm back now and good things are gonna happen. Gerry's talking to some major record companies in the States about releasing the last album over there, and for us to tour."

Janine and Judy had walked in while Pete was talking – he turned around and noticed them.

"Hey ladies, come and join us. What d'you say we have some beers to celebrate having the guys back together again?"

Janine went to say something but Pete held up his hand. "Yeah, I know what you're gonna say, but the doctors said I can have the odd beer so long as I don't go crazy. And let's face it, booze wasn't the problem, was it? So come on, beers all round!"

Janine nodded to Judy, who went behind the bar passing out bottles of cold beer to Pete and the band. Janine joined her and opened a bottle of champagne, pouring a glass for them both. They clinked glasses with the guys and toasted, "The Flames!"

"Where's the leather jacket Pete?" Janine asked, weighing up the new look.

"Thought I'd have a change," he said, swigging his beer. "What d'you think?"

"I prefer the leather, it's more you," she replied. "Guys! Denim or leather?"

"Leather!" they all answered as one voice.

"Leather it is then," Pete said, laughing. It felt good to be back with the guys again.

Over the last couple of months, Gerry had been working non-stop on the renovations at the Warwickshire property and the new club, which was going to be called The Lexxicon. Once the team of builders had finished at the mansion, Janine had moved out of their apartment and taken over the completion of the interior decoration, fixtures and fittings, while Gerry stayed on to oversee work on the club. Janine had big plans for the kitchen and her own gym, which she would install in one of the bedrooms.

The one problem with living out in the countryside was that she couldn't see Ray Law as easily as before. Previously, it had been just a quick taxi ride to his flat. Now she was about thirty minutes away, so in future she'd have to think about how to see him without Gerry suspecting. At the moment, Gerry was too busy with his precious club to be bothered, but once it was finished she would have to be more careful.

True to his word, Ray had been out and bought two expensive crystal champagne flutes and he and Janine were lying in his bed enjoying a glass of Bollinger. Their lovemaking had been urgent but fulfilling, and Janine was reflecting on her feelings as she watched him in the flickering candlelight.

There had been the others of course; Pete Peterson was exciting but a liability; Richard Kennedy had been opulent and rich, and she was sorry that he was dead. Then there was Gerry. She loved him, but she wasn't in love with him. Was that possible? He'd just surprised her by buying the fabulous mansion in the country. Who could resist such riches? But sometimes they felt like hollow gestures. She remembered how she'd laid down the rules with Pete and Richard. It was just fun, nothing serious and certainly not love. But with Ray it was different. With him it felt real. She knew he'd gone to a lot of trouble choosing the right glasses to impress her, and she was flattered, but he didn't have to – she would happily drink from a mug as long she was sharing the moment with him. She hoped he felt the same.

Back in the city, the club had taken shape really quickly, with construction of the two main rooms finally finished. No expense had been spared on the décor including huge, specially commissioned, hand-painted murals lining the walls throughout. Gerry had also managed to incorporate some of the chains that had been left, by turning them into surreal sculptures. The place almost felt like a gallery of modern art. The latest in sound and lighting systems had been installed in the main concert room - Lexx1 -and a brand-new grand piano, chosen especially for Alex Mitchell, took centre stage in Lexx2, the smaller more intimate room where he would play regularly.

As in all of Gerry's clubs, special attention had been paid to the bar. Gerry knew booze was business and Lexx1 would boast an impressive copper-topped bar, stretching the whole length of the room. In the publicity material, Gerry made the bold statement that no one in The Lexxicon would have to wait longer than thirty seconds to be served. He wasn't sure it would go down well with the bar staff, but it had certainly gained attention and created a buzz around the city.

The opening night had been set for Friday, 24th October, and the countdown had begun. Gerry launched a huge publicity campaign, with all the papers picking up on his outspoken claims that no drug cartels would take over his city. Gerry's promise that his clubs would be drug-free were given large headlines, with pictures of him standing outside the brand-new entrance to The Lexxicon. It had raised a few eyebrows at police headquarters.

Now that Pete was back and fit again, Gerry had asked him and The Flames to play on the opening night, so Pete had got the guys together for rehearsals at The Hideout.

Gerry had also asked Alex Mitchell if he would be interested in becoming part of the management team again. He'd been impressed with the way he'd run Rudi's, and there was a possibility he could be involved in booking the artists like he had done previously.

Janine had been furious and argued with Gerry about involving Alex in the business. She had always been suspicious of him – and had mentioned it to Ray one night.

"We've been keeping him under surveillance for a while and to be fair he looks squeaky clean," Ray said, as they relaxed in his flat. "Matt and I have been talking about getting him in for another interview. What bothers me is why Frank Kelly would mention him during questioning? There's something linking Alex to that whole situation at Rudi's and we can't find it. His drummer Thomas, Frank Kelly, Mr. C – they knew something but they're all dead, and old Errol refused to be drawn when we spoke to him at Mr. C's funeral. What does Gerry want him to do?"

"Nothing major – I think it's something to do with booking the bands," she replied. "But he gives me the creeps and I just sense he's up to something."

Matt Burgess had called Alex Mitchell the next day and asked if he would come into police headquarters for a chat. Alex was reluctant at first, making excuses that he was too busy now he was involved in the new club with Gerry. But as soon as Matt suggested they would come down to The Lexxicon and speak to him there, he suddenly found time and said he would call in later that morning.

Ray had decided to let Matt take the lead while he watched on in the observation room. They didn't want to alarm Alex, and Ray hoped that in his absence Alex would relax and drop his guard.

Alex turned up at eleven thirty, dressed in a smart suit with a collar and tie. Matt apologised for the overpowering odour of stale sweat in the interview room, and offered Alex tea or coffee, which he declined. He appeared nervous and slightly on edge, so Matt complimented him on the wonderful music he'd played at Mr. C's funeral – appealing to his ego seemed to calm him down.

Matt opened his notepad. "It's just something that came up recently and we wanted to have a word with you about it," he said in a matter-of-fact way. "Frank Kelly, the man responsible for the bomb that destroyed Rudi's, happened to mention you when we were interviewing him, and we wondered if you knew him?"

Alex leaned back in his chair. "No, I never heard of him. I mean, I heard his name on the news in connection with the shooting, but that's all."

"So can you think of any reason why he'd want to kill you, along with the American cartel responsible for importing the drugs?"

Alex was now sitting up rigidly straight. "No, not at all. I mean, I wasn't involved in any way with the cartel."

"But Thomas Wilson was. And according to reports, he was using Rudi's to bring in the drugs. Are you telling me you weren't aware of that?" Matt was a little more aggressive now, pushing him.

"Of course not. I mean, yes. I wasn't aware what he was up to. He told me they were records from the States."

The door opened and Ray walked in and sat down opposite Alex.

"Hello, Alex. Thanks for coming in. I'd like to clarify something you just said, if you don't mind. You're saying that you were unaware of what Thomas Wilson was doing and that he told you the deliveries were records from the States. Is that correct?"

"Yes, that's what he told me, I never saw what was in the packages." Alex fidgeted nervously.

"Thanks for that, Alex. I think that's all for now."

Ray stood and left the room. George Williams was waiting for him in the observation room with Gerry Fortuna.

"Hello Gerry, thanks for coming in. I assume you heard that?" Ray said, shaking Gerry's hand. They watched as Matt Burgess escorted Alex out.

"He's lying," said Gerry. He was calm, but Ray could tell he was angry. "The day you and I met him and Mr. C at Rudi's, he said they were his records. Imports from the States and even asked if I would like to borrow some. Miles and Coltrane – I remember because I can't stand jazz!"

"So what's your next move?" George Williams asked Ray.

"Well, he's definitely got something to hide. It's not enough to get him on a charge though."

"I've been doing a bit of digging as well," Gerry said. "Janine has always made a point of saying she had suspicions about him, and recently I was talking to an old friend who has an agency that books bands. He was telling me how he used to deal with Alex to book reggae and soul acts into Rudi's. He said all the money went direct through a small agency and then to Alex who paid the acts. So he checked up on this agency, and it turns out it's completely bogus. There's nothing at the address where the agency was registered."

"So Alex was running a scam?"

"Exactly. Every time he booked an act into Rudi's, he was creaming off the top for himself." Gerry said.

"Explains how he could afford to be looking at apartments with Richard Kennedy." Ray said. "Janine told me that Richard had shown Alex a couple of apartments that were well out of his price range. Richard wondered at the time how Alex was going to pay for them. This explains it."

"And when Rudi's was blown up, that put a stop to his little fiddle," Gerry said.

"It still doesn't explain why Frank Kelly mentioned him though," George Williams said.

Ray thought for a moment. "It does if he knew all along about the drugs coming in. Possibly he was being paid by Thomas Wilson. He must have been making a fortune on top of what you were paying him, Gerry."

Gerry had gone quiet. "I have to get back to the club. Keep me informed," he said.

George Williams followed him out, leaving Ray on his own.

Matt Burgess came back a few minutes later. "Well, that was interesting," he said. "What did Gerry Fortuna have to say?"

"Not a lot, and that's what worries me," Ray replied.

Gerry was just about managing to keep his anger under control. He was weighing up what he'd heard as he made his way back to the FAM office above the Hideout. Alex had been creaming off the top of every deal he'd done for artists appearing at Rudi's. *I trusted him, leaving him on his own to run the club, and this is how he repays me. But worse than that, he lied to me when he said he knew nothing about the drugs and he was involved all along! And I spent yesterday arranging for a grand piano to be delivered for him. How could I be so blind? Janine was right all along.*

As soon as he arrived at the office he sat down behind his desk and calmly worked out what he was going to do.

Ray had contacted Julia Davies and arranged for Michael Brennan to come into police headquarters for an off-the-record interview with him and Matt. Ray felt certain that there must be a reason why Frank Kelly had been almost arrogant in mentioning the club manager in the same breath as the Americans. Perhaps the members of the Association would know why.

Julia turned up directly after lunch with her client, and they were shown into a free interview room, which happened to be the newly refurbished one.

"Well it's nice to smell something fresh for a change," Julia observed as she sat down. She was wearing her grey, pinstriped business suit, glasses and high heels, although Ray noticed she wasn't smoking this time. He acknowledged her comment with a slight nod of his head, and then addressed Michael Brennan.

"Thanks for coming in Mr. Brennan. We fully understand you signed the Home Office contract, but there's something that's cropped up recently and we hoped you might be able to help us."

"If I can," he replied, a little tentatively.

Ray carried on. "You see, when Frank Kelly was interviewed, he made a reference to the Americans and the club manager needing to be taught a lesson. Do you know why he'd say that?"

Michael thought for a moment. "I think you should speak to Joe Burke. He has some photographs that might explain it."

Ray spoke to Matt. "Can you get hold of Patrick Bloom and ask him to get Joe Burke in here? Thanks."

He turned back to Michael Brennan and Julia. "Thanks for your time Michael. You've been very helpful, and you too, Ms. Davies."

Julia stopped as they were leaving and leaned into Ray. "I'll call you," she said, and briefly touched his hand. There was that perfume again.

Ray wondered how long he could keep this dangerous game going with both Julia and Janine. But right now he had to concentrate on the case and the possibility of a lead from Joe Burke.

In his office, Gerry phoned his friend at the agency, and explained what had just happened with Ray and George Williams. Gerry asked him to arrange a meeting with Alex in The Lexxicon, on the pretence that he wanted to see inside it. Gerry knew that Alex had his own key so it wouldn't be a problem, and he told the agent to make sure he asked to see the stage and dressing rooms. Once there, he would suggest to Alex about them booking acts together, suggesting they could make a bit of extra cash. Gerry was sure Alex wouldn't be able to resist telling him about his little scam at Rudi's.

The agent called back to say Alex had agreed to meet him at eight o'clock, and Gerry immediately put his plan into action. He called Bobby McGregor and arranged to meet him at the back of The Lexxicon at seven-thirty. They would sneak in through the rear door that led directly to the dressing rooms, making sure they were waiting when Alex and the agent reached the backstage area.

Patrick Bloom had called Ray to say he would bring Joe Burke into police headquarters at eight o'clock. Joe was happy to help in any way he could. Ray had outlined the details to the solicitor, explaining that Michael Brennan had said Joe had photographs that could be of interest.

George Williams was waiting with Ray in the observation room, when Matt escorted Patrick Bloom and Joe Burke into the interview room. Ray had managed to make sure they were in the best room again.

"Mr. Bloom, Mr. Burke; thank you for coming in. We acknowledge that you signed the Home Office agreement, and as such, respect your right to refuse to discuss the case any further. But recent information has come to our notice, and we're trying to establish new facts that could result in a further arrest. Joe, may I call you Joe?" Joe Burke nodded his assent. "Michael Brennan suggested you might have photographic evidence that Alex Mitchell was involved in the receipt and distribution of drugs at Rudi's nightclub. Is this true?"

Ray waited while Joe Burke opened a folder and carefully spread out a selection of black and white prints, clearly showing Alex and Thomas coming out of Rudi's. Alex had also been photographed receiving packages from a delivery company, which he had taken into the club. Thomas always left with a package, and on one occasion had blatantly handed over an envelope, which Alex could be seen opening; he was then photographed counting the money it had contained. The dates on the back of the photos showed it had been happening on a weekly basis.

"Thank you Joe, these seem to prove, without doubt, that Alex Mitchell knew what was happening. He can even be seen counting his payment. Can I keep these?" Ray was trying to conceal his excitement.

"Of course, help yourself," Joe replied. "How's my daughter?" He gave Ray a knowing smile as he asked the question.

Ray looked puzzled for a moment. "She's fine I think," he replied.

"Look after her; she a good girl." Joe shook Ray's hand and left the room with his solicitor.

"What was that about?" Matt asked as they joined George Williams back in the observation room.

Ray ignored him. "Well, I think these photos give us enough evidence to bring Alex in for more questioning. Matt and I will do it first thing tomorrow morning."

"I assume you're going to the big opening on Friday?" George asked Ray, as he headed back to his office.

"Wouldn't miss it for the world," said Ray.

CHAPTER TWENTY-SIX

AT THE same time Ray and George Williams were discussing Alex Mitchell, Gerry Fortuna and Bobby McGregor were standing silently in the dark, listening to Alex explain to the agent, how they could book artists and receive money from The Lexxicon, while taking a cut of the fee for themselves.

Gerry and Bobby were in the second of the two dressing rooms backstage, where Alex had taken the agent to show him the brand-new facilities in the club. They heard every word as Alex bragged about how much money he'd made from Rudi's without anyone knowing; how Gerry had never suspected what he was doing, and why there was no reason why they couldn't do it again. He was unaware of the door opening between the two rooms until Gerry coughed and Alex spun round in horror, realising he'd been set up.

"Well I have to say, that's a very interesting story you've been telling," Gerry said. "Why don't you tell me how much you were getting from the Americans while you're at it?"

"I...I don't know what you're talking about," Alex stammered. "I never knew what was going on, I swear."

"Alex, please don't treat me like a fool," Gerry glowered.

"Look Gerry, I can explain. You've got it all wrong."

"I don't think so. And you're gonna pay for what you've done."

As Gerry started to take his coat off, Alex reached into his jacket pocket and pulled out a revolver, pointing it straight at his employer.

Gerry stood where he was, an evil grin on his face. "Oh dear son, you shouldn't have done that. I'm really disappointed. After all I've done for you."

Alex was holding the revolver with both hands trying to keep it steady. "I'll shoot, I mean it!" His voice was shaky. He was staring at Gerry so intently, he hadn't noticed Bobby.

Suddenly, a massive bolt of pain exploded in Alex's head, as Bobby punched him from the side. Alex fell to the floor, letting go of his father's old service revolver which skidded across the floor as Gerry walked across and stood over him.

"Get him up," he said to Bobby. "I think we need to teach him a lesson."

Bobby lifted Alex up, and sat him down in one of the chairs in front of the large illuminated mirror. Alex tried to focus, but before he had chance to clear his head, Gerry pulled the chair round and hit him across the nose with a piece of wood left by the carpenters. Alex's nose erupted and all he could do was plead for Gerry to stop.

"Stop?" Gerry shouted in Alex's face. "I've only just started, you piece of shit." He slammed the wood down on Alex's left hand, which was wrapped around the arm of the chair.

Alex screamed.

"Scream all you want. Nobody fucks with Gerry Fortuna!" Gerry's growl came from deep inside him, as he smashed the wood down on Alex's other hand. Alex was on the verge of passing out, and Bobby grabbed Gerry's arm. He could see that both of Alex's hands were really badly damaged.

"Think that might be enough now, Gerry," Bobby said. "He's done."

Gerry was breathing hard. He started to walk away, until seeing the revolver lying on the floor, he bent and picked it up, calmly turned around and shot Alex between the eyes.

"Fuck! Oh Fuck! What did you do that for?" Bobby was shouting at him. "For God's sake Gerry, you didn't have to kill him!"

Gerry gave his best friend an icy stare. "I warned him, don't ever fuck with me or I'll kill you."

"Oh shit Gerry, what are we gonna do now?" Bobby was panicking.

Gerry on the other hand, remained placidly calm, the explosive temper drained away. He looked around him. "Help me with that plastic sheeting over there." He pointed to a roll the decorators had left. "We can wrap him in it and dump him in the canal out the back."

Bobby was agitated but did as Gerry said. Between them they wrapped the body in the sheeting and manhandled it through the back door.

The canal ran alongside the rear of the old factory, and there was a wooden dock where barges used to load in times gone by. It hadn't been used for years, and was in a state of decay with weeds growing over it. Gerry and Bobby carried the body along the towpath and carefully stepped onto the rotting wood. One of the timbers gave way with a loud crack and Bobby almost fell in the water. He managed to grab hold of the rail around the dock but he let go of his end of the roll, and Alex's head slid out, hitting the deck with a thud. Fortunately, the area they were in had been long deserted, but Gerry snapped at his friend. "For fuck sake Bobby, look where you're going!"

They managed to slide the body to the edge, and unrolling the sheet they dropped Alex into the canal, where he slowly sank into the murky water. Gerry leaned over and dropped the revolver into the water. Bobby folded the plastic sheeting up, and as they walked back, he dropped it into a skip full of building materials.

"What about that agent friend of yours. Do you trust him to keep his mouth shut?" he asked as they locked the club up.

"Don't worry about him," Gerry said. "He's gonna be receiving a nice wad of cash to ensure a loss of memory. He won't even remember coming here."

They got into Rollie and drove away.

Ray Law had spent the rest of the evening with Janine at his flat. She'd called just as he was leaving police headquarters, to say she would be there at nine o'clock. They were in bed finishing off the bottle of champagne he'd picked up on his way home.

"Where did you tell Gerry you were going? Another night out with the girls?"

Janine sipped her champagne. "He wasn't in. He called to say he was going out with Bobby and would be back late, so I called you and came straight here."

"You know your hunch about Alex Mitchell turned out to be right," he said. "Turns out he was involved with the drugs at Rudi's, and he was creaming off the top of the acts he was booking. Gerry was there when we interviewed him. He was livid when he went back to the office."

"I didn't go to the office today," Janine said. "I spent all morning and most of the afternoon waiting at the house for a delivery of kitchen tiles."

"Well, Matt and I are going to pick him up tomorrow morning first thing," Ray said yawning.

"Hey, don't be falling asleep on me," she said, reaching beneath the sheets to make sure he was still wide awake.

Later, as she was getting ready to leave, Ray came up behind her and kissed her neck. "Will I see you before the big opening night on Friday?"

"I hope so," she replied. "Although it's gonna get really busy, but leave it with me." She turned and kissed him.

Ray Law and Matt Burgess visited Alex Mitchell's flat early the next morning, but he wasn't there. They'd tried The Lexxicon later, and were told he wasn't there either. It was when they contacted one of the restaurants where he played, that they started to become suspicious. He hadn't shown up to play his usual set at ten o'clock the previous night, and when the owner called him there was no answer. Evidently, this was most unusual - he never intentionally missed a free dinner.

Ray and Matt spent the rest of the day back at police headquarters calling various contacts associated with Alex, with no luck.

They finally called it a day at seven o'clock.

Gerry meanwhile, had spent the day with Bobby making sure they had an alibi for the previous night, and had arrived at The Lexxicon shortly after Ray and Matt had left.

They set about making sure any evidence of their visit was removed. Bobby spotted a few drops of blood on the carpet in the dressing room, and made sure he cleaned them up before anyone else noticed. Then, he took a walk by the canal, and was relieved to see that the skip containing the plastic sheet had been removed.

There was no sign of anything in the water down by the wooden dock, and he made his way back to the club, unaware that Alex's body had floated further down the canal towards the lock leading into the busy central canal basin.

The next morning, Ray had just arrived in his office when his phone rang. It was Matt Burgess.

"Where? When? I'll ring George Williams" said Ray, trying to take in the news.

George Williams picked up his phone on the third ring. "Yes Ray. OK you get down there straight away. I'll wait to hear from you."

Ray and Matt arrived at the canal basin within minutes. A member of the public on an early morning walk with his dog, had spotted the body floating in the canal and called 999. He was standing over by the lock gates looking shaken. Ray tasked one of the constables with taking his statement, and making sure he was all right to go home.

The police surgeon called Ray over. "Pretty messy this," he said, "Look, he's been badly beaten and then shot in the head. Quite vicious, the way his hands have been smashed."

"Any idea how long he's been dead?"

"Difficult to say because he's been in the water for a while, and things have had a go at him. As a rough guess, at least a day possibly two, but don't quote me. I'll know more after the post-mortem." He moved aside to allow the police photographer to take the shots he needed.

Matt came over to Ray. "Does the fact that his hands have been beaten, make you think that whoever did this, knew him? An act of revenge?"

Ray looked at Matt. "Are you thinking what I'm thinking? Who do we know, who would want revenge on Alex Mitchell? I need to get back to the office and speak with George."

George Williams was in his office when Ray got back. "Sit down Ray. Coffee?"

Ray told George what they'd seen, and how he and Matt had both had the same thought.

"Jesus, Ray, you're playing with fire here," George said, scratching his head. "I mean I know Gerry's a tough character, and I've witnessed him in action a couple of times, but murder?"

Ray sipped his coffee. "You saw how he reacted the other day when we had Alex in here and he also told us about the bogus agency. He was furious Alex had ripped him off.

"Yes but would he kill him? I can't think he'd stoop so low. Hurt him maybe, but a bullet between the eyes! That's cold, calculated execution." George thought for a moment.

Ray finally interrupted. "We have to get him in."

"OK. But I think you should let Matt ask the questions. You know how you've already ruffled Gerry's feathers by talking to his wife behind his back. He's still touchy about that, and we don't want to antagonise him. Did you see his reaction when you mentioned her and Richard Kennedy? No, let Matt lead on it. He's good, and you know he'll do the job."

Ray considered George's reasoning. "All right, but I want to be in the room."

Ray was sitting in his office with Matt Burgess at ten o'clock the next morning, when his phone rang. "Gerry Fortuna and his solicitor are here to see you," the receptionist said.

"Can you get someone to escort them to Interview Room One?" Ray asked. He looked at Matt. "Might as well make it seem like we're making him comfortable."

They left it for ten minutes before going in. Ray was behind Matt, and he saw Gerry sitting at the table with his solicitor, who looked up as they entered. Julia Davies. Ray's stomach dropped. Was this some kind of joke?

She smiled as they sat down opposite them. "I was beginning to think you'd forgotten we were here," she said with her customary sarcasm. She was wearing another of her expensive business suits. This one was chestnut-brown with a fine, cream stripe. Her skirt was shorter than usual Ray noticed, and she wore dark-brown, high-heeled pumps. Her hair was immaculately plaited, her make-up perfect, and her sensual perfume pervaded the oppressive atmosphere in the room.

Matt ignored her and switched on the tape recorder after which they all identified themselves for the record.

"Thank you for attending, Mr. Fortuna. As you know, we are investigating the murder of Mr. Alex Mitchell. He worked for you. Is that correct?"

"Yes," Gerry answered.

"Was he currently employed by you?"

"Yes, he was going to play in the new club. I had recently acquired a grand piano for him."

"Would you say you were on good terms with Mr. Mitchell?"

Matt's question caused Gerry to look at Julia, who was writing in her leatherbound pad.

"Is that relevant, DS Burgess?" Julia asked.

"I think so," he replied. "What was your current relationship with Alex Mitchell, Mr. Fortuna?"

"Define relationship," Julia replied.

"Were you on good terms with Mr. Mitchell?" Matt countered her question. "I'm led to believe you were less than happy with Mr. Mitchell when you left here the other day."

"I think that's supposition on your part, DS Burgess. Do you have any proof my client was unhappy with Mr. Mitchell?" Julia was speaking to Matt, but watching Ray.

Matt ignored Julia. "Where were you on the night of Monday 20th October, between seven and eleven Mr. Fortuna?"

Gerry thought for a moment. "I was with Bobby McGregor and an agent who's an old friend of mine."

"Would this be the same agent you referred to, when you were describing how Mr. Mitchell had been, and I quote, creaming off the top for himself?" asked Matt.

"He brought it to my attention; that's correct."

"And will this agent confirm he was with you and Mr. McGregor on Monday night?"

"Yes of course," Gerry said, looking at Ray with a slight smile.

"We will of course be speaking to both him and Mr. McGregor."

Julia stood up. "I think that's all for now. As you well know, my client is a busy man." She smiled at Ray as she accompanied Gerry out of the room.

Matt slumped back on the chair. "What do you think?" he asked Ray, who was sitting quite still, staring at the empty space where Julia had just been.

"I think he killed Alex, but I don't know how to prove it. I'm sure both his agent friend, and Bobby McGregor, will give him a perfect cast-iron alibi, so in the meantime we just watch and wait. He's not that clever; he'll make a mistake, and we'll be waiting."

CHAPTER TWENTY-SEVEN

THE BIG day had finally arrived. It had all started early that morning, when Janine had rolled in at some ridiculous hour after one of her nights out. Gerry had got in late himself but had gone straight to bed, knowing that today was going to be really busy.

Janine had woken him when she came crashing into the bedroom. She loved her nights with the girls, which she had at least once a week. And who was Gerry to complain? As long as she came home to him every night that was all that mattered. But she was out of order on this particular occasion, especially as she knew how important today was. He was glad she was independent; as ten years her senior, he preferred a quiet night in watching a film. Their's was a marriage that many of his friends had doubted would last, but much to everyone's surprise, four years down the line they were still together, going strong.

Usually, Janine was first up and in her private gym even after a late night out. But today she'd woken in a strange mood, and seemed almost annoyed when Gerry insisted that she come into the office to oversee the signing of Pete's record deal.

It was the deal Gerry had been negotiating with American record giants Westoria, ever since Pete had left Anders Neckermann. Once Pete signed, they would earn a cool quarter of a million dollars from their percentage of Pete's management agreement.

For some reason, Janine was taking forever to get ready, and Gerry, who hated being late, was having difficulty controlling his temper. He'd sat on his own in their enormous kitchen, and eaten his usual breakfast of cereals and toast, washed down with a large mug of tea. Decorated with stripped pine on the walls and Mediterranean terracotta floor tiles, the kitchen was something straight from the pages of Homes & Gardens magazine. Gerry hated cooking, but Janine had spent a fortune equipping it with the latest must-have culinary items. A shining set of copper pots and pans hung from a rack in the middle of the ceiling, an extortionately expensive set of razor-sharp Japanese knives – so sharp he was afraid to touch them – stood in a huge wooden block on the island in the centre of the room, and a gigantic American fridge-freezer she'd had shipped over from California, hummed in the corner.

Some people lived to eat, but Gerry just ate to live – and the simpler the better, which was strange considering his father had been a waiter in an Italian restaurant. He couldn't understand the attraction of spending hours in front of a cooker, but it clearly made Janine happy.

He looked at his watch again, and realised he'd been sitting there for half an hour waiting for Janine to come downstairs.

"For God's sake, babe, will you get your arse into gear," Gerry shouted from the bottom of the stairs. "We need to be in the office ready for the call from Los Angeles. You know what those guys in the States are like."

Janine called from the bedroom. "Just give me a minute Ger; nearly ready."

"I'll wait for you in Rollie then," he called back as he walked through the oak-panelled hallway, stopping briefly at the bottom of the curved staircase to tap the imposing suit of armour on the helmet. Gerry loved the idea of owning his own piece of English history.

Upstairs in the master bedroom, Janine was sitting on their huge four-poster bed, pulling on the black leather jacket that matched her skin-tight, black leather trousers. She'd chosen the bedroom decor herself, to reflect the style of the house, with sumptuous furnishings and matching curtains. The medieval-style wall coverings had cost a small fortune, but along with the bed they finished the room off perfectly.

The phone rang on the bedside table, and she picked it up on the second ring. "Hello?" she whispered into the handset.

She'd convinced Gerry to install one of the latest cordless systems, so she could walk around the bedroom while she was talking; slipping into her dressing room to continue her conversation in private if need be.

"Hi, just checking you enjoyed last night," said Ray.

"I thought I told you not to call here when he's about."

"Yeah, sorry. Will I see you today?"

"Of course," she replied. "Now I have to go, before he suspects. See you later."

She emerged from her dressing room and put the phone back on its charger, just as Gerry walked into the bedroom.

"Will you come on," he said impatiently. "If we don't go now we'll miss that call with the States."

"Ready Ger! How do I look?" She twirled round, her wavy shoulder-length red hair accentuating her piercing emerald-green eyes. Her well-toned body could easily be that of a model.

Gerry put his arm around her waist and gave her a squeeze, "Gorgeous as always, babe!" And kissed her cheek.

Janine finished off with a spray of Chanel No.5 as she left the room. They walked swiftly down the staircase, out through the hallway past the suit of armour - which Janine secretly hated - and across the gravel drive to the car.

It was a bright crisp day, and the leaves on the trees had taken on the autumnal reds and yellows Janine loved so much. The ivy and Virginia creeper covering the front of the house looked fantastic, and the air felt so clear. On days like today, living in the countryside definitely has its advantages, she thought.

Sitting in the opulent luxury of Rollie's heated leather, Janine thought back to the events of last night. She was still aching and a little sore from the passion she'd enjoyed with Ray. She knew it was wrong, but the trouble was it always felt so right.

She was brought back to the present as they pulled into the car park at the back of The Hideout; she'd been wrapped up in her thoughts for the entire thirty-minute journey.

While Gerry and Janine were driving into the office, Pete Peterson was getting himself together in his city-centre apartment.

Pulling on his snakeskin cowboy boots and trademark leather jacket, Pete checked himself in the floor-to-ceiling mirrored wardrobe doors that ran alongside his king-size bed. He'd had some fun with that feature over the time he'd lived there. He smiled to himself. His long, straight, black hair and slim six-foot frame, gave him a distinctive look, which he'd used to his advantage – especially where the opposite sex was concerned. As he straightened the sheets on his bed, the sweet, lingering smell of perfume momentarily took his mind back to the previous night.

He picked up the phone on the bedside table and dialled the number he knew so well. A few moments later, he went out onto the balcony and lit his first joint of the day to help him relax ready for today's events.

Since moving back to Birmingham, he'd managed to cut down his daily drug intake to just a small amount of weed and the odd line of coke. He knew that the most sensible course of action would be to stop altogether and he'd tried, but in his mind, he didn't think a little would hurt. The last tour had been a disaster, and it was all down to his excessive drug-taking. Financially it had made money, but Pete's relationship with the band had suffered. He needed to be careful now that Gerry was becoming fanatical about drugs, after all the trouble with Rudi's.

He locked the door to his apartment and took the lift down the three floors to the entrance lobby. He was fortunate that his building had a twenty-four-hour concierge, which kept the twelve apartments secure and private. It was an expensive luxury, but it had its advantages. Especially in keeping away unwanted visitors.

It was only a ten-minute walk to Gerry's office, along the canal and across on the other side of town; he enjoyed the exercise and fresh air. It was a chilly morning, but he didn't really notice – his thoughts were preoccupied with what was about to happen to his career, once he'd signed the recording deal with Westoria Records.

When Pete arrived at The Hideout, Judy buzzed him in. At just twenty-one, Judy was the youngest member of the team. She was a petite, five-foot-four blonde, with the latest Farrah Fawcett hairstyle, framing high cheekbones and cornflower blue eyes.

Pete leaned over her desk and gave her a quick kiss on the cheek. "Hey babe, you're lookin' gorgeous as usual."

They exchanged a knowing smile, before he took the stairs two at a time, to the plush suite of FAM offices where Gerry and Janine were already waiting.

"Morning both," he said as he breezed in. "Are we ready to rock?"

"Speak for yourself," mumbled Janine from the kitchenette, stirring the cup of coffee she'd just made for herself.

Pete looked in the doorway. "Couldn't make one for me while you're there could you, Jan?"

Gerry was sitting behind his desk. "You know, considering you're about to become very rich and famous, with one of the most recognised faces on the planet, you might have had a shave before you left home this morning," he said with a frown.

"Mate, it's the cool new look. Haven't you seen all the guys now, with the designer stubble?" said Pete, striking a pose.

"Looks bloody scruffy to me. What do you think, babe?"

Janine stroked Pete's face as she passed him his mug of coffee. "Mmm. Feels all sexy."

"Come on Gerry," said Pete. "Get with the times man – it's not as if I'm gonna be on the telly is it?"

"No, but there's a photographer from the NME coming in later to get a photo of you signing the deal. And don't forget, you're playing a set at the opening tonight. Or had it slipped your mind?"

"Of course not, how could I forget? We've been rehearsing all week," said Pete. "Oh and by the way, the lads were asking if they're going to get paid for tonight."

"Of course they are," snapped Janine. "We always make sure the band are looked after; you know that!"

"Yeah, I know, but I don't want them worried about what might happen once this deal is signed. Don't forget, it's only Pete Peterson signing the deal, not The Flames – they're not gonna be happy about that."

"Well, until the deal's done and we've met with the guys over in the States, I honestly don't know," replied Gerry. "Listen, nobody appreciates the work those guys have put in more than I do."

Pete sat down in front of Gerry's desk. "Yeah, but I'm not gonna do a Bowie on them and just get rid once things start to happen. They were there at the beginning and helped create what I'm signing today – I don't want to lose that. We may have had our ups and downs recently, but they're still part of what I am."

"OK, point taken, but remember what I always say: Whatever it takes babe!"

"What do you mean by that? Whatever it takes babe?" Pete snapped back.

"Look Pete," interrupted Janine, "you're just about to sign a deal that will change your life, so let's leave it for now eh?"

Pete was about to reply, when one of the lights on Gerry's phone started to flash.

"This is it guys," said Gerry, picking up the receiver.

Pete and Janine gathered round the desk.

Manny Oberstein, head of Westoria Records in Los Angeles, was on the line. "Hey, Manny, how's things?" Gerry enthused into the phone. "We've had all the paperwork checked and double checked this end. How about you?"

Manny started to talk, but realising the others couldn't hear, Gerry stopped him. "Hang on a sec, Manny, let me put you on speakerphone."

"Hey, guys." Manny's American drawl came out of the small speaker loud and clear. "How's it going over there?"

"It's great," said Pete trying to sound cool.

"OK then! We're happy here, so if you've got your documents in front of you, all we need is for Pete to sign his name on the bottom. I'll do the same here and we have a deal!"

Gerry slid the contract across the desk to Pete and passed him his treasured Montblanc Meisterstück fountain pen. It had belonged to his late father, and he'd used it to sign the deal on The Hideout. He noticed Pete's hand was shaking slightly as he took it. *Strange*, thought Gerry. *Pete is usually so cool and calm, but then it's understandable when you think that signing this piece of paper will change his life forever.*

But after a split second, the super-professional persona returned, as Pete signed his name with a flourish.

"We're done this end, Manny," said Gerry. "How about you guys?"

"We're all cool here, Gerry." Manny's voice boomed out of the speaker. "Welcome Pete Peterson to the Westoria family – I've a feeling this is gonna be big!"

"We'll get the paperwork completed, and Janine will get it wired over to you today. Then we can start planning a trip over there for Pete and his band as soon as possible."

"That all sounds cool, Gerry. We'll be in touch next week. We like to take things one step at a time here at Westoria, so we'll call you on Monday with our thoughts. Congratulations guys!"

And with that there was a click and suddenly the room was silent. No one said anything for what felt like an age. Then suddenly Gerry stood up and shouted at the top of his voice, "Judy, fetch the Champagne!"

Janine was smiling and hugged Pete. Then Gerry hugged Pete and Judy appeared with a bottle of Vintage Bollinger and glasses. Although a sworn teetotaller, Gerry always kept a top selection of fine wines and champagne; he skilfully removed the cork from the perfectly chilled bottle and filled their glasses which he exchanged for the usual glass of Coca-Cola Judy had also brought him.

Their glasses charged, they all clinked them together, toasting in unison; "To Pete Peterson, superstar!"

Pete had left Gerry and Janine upstairs attending to the paperwork, and followed Judy downstairs. As they reached the bottom, he put his arms around her and pulled her towards him. He was so much taller than she was, but he bent down as she lifted her face up, and they kissed. It was a long passionate kiss and they hadn't heard Bobby McGregor come in. He coughed and they pulled apart quickly.

"Hey don't worry guys," Bobby said. "Your secret's safe with me." He winked at Pete and went up the stairs.

"You coming back to mine after the gig tonight?" Pete said.

"Try and stop me. Love you baby," she said as Pete walked through into The Hideout.

"I love you too," he said back.

The Flames were just arriving for a final run through before the big gig later that night at The Lexxicon. Pete was going to wait until the official announcement, to tell them about the deal in the States. He wasn't altogether happy about not knowing whether Westoria would take the band as well, but for now he had a gig to do, and he was not going to let it bother him.

Janine was sending the completed contract over to the Westoria Records office, when Bobby came into the office. He gave her a hug and kiss on the cheek like he normally did, but she noticed he seemed a little tense. She put it down to the big show tonight. He'd taken on more responsibility at the club since Alex's death, and he looked tired. She needed to do some last-minute shopping for new tights to wear at the gig, so she left him and Gerry to it, and went downstairs. Judy had already left to get some lunch.

Bobby waited until she'd gone before turning to Gerry. "They had me in for two hours yesterday, asking me loads of questions," he said.

"Didn't the solicitor woman sort it?"

"Yeah, but I don't like all that police shit. I think they know something and they're not saying." Bobby was on edge.

"Don't worry. Just stick to the story and we'll be fine," Gerry said, trying to calm him.

"What about that agent? You sure he'll keep shtum?"

"He's sorted, I told you. Just relax."

Neither of them had heard Janine come back up the stairs – she'd forgotten her purse. She was on the top step and caught the essentials of their conversation. She froze. Was she hearing correctly? Gerry and Bobby? She waited for a lull in their conversation, then loudly stamping her feet on the stairs, came back in the office.

"Sorry, I forgot my purse," she said, going over to the desk and picking it up. "See you later."

She gave Gerry a peck on the cheek and ran out of the building with her mind in turmoil. She should tell Ray? But she couldn't betray her husband. If what she heard was true, they were responsible for Alex's death. What was she going to do? Who could she turn to for help? Who could she trust?

She was walking aimlessly, when she saw Pete and Judy holding hands in a coffee bar, just up the road from The Hideout. She must have walked in a circle. Could she trust Pete? She had done in the past – when they were having 'their scene'. They hadn't fallen out, and it had been Janine's quick thinking that'd saved him at the end of the tour; but could she really trust him? And what about Judy? Pete was really tight with Judy now, and she got the feeling that whatever Pete did, Judy would be there too.

Janine knew she had to speak to someone, so summoning up all her courage, she walked into the coffee bar.

Half an hour and two cups of coffee later, Janine had told them what she'd heard Gerry and Bobby discussing, and what Ray Law had told her about Alex. Adding two and two together, they concluded that

Gerry and Bobby were responsible for the murder but had decided it was wiser to say nothing for now. Once tonight's event was over and the dust settled, they would tell Ray Law what they knew. After all, what difference would twenty-four hours make?

CHAPTER TWENTY-EIGHT

AT LAST, they were standing on stage; Gerry in the middle, Janine on one side, Pete on the other. The club was packed to the rafters. Gerry had insisted Janine accompany them on stage, and she stood looking out at all the expectant faces. Pete looked so calm – he was used to it. Even Gerry had a confident air, standing there in his new suit. Janine couldn't believe he was so relaxed, considering what he'd done – but she knew she had to play the part, so she smiled and waited for him to speak.

Gerry walked forward and took the microphone from the stand in front of him. He glanced at Janine and then at Pete, before addressing the crowd. "Good evening, ladies and gentlemen."

There was a tumultuous roar.

"Before I go any further, I'd like to pay tribute to a very talented young man, who sadly is not with us tonight. As you may know, Alex Mitchell was found murdered this week, and I would like to dedicate tonight's show to his memory."

The audience burst into more applause.

Gerry waited until it died down. "I would like to thank my beautiful wife for her continued support and tireless energy."

He paused as the crowd cheered and wolf-whistled. Janine acknowledged them with a coy wave.

"And now, I would like to make a very special announcement regarding the man standing here on my left." There was a huge cheer from Pete's fans. "Today, Pete Peterson signed an exclusive record deal with Westoria Records in the United States of America, which will see his album released worldwide." He paused. "Ladies and gentlemen, you are looking at a future global superstar – Pete Peterson!"

The crowd was ecstatic and the noise deafening. Once again Gerry waited for calm. "So without further ado, welcome to the greatest club Birmingham has ever seen…The Lexxicon!"

The curtains behind them opened and The Flames blasted into the intro of their opening number as Gerry escorted Janine to the side. Pete took his guitar from the stand in front of the drums, and ran to the front of the stage. The crowd was bouncing as Pete approached the microphone and started to sing, accompanied in perfect unison by his fans; they knew every word. The place was already rocking, and as Janine elbowed her way over to the bar, she spotted Ray Law with George Williams who was grimacing at the volume of the sound system.

She ended up standing next to Ray.

"Great speech!" he shouted in her ear.

Janine looked around but couldn't see Gerry. He was with her when they came off stage, but had disappeared.

"Let's go in the other room," she shouted at Ray. Ray tapped George Williams on the shoulder, and they followed Janine into Lexx2. Mercifully, it was much quieter.

"That's better. I couldn't hear myself think in there." George Williams was rubbing his ears.

Janine took hold of Ray's arm, pulling him away from the bar so the barman couldn't hear. "Ray, there's something I have to talk to you about; it's about Alex's murder. I think I know…" She faltered as Gerry and Bobby walked into the room.

"Ah, I see you've had the same idea," Gerry said. "Does it have to be that loud? It's a wonder some of those kids aren't deaf! Now what are we having to drink? Champagne?" He turned to the barman. "There's a bottle of Bollinger in the chiller, and I'll have a glass of coke."

Janine glanced at Ray, but he gave her a tiny shake of the head. Gerry didn't notice, but Bobby certainly did.

"Have there been any new developments in the case?" Gerry spoke directly to George Williams, deliberately ignoring Ray.

"Nothing that I can tell you yet, Gerry. I'm sure you understand I can't discuss an ongoing investigation. I'm impressed with the club though; what an amazing venue." He changed the subject. "A bit too loud in the other room for my liking, but it's very nice in here."

"Yes, thank you. We should have been listening to Alex playing the piano tonight. It's a terrible shame. I've been thinking about calling it The Alex Mitchell Room, in his honour. What do you think Janine?"

He gave Janine a strange look she hadn't seen before; almost challenging her. He knew she hated Alex; she'd made no bones about telling him. And he hardly ever called her Janine.

"I think that's a wonderful idea, Ger," she replied. "He was a brilliant musician."

She looked at him; he was feigning sadness. *He's playing mind games with us*, she thought. *The arrogant bastard thinks he's got away with it. But does he know I heard him and Bobby?*

"Sounds like The Flames have finished," Gerry said. "Come on, babe, we ought to go backstage and congratulate Pete. Don't mention that we didn't stay in the room though. It might upset him." He laughed, turning to George Williams and Ray. "You coming too gents? Always good to have the law around."

They followed him and Bobby, weaving their way through the crowd, into the dressing rooms at the back of the stage.

Pete and The Flames had come off stage to absolute bedlam. The crowd was going wild, shouting for more, and Pete was about to go back on stage again, when Tony Waters stood in his way.

"So, when were you going to tell us about the Pete Peterson record deal then?" He emphasised Pete's name with air quotes.

"Look guys, I'm sorry, but that's the way the company wanted it. I've already told Gerry, I'm not doing it without you. Nobody appreciates how you stood by me more than I do. You'll still be there with me, but there was nothing I could do." Pete was doing his best to keep the situation calm, but Tony was obviously annoyed.

"So, no more Flames then! That's fuckin' great. The next thing will be the American musos taking over I suppose," he said, turning to the others for support. "Are you lot just gonna sit there and take this shit?"

Gerry waded straight into the argument. "Sorry guys, just thought we'd come and congratulate you on a great show," he said, trying to ignore the atmosphere. He turned and spread his arms wide to usher the others back before they had chance to get through the door. "Let's get another drink folks. I think they're a bit busy."

Bobby stayed, anticipating trouble.

Tony, who was drinking from a bottle, turned round to Pete pointing it at him. "Well I for one don't believe you, and as for that bastard manager of yours…"

Bobby stepped in front of Tony. "I think you need to calm down," he said, but Tony had been drinking before the show and was now becoming unreasonable and made the mistake of taking a swing at Bobby. Before anyone else had a chance to move, Bobby had sidestepped him, and with one swift punch knocked Tony flat on his back, the contents of his bottle spraying everywhere as he fell backwards.

All the other band members jumped into the argument with Pete, who was trying in vain to restore order. Within a few seconds, the band had descended from celebrating a triumphant gig, into utter chaos. Beer bottles, chairs and equipment were flying around the room.

Bobby found himself standing in a corner watching the demise of The Flames unfold in front of him, and wondering how on earth he was going to explain all this to Gerry in the morning.

Back in the club, Gerry had managed to get them all to the bar again, and dismissed the scene in the dressing room as high spirits. "Janine will tell you what they're like," he said. "She's dealt with them before haven't you, babe?"

Janine smiled and nodded. There was no way she'd be able to speak to Ray on his own now, and she'd had enough – she wanted to go home to bed. Unfortunately, it would be with her husband and not with the man she really wanted, but there would be another time; she would make sure of it.

"I'm tired Ger, can we go?" She gave Ray and George Williams a smile, and a peck apiece on the cheek.

"No problem, babe," he said, shaking hands with George and Ray. "You'll keep me informed won't you?"

"Of course, Gerry, you'll be the first to know of any developments," George said.

Gerry left holding Janine's arm but she was able to manage a glance back over her shoulder and a quick smile for Ray before disappearing through the door.

George shook his head. "I fear all my advice might have been wasted; I hope you know what you're doing," he said, finishing his glass of champagne.

Gerry and Janine left the club through a mass of people gathered outside. Gerry liked protection when there was a crowd, but Bobby was otherwise engaged with Pete in the dressing room, so Gerry and Janine were forced to push their way through the hoards to reach Rollie impeded by all the well-wishers grabbing Gerry's hand to congratulate him on the club, Janine smiling, thanking everyone and pulling Gerry on towards the car.

As they reached it, a thickset man, about the same height as Janine and wearing a black overcoat, stepped out in their way.

"Mr. Fortuna?"

Gerry stopped as the man leaned towards him.

"Here's a present from Rota Bocan. Benny Mulligan sends his regards."

Janine noticed only the glint of steel as the man plunged the knife into Gerry, stared at her for the briefest of instants and disappeared into the crowd.

Gerry fell back onto Janine. He gripped the hilt of the blade protruding from his chest. Blood poured from the wound and Janine let out an ear-piercing scream as reality struck.

Inside the club George Williams and Ray Law had just collected their coats from the cloakroom and were beginning to make their way out, when they heard Janine screaming.

In a split second, Ray leapt into action. He barged his way towards the Rolls. He could see Janine on the ground, nursing Gerry's head in her lap. Gerry's white shirt had turned crimson as blood continued to ooze from the wound.

Ray squatted down next to Janine who was sobbing uncontrollably. "Ger, don't leave me," she cried.

Ray tried to comfort her. She was stroking Gerry's face, her tears dripping on to his cheeks. "What am I gonna do Ger? What am I gonna do?"

Gerry looked up at her, his eyes brimming with pain. He swallowed and said something. Janine could barely hear him.

"Whatever it takes, babe," he whispered. "Whatever it takes."

Acknowledgements

Thank you so much for reading my first book. I hope you enjoyed it and are ready to join me in the ongoing journey with Pete and Janine.

I've had a fantastic time writing *Whatever It Takes Babe*, but it wouldn't exist without the help of some very special people.

Don't worry, I'm not going to launch into one of those epic Oscar winning speeches. More the Ricky Gervais, 'Thank your agent, your mum and get off' kind!

I'd like to thank my publisher Andrew Sparke and his team at APS Books for their faith and tireless work.

My friend Nic Perrins for her proof reading.

Wendy Eckhardt who advised me on Police procedure and aspects of the law.

My wonderful friends and family whose feedback was so welcome. Beth, Steve, Tracey and Chris.

And last, but not least, my best friend and inspiration, Cissy Stone. Whose never ending support and encouragement got me here.

Des Tong.

FICTION FROM APS BOOKS
(www.andrewsparke.com)

Davey J Ashfield: Footsteps On The Teign
Davey J Ashfield Contracting With The Devil
Davey J Ashfield: A Turkey And One More Easter Egg
Des Tong: Get It Done
Fenella Bass: Hornbeams
Fenella Bass:: Shadows
Fenella Bass: Darkness
HR Beasley: Nothing Left To Hide
Lee Benson: So You Want To Own An Art Gallery
Lee Benson: Where's Your Art gallery Now?
Lee Benson: Now You're The Artist…Deal With It
Lee Benson: No Naked Walls
TF Byrne Damage Limitation
Nargis Darby: A Different Shade Of Love
J.W.Darcy Looking For Luca
J.W.Darcy: Ladybird Ladybird
J.W.Darcy: Legacy Of Lies
J.W.Darcy: Love Lust & Needful Things
Paul Dickinson: Franzi The Hero
Jane Evans: The Third Bridge
Simon Falshaw: The Stone
Peter Georgiadis: Not Cast In Stone
Peter Georgiadis: The Mute Swan's Song
Milton Godfrey: The Danger Lies In Fear
Chris Grayling: A Week Is…A Long Time
Jean Harvey: Pandemic
Michel Henri: Mister Penny Whistle
Michel Henri: The Death Of The Duchess Of Grasmere
Michel Henri: Abducted By Faerie
Laurie Hornsby: Postcards From The Seaside
Hugh Lupus An Extra Knot (Parts I-VI)
Hugh Lupus: Mr. Donaldson's Company
Lorna MacDonald-Bradley: Dealga
Alison Manning: World Without Endless Sheep
Colin Mardell: Keep Her Safe
Colin Mardell: Bring Them Home
Ian Meacheam: An Inspector Called

·

Ingram Content Group UK Ltd.
Milton Keynes UK
UKHW020638220523
422140UK00014B/495

9 798223 258698